THREE WOMEN

www.transworldbooks.co.uk
www.transworldireland.ie

THREE WOMEN

Marita Conlon-McKenna

TRANSWORLD IRELAND

TRANSWORLD IRELAND
an imprint of The Random House Group Limited
20 Vauxhall Bridge Road, London SW1V 2SA
www.transworldbooks.co.uk

First published in 2012 by Transworld Ireland,
a division of Transworld Publishers

A CIP catalogue record for this book
is available from the British Library.

ISBN 9781848271210

Addresses for Random House Group Ltd companies outside the UK
can be found at: www.randomhouse.co.uk
The Random House Group Ltd Reg. No. 954009

The Random House Group Limited supports the Forest Stewardship
Council (FSC®), the leading international forest-certification organization.
Our books carrying the FSC label are printed on FSC®-certified paper.
FSC is the only forest-certification scheme endorsed by the leading
environmental organizations, including Greenpeace.
Our paper procurement policy can be found at
www.randomhouse.co.uk/environment.

Typeset in 13/16pt Erhardt by
Kestrel Data, Exeter, Devon
Printed and bound by
CPI Group (UK) Ltd, Croydon, CR0 4YY.

2 4 6 8 10 9 7 5 3 1

For my wonderful mother,
Mary

Acknowledgements

Thank you to my amazing family: my husband, James, and our children Mandy, Laura, Fiona and James and my son-in-law, Michael Hearty, and my two little sweethearts, Holly and Sam.

To my sister Gerardine. Thanks for being there – the two of us sharing so much.

And to Michael Fahy – almost part of the family.

To Anne Murphy for her understanding and for making me laugh so much in Canada.

To Fran Leach, for her constant encouragement, friendship and fun and all those sunny days in Baltimore.

To my friends Catherine Harvey, Anne O'Connell and Joyce Van Belle.

My special thanks to my wonderful editor, Linda Evans. Also thanks to Joanne Williamson, Vivien Garrett, Bella Whittington, Aislinn Casey, Kate Green and Sarah Whittaker, and to everyone at Transworld's London office for their immense support, encouragement and work on this book. And to Eoin McHugh in Transworld Ireland's Dublin office.

To my agent Caroline Sheldon, for her constant belief in my writing and the excitement that working together on every new book brings!

To Simon, Gill and Sophie Hess, Declan Heaney and Helen Gleed O'Connor and everyone at Gill Hess, Dublin, for making it all seem easy and for looking after me and my books so well!

To bookshops and booksellers everywhere – thank you for bringing my books and readers together.

To Sarah Webb, Martina Devlin and Larry O'Loughlin, and all my fellow writers – thanks for just being there!

To my readers – thank you for making me enjoy writing so much.

Chapter One

ERIN HARRIS STUDIED HERSELF IN THE MIRROR. LONG LIGHT-brown hair with an undeniable tint of red and gold, pale skin, freckles, weird blue-green eyes that seemed to change colour with her mood, long limbs and an okay figure. At twenty-six years of age she guessed she was kind of attractive – not beautiful, not pretty, but definitely attractive for someone who had just completed the first quarter of her life.

Her mum and dad and brother Jack had already texted her their birthday good wishes, and later they would all get together for a family dinner at home. Today was going to be a good day. Even though it was only early March it was sunny and bright outside and, judging by the banging around in the kitchen, her two flatmates were busy making her a birthday breakfast before they all set off for work.

She dragged the hairbrush through her thick, wavy hair and, grabbing her dressing gown, joined Nikki and Claire in the kitchen.

'Hey, we were going to bring a tray into the bedroom to you!' laughed Nikki, giving her a hug.

'The scrambled egg and salmon will be ready in a min,' added Claire, 'and I've made us all a pot of proper coffee.'

'I prefer eating here,' Erin assured them as she curled up on to the old leather armchair that had pride of position at their kitchen table.

'I'll get the pressies,' said Nikki, as Claire poured Erin a big glass of orange juice.

'You two are spoiling me,' sighed Erin, glad that she was sharing her apartment with two of her best friends.

'That's what birthdays are for,' replied Claire, giving her a hug. 'When you're a kid it's all parties and presents and no homework, but us grown-up girlies still deserve a bit of pampering from our best friends on our birthdays.'

'I can't believe I'm twenty-six!' Erin marvelled. It sounded so old. Yikes – thirty was only around the corner!

'Sssh!' hushed Nikki. 'We won't mention ages or years at this table. Agreed?'

'Yes,' nodded Claire and Erin, both aware of how obsessed Nikki was with age and beauty and looking good.

'Here's my pressie,' said Nikki.

Erin opened the pink-and-white-wrapped package. It was a bottle of her favourite perfume and a voucher for a facial at L'Esprit, the expensive salon that Nikki always went to in nearby Ballsbridge.

'Nikki – you spent far too much!'

'I'm a good customer there, so they give me a bit of a discount for my friends,' Nikki confessed.

Claire's present was wrapped in zany Quentin Blake printed paper and contained a cute pair of pale-blue pyjamas decorated with little white rabbits.

'Oh, I love them!' said Erin.

'Open the other present,' urged Claire.

Erin laughed when she saw the latest Rachel Allen cookery book. 'You two are just trying to get me to do some of the cooking round here.'

'True, but there's some really great recipes in it and they're easy – even for someone like you or Nikki,' replied Claire, a natural cook, as she served them creamy scrambled egg and salmon on toast along with their coffee.

The sun poured in through the window as they ate and, just as she was finishing, her phone went.

'Hi Mum!'

Erin listened as her mum's voice broke into the familiar refrain of 'Happy Birthday to You'. Claire and Nikki both joined in the singing too.

'Mum, thanks for phoning. Listen, I'll see you and Dad tonight.'

Her mum was big into birthdays. Erin guessed that's where she got it from too, wanting to celebrate and mark birthdays and special dates and traditions.

'Hey, I'd better rush.' Nikki jumped up from the table. 'We've a client meeting first thing. You and Luke enjoy tonight!'

'Thanks, Nikki.'

'Nikki – you've hardly touched a thing!' complained Claire.

'You know I'm not a breakfast person!' called Nikki as she disappeared.

'Talk about understatement. She has literally just had black coffee and a finger of toast and hasn't touched her egg.'

'You know what she's like,' said Erin. 'She just wants to be stick thin like a super-model.'

'I'd better get going too.' Claire drained the last of the coffee. 'Old Mr Stevens and his bad knee are my first appointment today. Wednesday always seems to be my OAP day at the surgery – they all seem to need physio for something or other!'

Ten minutes later Erin was on the DART train heading into work. She smiled as she read Luke's text. He was in London for the day at a meeting, but promised to be back in time for tonight's dinner. Sometimes she could hardly believe that she was going out with someone as cool as Luke, who also happened to be as nice and kind as they come. Three years older than her, he worked on the finance team in Hibernian Stockbrokers, which impressed her parents and friends but also meant that they could still afford to eat out and go away for the odd weekend. So many of her friends had lost their jobs or were in pretty dire financial straits, but thank heaven Luke's firm was okay. He might have to work crazy hours but at least he had a job, and a good job at that.

Erin's own salary had been cut by more than twenty-five per cent in the past two years, and she knew that De Berg O'Leary Graphics were hanging on by a thread. This year no graduates had been taken on and a few of the staff were on a three-day week. Monika De Berg and her husband Declan O'Leary had built up a wonderful business over the past fifteen years in Ireland, and had worked on some amazing campaigns, but the firm now spent a lot of time pitching for smaller jobs and tendering for design contracts that might never happen.

Erin tried not to get disheartened. At least she had a job when so many graphic designers didn't, and she was doing something she loved. She had to stay positive and believe that, career-wise, things would improve.

She walked briskly to the office, where Alice, their recep-tionist, let her in. Sliding into her desk on the second floor of the old Georgian building, she switched on her computer. Today was going to be a good day, she resolved . . . a really good day.

Chapter Two

KATE CASSIDY STOOD IN THE KITCHEN TRYING NOT TO GIVE into the overwhelming sadness she felt. Every year it was the same, the date imprinted on her mind for ever. No matter how much she tried to forget it, to put the past behind her, the date on the calendar always rekindled that sense of panic and pain that she still remembered so acutely.

She'd been only twenty years old when it happened, and so naïve and stupid it was beyond belief. One mistake that had cost her so much and changed everything. One mistake that she could never forget, or undo, no matter how hard she tried. She steadied herself and gazed out in the garden. It was covered in yellow daffodils. She'd planted the bulbs under the trees, in the flowerbeds and crowded them into pots. She loved their colour and sense of joy. They symbolized the arrival of spring . . . new beginnings.

The daffodils always evoked that period when her life had changed and she had given up her baby for adoption. At the time it had seemed a solution to her problem, but what kind of woman was she that would allow her own flesh and blood, her daughter, to be raised by strangers? Somewhere out there people she had never met had raised her child and made her their own.

Over the years she had somehow learned to accept it. Still, it didn't stop her from thinking about her daughter and wondering what she might be like now.

Her phone went. It was her sister, Sally. She smiled – good old Sally was wonderful.

'You okay, Kate?' Sally asked, her voice full of concern.

'Yes.'

Sally was the only one in the family who knew her secret, who had helped her at a time in her life when she was desperate and felt so alone. And, like herself, Sally never, ever forgot the date. Every year her sister would phone to talk to her and later they would meet up for a chat or a walk and lunch. It was almost a ritual by now. A ritual that Kate valued so much – the only acknowledgement there was of what had happened.

She looked around her kitchen, neat and clean with good, hand-painted cream units and a top-of-the-range Neff cooker. She had a lovely home, a good husband, three children – and yet she always felt that something was missing, something that she could never have, could never regain . . . ever . . .

Chapter Three

NINA HARRIS WHISKED THE EGGS TOGETHER BEFORE FOLDING in the rest of the ingredients to make the chocolate almond cake. She poured the mixture carefully into the cake tin and popped it into the hot oven. Now she could set about making the creamy chicken and mozzarella dish that was one of Erin's favourites. She and Tom had offered to treat Erin to a birthday dinner down in the village tonight, but their daughter had said she'd far prefer dinner at home if that was okay.

Nina had phoned Erin at breakfast time to wish her happy birthday and, as she listened to her daughter's excited voice on the phone, Nina still couldn't credit that it was twenty-six years since Erin had been born. It seemed like only yesterday that she had held in her arms a beautiful, blue-eyed baby with a steady gaze and a fuzz of reddish-gold hair.

Every year as they celebrated Erin's birthday Nina remembered the past, and the other woman who had given birth to their daughter on that date and then somehow made the difficult choice of giving her up for adoption.

When Erin was small Nina had been nervous that one day

this woman would turn up and demand her child back – even try to steal her back. But as the years went by the fear had eased and she had been so busy, always organizing birthday parties with cakes and balloons and bouncy castles and face-painting and magic shows and trips to the puppet theatre, that gradually the worry of this other woman had passed.

Erin had been almost twelve weeks old when all the complex legalities and stringent interviewing processes and assessments were finally overcome and they received the good news from the social workers for the adoption agency that they could collect their baby from St Raphael's Children's Home. After so many years of trying to become parents they couldn't believe it and were totally overwhelmed finally to be handed a baby girl to take home. They had been scared as anything coming home with Erin, worried they would somehow harm or hurt her, this precious baby they had been given, and neither of them had slept a wink that first night as they watched her sleep in the antique wooden crib they had bought for her.

It had taken them a while to learn to relax and enjoy being parents, but from the first minute when Erin Grace Harris had grasped her finger fiercely in her tiny hand, Nina knew that Erin was hers for ever. She was her mother and that's what mattered . . .

Motherhood was such a complex issue, as Nina had discovered. One did not have to give birth physically to a child to love and bond with it and become a mother. Giving birth was the least of it! Every day you concentrated on doing your best to love your children, to help them to grow and become warm, rounded, good people capable of loving and being loved. From coping with sleepless nights and childhood temperatures and illnesses, and cooling down hot, teething gums, to teaching

17

them how to talk and walk and cycle their bikes and learn to read and write and study and think and become decent human beings. As far as Nina was concerned, it had always been a case of nurture, not nature, with Erin and their son Jack. Tom and she had done their utmost to be good parents and make Erin and Jack feel totally loved and wanted. They'd encouraged each of them to learn, explore and enjoy the things that held their interests and gave them pleasure and joy.

On days like today she thought of the scared young woman who had given them such a gift when she had signed the agreement to let Erin be adopted. She hoped that, wherever that girl was now, she was happy and had a family of her own.

They were quite a crowd for dinner, as Nina's sister Lizzie – who was also Erin's godmother – and her husband Myles were coming and Tom's brother Bill and his partner Charles. Her mum May would join them for dinner too; Myles and Lizzie would collect her en route. May Armstrong was eighty-six years old and had her good and bad days, though she had seemed chirpy enough when Nina spoke to her earlier. Between them, Lizzie and she kept a good eye on their mother, who unfortunately was beginning to suffer with failing physical health and worrisome early signs of dementia. Her geriatrician had advised two years ago that their mum should consider moving into a home, but May had refused point blank, saying she could manage and that she would far prefer, when the time came, to die in her own home than to be incarcerated in a nursing home surrounded by old people she didn't know.

All they could do for the moment was try to be around as much as possible to help, and to keep things to a balanced routine that worked best. Her mum had a home help who came in three mornings a week and she went to the Silver Seniors Lunch Club every Thursday, which was held in Glenageary's local parish hall and was something May really enjoyed. Weekends they took turns, and once a month their brother Mark came up from Kilkenny and stayed with his mum for two nights.

Nina set the table then hurried upstairs to change before everyone arrived.

'Nina, what will you have?' Tom asked when she came back down. Her mum was ensconced in the armchair near the fire, enjoying a sherry, while Lizzie and Bill and Charley were downing gin and tonics. Her brother-in-law Myles, a teetotaller, was on his usual Ballygowan with ice and lemon.

'I'll have one of those too, please.'

Jack and his girlfriend, Pixie, came into the sitting room with bottles of chilled Corona in their hands.

'What are we eating?' Jack asked.

'Wait and see!' teased Nina, who was used to her son constantly enquiring about what he was going to be fed. At six foot three he always seemed to be ravenous.

'Any sign of Erin and that lovely boyfriend of hers yet?' asked her mother.

'No, Mum, they must have got delayed,' she said, going to check on the meal.

Erin arrived in a flurry of long legs encased in fine black leggings and knee-high boots, wearing a grey-and-orange striped top – or dress or whatever they called it – that picked up the colour of her long, glossy hair.

'Mum, sorry I'm a bit late, but I was hoping that Luke could make it too.'

'Where is he?' Tom asked.

'Stuck in London; he couldn't get back as all this evening's flights were grounded because of fog at Heathrow. I'm sorry.'

'All the more food for us!' crowed Jack.

'I'd prefer he was here,' Erin said, taking a swipe at her younger brother.

They all sat around the huge oak table in the kitchen as Nina and Tom served the meal. May insisted on sitting beside her granddaughter.

'I want to find out when she and this Luke fellow are getting engaged and married,' she said loudly. Ever since she had gone slightly deaf, May spoke that bit louder, unaware that everyone could overhear her conversations now.

'Granny, we are just going out – he's just my boyfriend,' Erin protested, embarrassed and saying a silent prayer of thanks that Luke was not sitting beside her.

'Have you seen a ring yet?'

Nina and Lizzie couldn't help themselves and were in stitches laughing as poor Erin tried to handle her grandmother.

'Your grandfather took me to Weir's. He spent about four months of his salary on buying me this.' She showed the gold ring with its two diamonds and central sapphire to Erin. 'But it was worth every penny because I still wear it . . . never take it off me, and I might have forgotten some things but I will never forget Harry and this ring.'

'It's a lovely engagement ring, Granny, but Luke and I are not at that stage yet,' Erin stumbled on.

Uncle Bill and Charley regaled them with details of a trip they had just taken to Hong Kong, Singapore and Australia.

'We wanted to mark Charley's sixtieth birthday,' said Bill, 'and it was a trip we both wanted to do. We have friends in

Hong Kong and Sydney, so it was great. Exhausting going long-haul, but we both loved it!'

'Pixie and I are hoping to go to Oz when I finish my exams in the summer,' announced Jack.

Nina caught Tom's eye. This was the first time they had heard any mention of this from their son.

'Are you going on holiday?' asked Myles as he passed around the asparagus dish.

'No, we hope to go for a year and do that whole down-under thing!' laughed blonde-haired Pixie, squeezing Jack's hand. 'We've both got lots of friends out there, so it should be good fun!'

'Half the country is out there,' laughed Charley, 'judging by the number of young Irish people we met on our travels. They were everywhere . . . and they all seemed to be getting plenty of work and enjoying it.'

Nina got Jack to help her clear away the plates. He seemed besotted with this pretty Pixie of a girl, with her short, white-blonde hair and pretty face, and was obviously planning to spend the next year of his life on the other side of the world with her.

The butter icing was perfect, thought Nina, as she put ten candles on the top of the birthday cake. Lighting them, she signalled to Tom to dim the lights on their side of the room as she carried the cake over to where Erin was sitting and everyone sang

> 'Happy birthday to you,
> Happy birthday to you,
> Happy birthday, dear Erin . . .'

Their daughter's face was so happy as she blew out the candles and thanked everyone for coming. She is such a beautiful girl, thought Nina – beautiful not only on the outside, but also on the inside where it matters most.

They finished up about midnight. Jack and Pixie had already gone and got the DART to town to Pixie's place. Erin had decided to stay the night, while Myles offered to drive everyone else home.

'Mum, it was such a lovely night,' Erin said, hugging her. 'Thank you.'

'And thank you, Erin, for being such a good daughter,' Nina said, kissing her goodnight.

Lying in bed beside Tom, Nina couldn't sleep.

'You did hear what Jack said about going to Australia with Pixie?' she asked.

'Yes, I did,' said Tom patiently, 'like everyone else at the table.'

'Did you know anything about this? Had he said anything to you?'

'Nina, nearly every young person in Ireland is talking about emigrating or going to Australia or America or Canada . . . That's the way it is because there are no jobs here for them. You know that from all our friends. Why would you think it would be any different for Jack than all the other guys in his class?'

'I don't want him to go,' she said defiantly.

'Well we can't stand in his way or stop him,' Tom sighed, turning to face her. 'Jack'll go away, but he will come back, just wait and see . . .'

'What if he doesn't?'

'He will.'

'I couldn't bear it.' Nina was so upset. 'I couldn't bear to lose him.'

'Nina, we don't own them. Jack is twenty-three years old and Erin is twenty-six . . . . They have to make lives of their own. Erin is very keen on this Luke fellow – who's to say he won't end up working in London and then so might she?'

'Tom Harris, don't you dare upset me any more!' she pleaded as she slipped into the reassuring curve of her husband's arms.

Chapter Four

ERIN COULDN'T BELIEVE IT — LUKE WAS TAKING HER TO THE fanciest restaurant in Dublin. 'I told you that I'd make it up to you for missing your birthday dinner with your folks the other night,' he laughed, 'and I'm the kind of guy who keeps his promises.'

It had been a nightmare getting ready to go out, as Nikki had hogged the bathroom for nearly half an hour and Erin and Claire had been forced to beg the guys next door if they could use their bathroom. Next time they rented somewhere they were getting at least two bathrooms! As the doormen let them inside Gilbert's, the French restaurant, and she saw the style of the place, Erin thanked heaven she had decided to put on her new jade-coloured Karen Millen dress. Most of the fashionable couples were a good bit older than them and obviously wealthier too.

'Are you sure you can afford this?' she whispered to Luke. The Michelin-starred restaurant had a reputation for being super-expensive.

'Don't worry — I got a great bonus last week!' he grinned.

The waiter led them to a table near the window and was so attentive that Erin had to try to keep a serious face. The menu was incredible and it took ages for them both to decide exactly what they would like to eat, with the waiter taking great care to explain everything they wanted to know about the dishes that were on offer. Erin went for a mixture of seafood that included lobster, crab, Dublin Bay prawns and salmon, served with some kind of oyster foam; it was absolutely delicious. Luke ordered a really good wine and the waiter kept their glasses constantly topped up as they chatted away. One course followed after another: pork belly, seared tuna, champagne and elderflower mousse, and a berry tart. Neither of them could believe it as seamlessly they were presented with each gourmet dish.

'This place is amazing,' she said. 'Thank you for bringing me here.'

'Erin, I always want to do things to please you and make you happy,' he said softly, taking her hand. 'You know that.'

She nodded. Over the past few weeks their relationship had been getting more serious . . . they both knew it. Luke was becoming more and more a part of her life and she was structuring what she wanted to do around him, as his work schedule was kind of crazy. He was commuting back and forward to London a lot and it looked like this was going to become a regular feature.

'I'm back there Wednesday,' he said, sipping an Irish coffee.

'But I got tickets for us to go and see the Frames in Vicar Street.'

'I won't be here – maybe you can bring one of the girls or sell them on the internet?' he suggested.

'I'll bring Lilly from work. She's a massive fan and was

saying the other day that all the tickets were sold out and she couldn't get one.'

'There you go – no harm done!'

Erin tried to hide her disappointment. She had to accept that if she had a boyfriend with a high-flying career who could afford to take her to Gilbert's for dinner, then she couldn't expect him to be around all the time.

'Hey, let's get a last drink and then head to Club 55!' he suggested. 'I think Ronan and a few of the guys from the office are going there later.'

'Why don't we just head for your place or my place instead?' she suggested.

'I've had a hectic week, Erin – I just feel like blowing off a bit of steam. Besides, I want to show off my sexy girlfriend in her pretty dress on the dance floor.'

Erin laughed. He was such a bloody charmer . . .

The night club was packed and they had to push through the crowds. Erin would have been happy to stay at a romantic table at the rear of the club near the door, but Luke took her hand and guided her towards the area where his friends Ronan and Conall and Ritchie were sitting with their girlfriends. Michelle, Ronan's girlfriend, was nice and immediately said hello to Erin, but Conall was going out with an absolute wagon who was some kind of celebrity model who was on the new Dunne's Stores ad and thought she was Kate Moss!

They ordered some more wine and chatted for a while, then they danced, though there was barely room to stand and the floor was so sticky Erin's shoes felt glued to it.

'Let's get out of here!' Luke said eventually, so they hopped in a taxi to Grand Canal Square, where he shared an apartment with Dan, a guy he'd gone to college with. Tonight they had the place to themselves, and Erin was glad that they could finally be together without lots of people around. She loved his apartment, which was really streamlined and kind of masculine, with expensive designer couches and leather chairs and a massive glass dining table. Luke had the bigger bedroom and, as they stood looking out at the iconic Daniel Libeskind-designed theatre building with its giant red rods lighting up the night sky, Erin relaxed into his arms, feeling the broad width of his palm running down her back.

The next morning they had toasted bagels, fruit juice and coffee in bed as they read the Sunday papers.

'My folks have asked me to Sunday lunch later. Do you want to come?'

Erin had met the Gallaghers twice. His parents were hard going, but she supposed she had better make some effort to get to know them better.

'Sure – that will be nice. But I have to go home and change before we go there.'

Chapter Five

ERIN WAS SO ENGROSSED IN THE RE–DESIGN OF THE FRONT page of a brochure for a new hotel that was due to open in three weeks' time that she hadn't realized it was almost seven o'clock until she noticed Declan packing up his Apple Mac and grabbing his jacket to head home.

Work was scarce at the moment and she really appreciated Monika and Declan keeping her on and giving her projects like this to work on. The marketing budget for the Mount Clement's launch was cut to the bone, but that didn't mean the client didn't deserve their best effort. They were doing decent-quality printing and Erin wanted a glossy brochure that would reflect the high-spec build. There were also menus, guest advice leaflets, maps, wedding package sets to be done. She had spent two days down around the hotel with her camera and had got some great ideas in terms of the important design elements which she would use to create an instantly recognizable logo for the Mount Clement, the gorgeous old summer house in Kerry which was now about to become a five-star destination. She and Luke had stayed there and both really enjoyed it, Luke disappearing off to play a bit of golf while she worked and had discussions with David Mountjoy, the owner, about the exact image he hoped to create. It was a magical place, and David and his wife Heather deserved to see their hotel do well.

She checked her phone. There was a message from her flatmate Nikki: *'See you two Musketeers at home soon.'*

Erin had been thinking about heading to Dundrum to do a bit of late-night shopping, but she'd give that a miss and head home to the apartment instead. Girlie nights with her two flatmates on a Wednesday, with pizza or pasta and a bottle of wine, were far more important. The rest of the week the three of them always seemed to be rushing around and often didn't get to talk to each other for days on end. Her friends were important and she knew that, no matter how busy she was in work, she had to make time for them.

Funny – Nikki had been acting strangely for the past few weeks and both Erin and Claire were worried about her. She was barely eating and had got even thinner than usual. Claire said she could hear Nikki throwing up sometimes. Maybe she had anorexia? Whatever it was, it was definitely getting worse. Eating disorders were a nightmare to deal with, but if Nikki needed help, they would both do everything they could for her.

On her way home Erin grabbed a bottle of Sauvignon Blanc, a big bag of tortilla chips and three fudge brownies for dessert. Nikki normally loved them – if she didn't take the brownies, then there was definitely something seriously wrong with her.

Claire was in the kitchen already cooking when she got in.

'Smells good,' she said, grabbing a few slices of ham.

'Hey – that's for with our meal! I'm doing risotto with prosciutto and asparagus tips,' Claire explained, moving the chopping board out of the way of temptation. As she dumped the wine in the fridge to chill, Erin thought just how lucky she was, sharing with someone who was almost a professional chef.

'Where's Nikki?'

'She's in the shower.'

'Do you think we should say something to her tonight?'

'Erin, it's the perfect chance. We have to try to find out what the hell is going on with her.'

Erin sighed. She hated confrontation. She and Nikki and Claire had been friends for years, since they were all kids. She'd hung out with Claire since they were five years old. They'd started school together and grown up together and shared so many things. Nikki had become the third Musketeer when they had gone to St Louise's Secondary School and ended up sitting in the row of desks beside each other at the back of the class. The lunatic Irish teacher would give them constant detentions and bad marks for always talking and messing.

'You three!' she would say angrily. 'How can you still be talking?'

'Cos we're best friends,' they'd retort.

Best friends always talked and messed and hung out to-gether. They were now in their mid-twenties and still hung out together and shared the second-floor apartment on Sandymount Road. Best friends helped each other out and stood by each other and supported each other. Claire was right – they had to get this sorted.

Erin pulled on leggings and a grey knitted sweater and went into the living room. Nikki came in a few minutes later, her hair still damp.

'I got us two DVDs on my way home.' Erin glanced at Nikki, seeing just how washed-out and exhausted she looked as she curled up with a few cushions on the couch. Maybe Claire was right, there really was something up with her.

'Food's ready!'

Claire had excelled herself with the creamy risotto. 'I'm entering you into Master Chef Ireland next year,' said Erin, as she sprinkled some more parmesan on to her plate. 'You are such a brilliant cook.'

'Erin, it's just a hobby,' Claire smiled, 'and that's the way it is staying. I think it relaxes me after a hard day doing massages and exercises on my patients.'

Nikki was quiet and they were only halfway through the meal when she got up from the table and ran to the bathroom.

'I told you,' whispered Claire, concerned.

Nikki returned and sat down, but said nothing, pushing the remnants of her meal away. Erin cleared the plates and made coffee, bringing in the fudge brownies for them all. Nikki left hers untouched on her plate.

Erin couldn't hide her worry. What the hell was going on with her? They had to say something.

'Are you okay, Nikki?'

'What do you mean?' she asked defensively.

'You're not eating your brownie.'

'It's only a brownie. Anyway, I'm full.'

'Is that really true?' asked Claire. 'I heard you this morning and last night.'

'Are you spying on me, is that it?' Nikki shouted angrily.

'No, we're not,' replied Erin. 'We're both just worried about you.'

'Nikki, what's going on?' demanded Claire.

They were waiting for a tirade of anger and abuse, but

31

instead were greeted with utter abject misery as Nikki began to cry.

'I'm pregnant . . .'

'What?'

'I'm fecking pregnant! I'm twelve weeks gone.'

'Are you sure?'

'Of course I'm bloody sure! I did the stupid test thing three times to check. It's positive!'

Erin didn't know what to say.

'You're going to have a baby, Nikki! That's great news,' Claire said, trying to sound positive about it.

'When is the baby due?' Erin asked, attempting to hide her own shock.

'September. I still can't believe it! It's so fecking unfair,' gulped Nikki, her breath coming in shuddery, shaky gasps. 'I think it's going to be around mid-September.'

'Haven't you booked in with a doctor or hospital yet?'

'No,' she said firmly.

'How does Conor feel about being a dad?' probed Claire.

'I haven't told him yet,' she said, burying her head in her hands. 'To be honest, I don't know how he'll take it.'

Conor Lynch and Nikki had only been going out for about six months. They got on well together and Conor was a fun type of guy, loving nothing better than a few pints at the weekend before hitting a night club. However, Erin couldn't imagine him being a dad. Well, not for a few years yet! He was repeating exams and always seemed skint, paying back some loan or other.

'We're so pleased for you, Nikki, honest we are,' said Erin softly, giving her a big hug. 'I can just imagine you with the most gorgeous little baby.'

'I wonder will it be a boy or a girl?' laughed Claire.

'You'll be a wonderful mum, wait till you see,' Erin assured her, worried by Nikki's expression.

'I'm not ready to be a mum,' she wailed hysterically. 'Not yet.'

'But you love babies and they love you,' said Claire consolingly. 'You're great with kids.'

'They are other people's kids,' Nikki protested. 'It doesn't mean I want one of my own, not right now.'

'What do you mean, Nikki?' Erin was confused. What was Nikki trying to tell them?

'I mean that I might not have this baby,' she said, tears welling in her eyes. 'I really don't know if I want to do this. Having a baby changes everything!'

'Not have it?' Erin couldn't believe what she was hearing.

'I need to think about it. Talk to Conor.'

'What about your mum and dad?'

'What about them? This is my decision, not theirs,' she said angrily.

Erin was fond of Ruth and Malachy Byrne, Nikki's parents, and suspected they would be wonderful grandparents.

'Nikki, everyone cares about you. We'll all help out, honest we will.'

'You won't be on your own,' Claire added.

'We'll help you, Nikki,' they promised together. 'We're your friends.'

'I know,' said Nikki. 'I know that I have the best friends in the world. But I just don't know what to do. I'm only hanging on to my job by a thread and if Fergus O'Neill hears I'm pregnant he'll go mad.'

'Your boss can't fire you because you're pregnant,' Claire reminded her. 'That's discrimination.'

'He could make things very awkward for me.'

Claire went and opened another bottle of wine. She stopped pouring when she came to Nikki's glass.

'Maybe you shouldn't be drinking?' She hesitated. Nikki had already downed about half of the first bottle.

'Of all nights, I need a drink tonight, Claire. Don't be such a goody-two-shoes,' Nikki protested angrily. Claire refilled her glass.

'How are you feeling?' asked Erin.

'Crap. Tired, exhausted. I can't sleep. I can't think properly, and to top it all I keep puking. Not just in the morning but all through the day and night. It's a fecking nightmare.'

Erin reached automatically for her friend.

'Why did this have to happen?' bawled Nikki. 'Why am I the one to get pregnant? It must have been when I got that food poisoning a few weeks back from that chicken sweet and sour we got from the takeaway.'

Erin remembered both Claire and Nikki had been violently sick for twenty-four hours afterwards. Thank heaven she'd ordered a prawn stir-fry.

'It's not fair,' Nikki said.

'I know,' soothed Erin.

'When my period was late I kept hoping that it was nothing – stress, anxiety, dates mixed up . . . But then I did a pregnancy test. I nearly died! I kept thinking that it must be some kind of mistake, or that I had done something stupid with the test. But the results were all the same – positive. I'm pregnant whether I like it or not.'

They sat up curled up on the couch and squashy armchair for hours, talking and going over Nikki's various options. Claire was playing devil's advocate as Nikki went from wanting to have the baby to wanting to not have it. Have the baby! Don't have the baby!

'You have a boyfriend. A good job. You're healthy. You want to have kids.'

'You have an on–off relationship that might not last.'

'You are a workaholic and having a kid will make a massive dent in your career ambitions.'

'You are always stressed and tired.'

'You are definitely not ready to have kids yet.'

'Nobody knows about this baby except for the two of you,' Nikki said drunkenly, 'so nobody will know if I go and have a termination. I'll just say I'm going to London for the weekend and then – Abracadabra! Like magic, the baby is gone. *Phewt* – disappeared.'

Erin didn't know what to say. Claire, half asleep, was actually agreeing to go to London if Nikki really wanted someone with her to go to a clinic.

They went through three bottles of wine, a half bottle of vodka and some duty-free peach schnapps that was in the back of their drinks cabinet before eventually collapsing into their beds.

Erin could hardly sleep a wink. She kept thinking about Nikki and the baby – if there ever was even going to be a baby. The way Nikki was talking, there was a good chance that she was heading to London in a few weeks' time for a quick and easy termination, her problem solved. Who could blame her? But Erin felt especially uneasy about it. She was adopted, and being adopted changed everything . . .

Her own mother probably hadn't wanted her either, but at least she'd had the guts to go through with the pregnancy. If her

mother had taken the easy option, she wouldn't be here – Erin
Grace Harris wouldn't even exist. At least her birth mother had
given her the chance for life. Whoever she was, she'd chosen to
go ahead with the pregnancy and then had made the decision
to give Erin up to be adopted, agreeing for her to be handed
into the care of another woman and her husband to raise. She
was lucky! Her mum and dad had adopted her when she was
only a few months old.

She couldn't let Nikki go off to London and do something
that she would regret for the rest of her life. Getting rid of a
baby – how could anyone get over that? It could destroy Nikki.

Being a single mum wasn't easy, but Nikki would have so
much support and help from everyone, and besides, Conor
might actually be okay about becoming a dad.

Erin tossed and turned most of the night. She found
herself thinking about her own past – something she rarely
did; thinking of some strange young woman who had faced a
similar dilemma almost twenty-seven years ago and had made
her decision.

Hearing Nikki getting sick at about six thirty, she made her
a cup of tea and a slice of plain, buttered toast and brought it
into the bedroom to her.

'How are you feeling?'

'Crap.' Nikki looked awful.

'Did you sleep?'

Nikki shook her head.

'I couldn't sleep either,' Erin admitted. 'Don't get rid of the
baby, Nikki. This baby is part of you – a little you. I don't
want to miss seeing him or her crawling around or learning to
walk or talk. Please have your baby! So what if it's not the right
time, or things with you and Conor don't work out? You have

us! And the rest of your friends, and your family. We'll all help you, I promise.'

Nikki stretched out her skinny white arms and caught Erin in a big hug.

'I'm scared,' she admitted. 'But you're right, Erin, this is my baby and I just have to get used to it. I feel awful, but I'm not going to go anywhere. I couldn't do it . . .'

'You'll book into a hospital?' asked Erin.

'Yes. And I'll tell Conor tonight, and then go and tell Mum and Dad at the weekend.'

Erin was so relieved.

'What are you two up to?' interrupted Claire, hungover, in the doorway in her pyjamas, brown hair standing on end.

'Nikki's going to have the baby!'

'I know.' She yawned groggily.

'No – she's really going to have the baby and keep it!'

'What? Oh thank heaven!' Claire ran and hugged the two of them.

Excited, talking and planning, they forgot the time and got dressed for work in an utter panic.

'I look absolutely shite,' said Claire. 'I'm dying with a hang-over.'

'I feel like a zombie,' admitted Nikki. 'Do I look like one?'

'Yeah, we all look a bit like the walking dead!' agreed Erin as they left the apartment and made their way slowly to work.

Chapter Six

ERIN AND CLAIRE HAD GONE FOR A WALK DOWN ALONG SANDY-mount Strand. It was a beautiful evening, really warm, as they strolled along the seafront overlooking Dublin Bay. Nikki had finally gone to meet Conor and tell him about the baby.

'He'll drop me the minute he hears about it,' she sobbed hysterically before she left. Secretly, they both expected that she was right, but they made her calm down and re-do her eye make-up, and then wear one of her hottest dresses. Nikki was gorgeous – how could any guy resist her, even if she *was* pregnant?

'What do you think will happen?' Erin asked.

'God knows!' said Claire. 'Conor really likes Nikki and maybe he won't mind . . . Otherwise he is going to freak out and like most guys just walk away. We see it every day in the surgery.'

'I saw some statistic that almost twenty per cent of kids in Ireland are being raised by single parents, and they somehow seem to manage.'

'Would you do it? Have a baby on your own?'

'Yes,' said Erin. 'I definitely would. My baby . . . would be my baby, whether the father was involved or not.'

Erin had to admit that Nikki's pregnancy had sparked something she had never expected: it had made her think about her natural mother – the girl who had given birth to her and then had given her up to be adopted. It must have been desperate for her having to make such a choice.

They walked for about an hour. There were no phone messages from Nikki, so, turning back, they headed home.

They sat up waiting for her and were so relieved when she finally arrived in. She looked shattered, red-eyed, awful.

'What happened?' they asked in unison.

'What we expected . . . Conor is a little shit and wants nothing to do with the baby, but I told him that I was putting his name down on the birth cert for father's name whether he wanted me to or not!'

'Oh Nikki – we're so sorry!'

'Don't be! Imagine me wasting any more of my life going out with that creep?'

'Were you talking to him all this time?'

'No. We had nothing to say to each other, only shout. So I went over to Mum and Dad's. I was in a right old state!'

'You told them?'

'Yes . . . They were a bit shocked, but they were great. Mum is all happy that she is going to be a granny – most of her friends already are – and Dad said if the baby's father won't step up to the mark, then the baby's grandfather will . . .'

'Oh Nikki . . . I knew that they'd be great about it.'

'Dad says that I have to tell them in work on Monday.

He says that I have to stop hiding things, for the baby's sake.'

Erin and Claire were so relieved that Nikki was finally coming to terms with having a baby.

Chapter Seven

NINA GAZED OUT THE WINDOW AS TOM AND BILL AND JACK and Erin all were busy at the bottom of the garden. Today was Boat Day – the day Tom moved his beloved old boat down from the rundown coach house that served as a boat house to Dunlaoghaire Harbour, where it would be moored for the rest of the year, until it was lifted up again next winter. It was an all-hands-on-deck event as they lifted the heavy boat up on the tow equipment and attached it to the back of the Volvo, then tried to tow the whole thing down a windy, narrow back road without taking their wall and the neighbours' walls with them. Nina's job was to make endless cups of tea, soup and sandwiches for the hardy workers, and then have a big warming stew for when they all returned from having the first sail of the year and ensuring that the boat was safely moored in its annual berth.

She had learned to steer well clear of all the manoeuvring involved and instead enjoyed reading the Sunday newspapers flung on the couch beside her and sipping at her coffee. She loved days like this, when the family were all together, Tom and the kids in their jackets and gear, with even Bailey, their Labrador, out in the garden, caught up in the middle of it all as they finally managed to hoist the boat up on its wheels and got ready to move it down to the nearby fishing harbour. The work and fresh air would give them all an appetite. She was happy to stay here, content and cosy, keeping an eye on the food and just relaxing.

She must have dozed off, because when she woke Bailey was pushing to sit down on the rug in front of the fire and Tom was throwing a log of wood on the grate.

'It's windy out there,' he laughed, 'but we got her launched and took her for a bit of a run, then we got her moored.'

Jack looked wrecked, with bloodshot eyes, his skin sweaty and pale.

'He's seriously hungover, Mum,' teased Erin.

'We were all at Danny's farewell do. He's heading to Perth on Monday. He thinks he's got a job lined up there.'

'Well, I hope it all works out,' Nina smiled, knowing that Jack would really miss Danny, one of his oldest schoolfriends.

'You'll be lost without him!' interjected Erin, flinging herself on the couch beside Nina and grabbing the magazine part of the newspaper.

'How long till dinner?' yawned Jack.

'About thirty minutes,' Nina said, knowing full well that, like the dog, her son would be asleep in a few minutes.

She set the table in the kitchen and spooned out the stew on to their plates before calling the others to eat.

'Where's Luke this weekend?' she asked, as Erin helped to put the potatoes out in a bowl.

'Mum, he's my boyfriend,' she laughed, 'but that doesn't

mean that we are tied together . . . He's just gone to Liverpool
for the weekend to a match with a few guys from work.'

Nina bit her tongue. In her day couples spent all their time
together, but nowadays they seemed to live their lives separately,
each doing their own thing with their own friends half the time
and being together when it suited them. She and Tom both
liked Luke Gallagher. He was kind and charming, and fitted
in well with their family. But it was up to Erin to decide his
importance in her life, not them.

Finding the right partner was, to Nina's mind, the most
important thing in life. She was so lucky to have met Tom
and fallen madly in love with him on almost their first date.
The feeling, luckily, was mutual and after a pretty passionate
romance they had got married within about eighteen months,
once Tom had passed all his exams and accepted a job in
Grattan's Engineering Company. They had lived in a small
house in Harold's Cross for the first few years of their marriage,
until Tom got promoted. Like all couples, they had had their
fair share of ups and downs, joys and disappointments –
especially the heartache of discovering that they couldn't have
children, which had been an absolute blow to both of them.
But somehow they had managed to recover and decided to try
to adopt a baby if they couldn't have one of their own. First
Erin came along and then their little boy, Jack, both welcomed
into their lives with so much love. They became a family – a
proper family. She and Tom were both still mad about each
other and theirs was a good marriage. She had watched friends'
marriages fall apart over the past few years as their families
grew up. Even her best friend Vonnie and her husband, Simon,
had got divorced eighteen months ago and now barely spoke to
each other. It was heartbreaking.

*   *   *

Bill had brought along a bottle of their favourite Merlot and they all sat down around the table, Jack sticking to a large glass of iced water and Erin refusing any wine, grabbing a can of Sprite from the fridge instead, as she was driving. They ate and chatted easily about work and friends and all the news.

Erin told them all about the upcoming wedding of her best friend, Jenny, who was getting married in a castle in Cork in August and had all her friends demented with talking about budgets and costs and guest lists.

'I don't know why she and Shane just don't go off to some nice small place and get married with just the two families and a few friends, if they have no money. Who are they trying to impress?'

'You lot!' joked Nina. 'You all expect big weddings and dresses and bands, money or no money.'

'No we don't. Karl and Emma are getting married in the Registry Office in ten weeks and having the reception in Mere Zou, that lovely French restaurant on Stephen's Green, afterwards.'

'Good for them,' said Tom. 'I'm glad to see someone you know having a bit of sense.'

'Well, we all think it's great because we don't have to go and fork out to stay in a hotel and spend a fortune,' she admitted.

Nina smiled and wondered what would happen when Erin and Jack eventually decided to settle down and marry. Lord knows what kind of wedding Jack would want – probably something involving surfboards and beaches, if he had his way, whereas Erin was definitely more traditional.

Tom hushed her when she talked about Erin and Luke and the future. 'Give them a chance, Nina. They're young yet –

don't be letting that big heart of yours run away with you. Erin will make her own mind up when the time is right, like she always does!'

After dinner Tom and Jack and Bill sloped back to the living room to watch the replay of some rugby match and the rugby commentary from a panel of experts. Erin and Nina stayed in the kitchen, tidying up and having another mug of coffee each.

'Mum, I need to talk to you about something,' said Erin slowly. 'It's something I really need to know about.'

Nina could feel the heat of the mug against her skin as she took in the serious expression on Erin's face.

'I'm twenty-six years old and I need to know about myself . . . about before you and Dad adopted me. I suppose seeing Nikki pregnant and going to have her baby has made me think about it more—'

'Erin, we've told you everything we know already,' Nina said honestly, trying to disguise how perturbed she suddenly felt. 'Your dad and I have never tried to hide the fact that you and Jack are adopted. We've always been upfront with the two of you about it.'

'I know, Mum, but please tell me again,' pleaded her daughter.

'Why?' whispered Nina, trying to control herself.

'I don't know why – but I just need to know about the time when I was born and given up and about my birth mother. I've never really asked you and Dad too much about it before, but Mum, I really want to know. I'm entitled to know.'

'Of course,' said Nina, feeling the blood in her veins slow so much that it seemed almost frozen. She had always known this day would come, when Erin or Jack would demand to know more than what they had already told them – but not now, out of the blue after a perfect Sunday dinner! She wondered what had brought on this sudden desire to discover the past.

'Erin, it's only normal to be curious – totally normal to want to know more about your birth and what happened and how your dad and I adopted you.'

'And about my mother,' she insisted.

Nina tried not to show the pain inflicted by the dagger of her daughter's word – mother.

She was Erin's mother – no one else was. She loved her more than anyone else in the world did. She was the one who had cared for her from the day that Erin was handed into her arms – nothing and no one could change that. She was the one who had fed her, changed her, winded her, helped her to learn to talk and walk and read. Suffered endless sleepless nights when Erin wouldn't go to sleep or had nightmares or was sick. She had put up with toddler tantrums, and boldness, and teenage angst, along with the glorious hugs and cuddles and stories and the constant utter joy of having a beautiful, intelligent daughter as she went from toddler to schoolgirl to college to becoming this bright, confident young woman sitting across from her, building a life of her own.

'Erin, I'm not sure what more I can tell you than what you already know,' said Nina slowly, sitting down and trying not to give in to the rolling wave of despondency she felt coming towards her. 'Your mother was single. They told us that she was about twenty years of age when you were born. She wasn't from Dublin; the agency said she was from the country, but they wouldn't tell us where. She was from a good family, well educated, Catholic. She was a good person by all accounts, and the social worker said that she was very torn about her eventual decision to give you up.'

Erin sat hunched at the table, her chin on her hands, intense, listening.

'There must be something more, something more they told you, Mum. Think back.'

'I am trying to think back, Erin.' Nina racked her brain trying to remember. 'But it's a long time. Things were different then. There wasn't the openness there is now and obviously your mother wanted discretion, and the adoption agencies always guaranteed that. We all had to respect what your mother wanted. No contact is what she said, and that's what the agency told us.'

'That's crap!' exclaimed Erin. 'I'm a person too and entitled to know who I am and biologically how I got here. I'm fed up with all the bureaucracy and secrecy and claptrap. I know it's not your and Dad's fault, Mum, but surely I'm old enough to know who I am and about my biological mother.'

'Of course,' said Nina softly. 'Of course you are entitled. Your dad and I will do nothing to stop you and in fact are a hundred per cent behind you, whatever you want, Erin. I'm sure most young people in your situation want to know more about themselves,' she continued. 'It's only natural.'

'Thanks, Mum,' said Erin, flinging her arms around her. 'I knew you'd understand that totally. You are the best mum ever – this is the best family ever! But I still have to know about her, do you understand, Mum?'

'I understand, love . . .'

Nina could see the relief in Erin's eyes that she hadn't kicked up a fuss or got upset or anything. For years she had been waiting for this to happen, and she thanked heaven that she had somehow managed to retain her composure instead of breaking down and begging Erin to forget about it and be happy with the family she had.

'Mum, I've actually set up an appointment with the adoption agency and I am meeting someone there next week.'

'Well, hopefully they will be able to help you to get the information you need.'

'Mum, you've been great. Really great. Thanks.'

Nina said nothing, busying herself tidying the kitchen and packing the dishwasher, relieved when Erin disappeared off to join Tom and Jack.

Erin was going to find her mother – her real mother. Nina, upset, suspected that their relationship would probably never be the same once Erin and her natural mother were reunited. Where would she and Tom fit in? Just temporary substitute parents? She didn't think that she could bear the pain of it.

Chapter Eight

ERIN HAD SET UP THE APPOINTMENT TO MEET MARIAN KELLY at five o'clock. It was the adoption agency social worker's last appointment of the day and Erin had asked Declan if she could leave a bit early. Declan was such a great boss, and always tended to acquiesce with whatever his staff wanted. Whenever the time came to leave De Berg O'Leary Graphics, she knew that she would really miss the pleasant work environment that Declan and Monika had created.

The traffic was awful, but luckily when she arrived Marian was still with a previous client. Erin sat in the antiquated waiting room of the rather ramshackle Georgian building, skimming through ancient *Hello!* and *Homes & Gardens* magazines, trying not to be anxious. She was an adult, sane and normal, who was employed and was a good citizen, and she was entitled to information about her birth and its circumstances. Still, she could feel her stomach tumbling with nerves, which was so stupid. She had done nothing wrong, she repeated to herself over and over again.

'Nice to meet you,' said Marian, introducing herself. The social worker was a lot younger and more stylish than Erin had expected. 'Would you like a tea or coffee?'

'Coffee would be great, thanks.'

The office itself had been modernized – new desk and chair, all brown leather and cream, a tall vase of purple iris adding a splash of colour.

'Now, tell me what I can do for you,' said Marian kindly, sitting across from her.

'I want to find out about my mother – my birth mother.'

'Do you want to trace her? Is that it? Do you want to try to meet her?'

'I'm not really sure at this stage,' admitted Erin. 'But I do want to find out more about who I am and about my background. It's so strange – I know very little about what happened back then, the time I was born, and why my mother made the decision she did.'

'Do you disapprove of what she did?'

'I don't know. As I said, I don't know her circumstances or what happened to her. They were different times and maybe there was a lot of stigma compared to now. She probably felt that she couldn't keep me . . . I don't know . . .'

'Adoption and being adopted raise so many issues, and I understand how difficult it must be for someone who is an adoptee to have so little knowledge of their birth parents, no family tree, no history of their own, as such,' Marian agreed. 'But back in the nineteen forties and fifties and early sixties, being an unmarried mother in Ireland and other places was a total social taboo. Mothers were ostracized, often put in mother-and-baby homes, their babies considered illegitimate and treated as if they were second-class citizens. No wonder the girls wanted it all kept secret and so many gave their babies up for adoption.'

'But I was born in the eighties,' interrupted Erin, 'not then. Mothers surely could keep their babies if they really wanted to?'

'So why didn't your mother keep you? Is that what you're asking?'

'Yes,' said Erin, holding her breath as the question that had squatted like a big black stone somewhere deep inside her was finally revealed.

'Your mother had very valid reasons for giving you up, Erin, very valid. Things might have become far more liberal and tolerant and more open by then, but girls like your mother who found themselves with an unwanted pregnancy were still scared and alone and vulnerable. Many of them wanted to hide the pregnancy from their families or work colleagues and were faced with severe financial hardship in terms of trying to raise a child on their own. Single parenthood is an enormous challenge to take on and often it was felt it was better for the baby to be adopted by a loving family, a father and mother who really wanted a baby, rather than staying in a situation where often the mother was a young girl with little or no support and couldn't cope.'

'So I was one of those? My natural mother, for whatever reason, couldn't keep me and I ended up being adopted?'

'Yes,' said Marian, 'your mother made that decision. She wanted what was best for you at that time.'

'It did work out. My parents are great, and they adopted me and my brother, Jack, so it hasn't been a big deal ever for me about being adopted.'

'Well that's good to know, and believe me, most adoptions have worked out.'

'I really love my mum and dad,' Erin confided. 'They are the best in the world and have been so good to me and Jack. We are a very close family.'

'That's nice to hear,' smiled the social worker. 'Do your parents know that you were coming to meet me?'

'Of course.'

'That's good! So, Erin, tell me how you think I can help you.'

'I suppose I'm curious about it all – about her and where she's from, and about what kind of family she came from. Also, I've always looked so different from my mum and dad and their families that I kind of wonder, am I like her? Do I look like her or my biological father? I've allergies – did I get that from her? Most of the time I don't think about it, but now I'm getting older I suppose it matters more.'

'We find most adoptees come to us when they are getting married themselves or having a child, or facing some kind of pivotal choice in their own life.'

'I just want to know,' Erin insisted.

'What information have you already received?'

'Very little, only what Mum and Dad have told me – but they seem to know scarcely anything.'

'It was always the policy with adoption to protect the privacy of everyone concerned; that was paramount. The birth mothers wanted it and the families adopting children did too. They didn't want someone turning up on their doorstep a few years later, destroying their family and demanding the right to get their child back, or wanting to become suddenly involved in their lives. So you can see how delicate it all is.'

'I understand,' agreed Erin, 'I really do, but I want to find out more about my birth mother. I think I am sensible enough not to expect too much, but Marian, I do deserve to know at least who I am!'

'Do you have a birth certificate?'

'Yes, it's the copy of the one my parents have, which shows them as my parents and the date I was adopted. I also have my baptismal cert, but to be honest these aren't much use for me finding out about my mother.'

'I see.' Marian looked at the papers. 'So you want me to help you with the rest?'

'Yes. You are the professional and my parents both felt I should do this correctly and through the proper channels.'

'Very wise. So many people rush off and put two and two together and get five – they get it all wrong.'

'I don't want that. I've waited this long . . . I can wait a bit more.'

'That's good, Erin, because there are no quick answers.'

'What can you tell me?' Erin asked, looking at the file sitting on the social worker's desk.

'Well, you know that you were born on the tenth of March 1985. You were born in the National Maternity Hospital at five a.m. and weighed seven pounds and seven ounces. By all accounts a perfectly healthy baby girl.'

'I didn't even know that.'

'Your mother was single, and was twenty years old when you were born. She gave a Dublin address where she was staying, but the social worker at the time noted that she was from the country.'

'Do you know where?'

'No. We don't have that information. Probably she didn't want to divulge that.'

'Is there anything else?'

'Her occupation was listed as student, so I presume that she was studying at some college in the city.'

'What about my father? What happened to him?'

'There was no name registered – that was almost the norm then. But his occupation was listed as student also.'

'I see. Is there any other family mentioned?'

'Not officially, but the social worker in her notes said that her mother was dead and her father was a very strict Catholic and would be unsupportive to her situation.'

'Do you have her name?'

'Her name is Kate.'

Erin smiled. Kate. She liked it.

'Can I get a copy of my proper original birth cert?'

'Of course. I'll organize that for you.'

'Marian, thanks. At least I know more than I did before. My mum and dad just heard that she was temporarily living in Dublin and presumed that she was from the country and didn't want anyone to guess that she was having me.'

'Every bit of information we get about ourselves in these situations is precious.'

'If I did want to make contact with her – write to her or even try to meet her – how would I go about it?' asked Erin, suddenly curious about this Kate, who had only been a student when she was born.

'The best way is to go through us. We often suggest that you write a letter to your birth mother and then see if she will write to you before we progress things any further.'

'But I thought you didn't know where she is?'

'We have ways of finding people and making contact with them. We have lots of experience in bringing birth mothers and their grown-up children together, arranging for them to contact each other and often even to meet up and see each other.'

'Does it work?'

'It can be a bit difficult, but often it does. Seeing people reunited after such a long time can be very rewarding.'

'So what do I do?'

'If you want us to pass on a letter from you to your mother Kate, we will do that. However, we suggest no very personal details that would identify you, such as full names or addresses or telephone numbers, be used in the letter.'

'Why?'

'That's the way we work. We try to protect our client's privacy and yours. Many of the mothers have never told their husbands and families that they had a child, so discretion is needed.'

'I understand,' sighed Erin. 'Being adopted is such a major thing. Most people don't talk about it. A lot of my friends still don't even realize that I'm adopted.'

'That's what I mean, Erin – it is such a deeply personal issue for those affected by it.'

'Do girls still give up their babies?'

'Fortunately very few. It's such a hard thing for any woman to do. Single parenthood is a lot easier now. Most mothers have great support from family and friends and the state,' explained Marian.

'Well that's good!' smiled Erin, thinking of Nikki and her baby.

'The majority of the adoptions we handle now are overseas adoptions, as so few babies are given up by their birth mothers here in Ireland,' added Marian.

'If I write the letter . . . '

'You just send it in to me and I will do my best to get it to your mother. However, I cannot guarantee that she will respond to it – you do understand that?'

'Yes, but still it's worth trying.'

'I always advise take your time and don't expect too much.' The social worker passed her a card from the drawer. 'Here are my contact details if you need them.'

'Marian, thank you. You've given me so much of your time already and I really appreciate it.'

'All part of the job.'

'You know, I was dreading coming here today,' Erin admitted. 'I phoned a few times before and called into the office once a few years ago, and the person I dealt with made me feel like I had done something wrong or committed a crime!'

'There have been huge changes since then,' said Marian. 'Things have become far more open. Remember, if there is anything that I can do to help, please let me know.'

Back outside in the street, Erin felt relief wash over her. She had finally gone and done it, braved officialdom and all the red tape and begun to get some of the answers she desperately wanted. She was very curious about Kate now – and there was a real possibility that her curiosity would be satisfied.

Chapter Nine

ON WEDNESDAY ERIN GOT A COPY OF HER OFFICIAL BIRTH certificate from Marian Kelly in the post. Her hands were shaking when she opened it and spread it out on the table. This was a legal document stating officially who she was . . . Her mother's name, Kate Anne Flanagan, was written in loopy writing in one section, and 15 Granville Court, Rathfarnham, County Dublin, where she was staying when Erin was born, was written in another section.

Erin couldn't believe it, but her mother had registered her original birth name as Anna Mary Flanagan, whereas her parents had registered her as Erin Grace Harris. She had two totally different names on two birth certificates. It was bizarre. Anna Mary – that wasn't her . . . But a bit of paper said that she was Anna Mary Flanagan, daughter of Kate Anne Flanagan of Rathfarnham, County Dublin, and that she had been born on 10 March 1985 in the National Maternity Hospital, Dublin.

Obviously her mum and dad had changed her name when they adopted her . . . Maybe they didn't like the name Anna, or wanted to protect her identity in some way – or was it because her mum's brother Harry, who lived in Canada, had a daughter called Anna already? She hadn't a clue, but it was as if she had a double identity . . . a double life that she knew nothing about. It was intriguing.

She read and re-read the long certificate over and over again, hoping that it might reveal some other hidden piece of information. When Nikki and Claire came in she showed it to them.

'Very nice, Anna,' teased Claire.

'You must be so thrilled to finally have your proper birth cert – something all the rest of us just take for granted,' said Nikki, studying it.

'Yes.' She nodded dumbly as the girls hugged her. She'd been waiting for years to get this important document.

'Anna Mary Flanagan . . . It has a certain ring to it!'

'Shut up you two!' she giggled. 'That's my real name . . . well, the one she gave me.'

'You're Erin Harris,' said Claire firmly. 'This bit of paper can't change that and don't let it!'

Her mother's name was Kate, Kate Flanagan. Erin had no idea where she was living, or if she was even in Ireland. Was she married with a family? Maybe she had brothers and sisters? Erin couldn't put it from her mind and was distracted, unable to concentrate on anything. She decided to follow Marian Kelly's suggestion and write to her birth mother.

She spent hours and hours trying to compose a simple letter to Kate, a woman she didn't even know. Trying to find the right words to fill in for the twenty-six years of her life that this woman knew nothing about was almost impossible. She wanted the letter to be simple and direct and open – an invitation for her mother to establish contact with her if she wanted to. So she made it very clear that she felt no animosity or anger towards her and now, as her grown-up child, was ready to meet her. She drafted and re-drafted the letter again and again, trying to get the tone and the sense of it right. She printed it out so many times and then wondered if she should write it out longhand instead.

In it she told Kate about herself, her family and the things that she cared about and that made her happy. If nothing else, this letter would give her mother a good idea of how her life had panned out and the good family and education and up-bringing she had had.

Finally satisfied, she posted the letter on Friday morning on her way to work. She was so relieved that it was gone, and she wondered if she would ever hear back from Kate Flanagan.

Luke had arranged to meet up with her after work and when they met in Kehoe's pub on South Anne Street she bought him a pint.

'Drink is on me,' she smiled, passing him a pint of Heineken. 'I'm celebrating something.'

'What?'

'I've done something either very special or very crazy, and now I have to sit back and see what happens.'

'Now I'm curious!' he said, slipping his arm around her as she explained that she was initiating contact with her birth mother and had written to her.

'Erin, do you think that's wise?' he said, slightly dismayed.

'What do you mean?'

'What I mean is, you could end up with some awful woman landing herself on you and your family and saying she's your mother!'

Erin had told Luke not long after they met last year that she was adopted. It hadn't been an issue and she presumed that, because he never mentioned it, he was fine about it.

'Grant, a guy in my year in school, was adopted,' he told her. 'He traced his mother about five years ago and it was an almighty disaster.'

'They met?'

'Yes, and he could hardly get away from her and his so-called new family! They literally stalked him. I think they were trying to shake him down for money. He had to change his phone number and move.'

'You're exaggerating!'

'No, I'm not . . . and another friend of Mum's, her daughter Suzie traced her mother and discovered she came from a very dodgy background. Half the family were in prison.'

'Shut up, Luke, it's not like that. I'm just curious about her and I suppose my background.'

'Listen, if your mother was from any kind of normal family you would probably never have been adopted! It's far more likely that there were problems which meant she couldn't raise a child. Think about it, Erin – do you really want to find out?'

'Yes, I do,' she said angrily. 'I am entitled to know who I am and who my natural parents are. I thought you'd understand, Luke, instead of being so bloody patronizing.'

'I'm sorry, Erin. I'm just trying to protect you . . . I don't want anyone to upset or hurt you.'

'You've hurt me!' she said softly, staring at the top of her glass.

He could be an arrogant prick sometimes. Luke's family lived in such a protected, middle-class world. His parents – with their mock Edwardian house in Foxrock, their two cars and their apartment in Spain – were full of nonsense and, she suspected, were right old snobs, determined that their two sons would marry well when the time came. A daughter-in-law with any kind of a skeleton in the cupboard would certainly not go down well with them.

'What do Nina and Tom think of you digging this all up?'

'Mum and Dad understand, and fully support me. My mother, Kate, was only twenty when I was born. She was a student and probably panicked at the thought of minding a baby, so she did what she thought was best for me,' Erin said defensively. 'At least she had the guts to go through with the pregnancy when everyone else was heading off to London!'

'Okay, okay! She's probably going to be great and the two of you are going to really hit it off,' he said, giving in. 'She's probably beautiful like you and has a star-shaped freckle on her—'

'Luke Gallagher!' She nudged him in the ribs as the two of them burst out laughing.

Luke was just being overprotective of her, that's all it was.

'A few drinks here and then why don't we grab dinner in Milano's?' he suggested, pulling her into his arms.

Erin had to admit she was crazy about him. With his dark hair and handsome face, he was such an attractive guy. He was intelligent and assured, and yet had a good sense of humour and got on well with all her friends and all her family too. It made a change from Ben, her gym-obsessed previous boyfriend, who had been more interested in his latest marathon-training speeds than in her and had given her a running kit for her Christmas present which had annoyed her so much that she had dumped him in the New Year!

Going out with Luke had changed things. She'd met him at

a friend's party and they had just hit it off straight away. They'd gone to the cinema the next night and had been seeing each other ever since. They felt like a proper couple and she could imagine a future with him.

He was ambitious and a bit of a workaholic, but lots of the guys and girls she knew were just the same. Everyone was trying to impress everyone – that's the way things worked. Those who were fortunate enough to have a job worked hard and played hard, realizing how lucky they were actually to be employed.

'Another beer?' he offered.

'Sure, and then let's go and grab a table in the restaurant before they get too busy.'

She'd been so wound up all week that she just wanted to relax and unwind over the weekend and have some fun. Fate would decide if Kate Flanagan would respond to her letter or not.

Chapter Ten

ERIN STOOD AT THE DEPARTURE GATE. PEOPLE WERE ALREADY beginning to queue as the ground hostesses checked ticket print-outs and passports. Friday evening was always mega busy at Dublin airport and she had no time even to browse in duty free, let alone buy anything, as she had rushed through Terminal 2's crowded departure area.

She had been looking forward to a romantic Saturday-night dinner with Luke at their favourite restaurant, but he had decided instead to stay in London for the weekend as he had to be back there for an early Monday-morning business meeting anyway, and he had suggested that she join him there.

'Come on, Erin, we haven't been together in London for ages. It'll be fun and besides, the place I'm staying in is fabulous! Wait till you see it!'

'Okay,' she'd agreed and she went online and managed to get a ticket.

She liked London, and so many of their friends were working there. Luke was staying in a plush hotel near Canary Wharf. Tonight they'd grab a quick dinner and meet up with some friends, then tomorrow night Luke had managed to get them a booking at Le Cave, one of the city's hottest restaurants.

The flight was packed and Erin listened to some music as she wound down and tried to relax.

Two and a half hours later she was sipping chilled champagne in one of the fanciest hotel rooms she had ever been in, as Luke organized a taxi to take them to the Thai restaurant where they were meeting Lisa and her boyfriend Gavin, and Damien and his new girlfriend Hope.

London was hopping with restaurants and bars, packed with a Friday-night crowd, and the minute they walked into the restaurant Luke met two guys from the London office.

'Hey, Emil and Justin – this is my girlfriend, Erin. She's over for the weekend.'

'Bet Luke's glad to have you here, Erin, instead of sitting in his lonely hotel room working!' they teased, shaking her hand and inviting them to join them.

'Sorry, but we're meeting friends. I'll see you guys on Monday,' said Luke, steering her towards the back of the noisy restaurant, where Lisa was waving madly at them.

Erin hugged Lisa. She really missed her old college buddy.

'Wow, you look great!' she said, taking in the long, glossy hair, perfect smile and sexy but expensive outfit that Lisa was wearing.

'I'm earning good money here, so I've decided to take a bit better care of myself.' Lisa giggled. 'It's the first time in my life my hair has looked really decent and there's a fancy dental clinic near the office where the staff get a great discount, so now I've got a perfect smile.'

'Lisa, it's brill that the job is working out so well for you.'

'It beats being on the dole in Dublin any day of the week!

How are things going in your office?' Lisa asked as Erin sat in beside her.

'Things are pretty tight,' Erin admitted. 'A good few clients are gone.'

'Gone to another agency?'

'No, just gone – into liquidation or receivership. So many old clients and companies have just shut down or are really struggling, with no advert or media budgets really, so there isn't that much work and everyone is scrabbling for whatever they can get.'

'It sounds pretty grim!'

'I suppose it is pretty grim,' Erin said. Lisa was probably doing lots of high-end quality graphic work, whereas she was just trying to make ends meet.

'There are quite a few good jobs here,' suggested Lisa, glancing over at Luke.

'I'll think about it.'

'Gavin and I would love to have you two over here with the rest of the Irish posse.'

Damien, an old schoolfriend of Luke's, gave her a big hug and introduced his new girlfriend, Hope.

'We met in Hong Kong and she followed me back here.'

'Hey, tell the truth!' laughed Hope, a petite Chinese beauty. 'I got sent on a three-month placement in the London office and you begged and begged me to stay on or I would break your heart.'

'That's true,' he admitted sheepishly. 'I couldn't let you go. When "the Damo" falls . . . he falls hard!'

Soon the table was crowded with wine and beer, and everyone was chatting as they ordered a huge mixture of dishes. Erin was so glad that Luke had organized this get-together. They stayed till late, then all fell into taxis and Lisa and Erin arranged to meet for brunch on Sunday.

'Told you that you'd enjoy it!' said Luke smugly, slipping his arm around her as they took the elevator to their hotel room.

Erin yawned. She was tired, a little drunk, but so happy she'd come over. Falling into the massive bed with its aubergine-coloured throw and crisp white linen, she giggled as Luke flung off his shirt and trousers and joined her.

'I hate being away from you,' he said, nuzzling her bare shoulders and neck.

'And I hate it when you're not around too,' she admitted, pulling him closer and sliding her hands along his back.

Saturday was spent tasting and testing delicacies from the local weekend food market down on the wharf, before a quick lunch and heading off to see the big Matisse exhibition at the National Gallery.

That night they went for drinks to a wine bar before eating at Le Cave. Soft jazz played in the restaurant and the menu was divine. Erin opted for scallops to start, followed by the most delicious pan-fried sole with green beans and rosemary-roasted potatoes. Luke was being extra attentive and romantic as they ordered a bottle of Chablis.

As the evening went on, couples got up to dance and Erin slipped into Luke's arms as the rhythms of soul and jazz took over.

'I love this place,' she sighed as they smooched.

'We could become regulars.'

'What?'

'That's what I want to talk to you about,' he said, taking her hand and leading her back to their table.

'Visiting?'

'No, based here.'

'What are you talking about, Luke?'

He topped up her glass. 'There's a chance – a good chance – that I will be moved to the office here. I'm back and forward the whole time for the past six months, so I suppose it makes sense.'

'But things are okay in Hibernian in Dublin. You told me the company's doing fine.'

'It is. Fine is okay, but over here things are booming and I guess that's where you want to be career-wise, Erin – you must understand that.'

'Of course,' she said, trying not to show her sense of panic at the prospect of Luke moving to London.

'Obviously, if I do move over here, I'd want you to move too, Erin – come over here, move in together, whatever it takes. I don't want us to be apart or doing that deadly Dublin-to-London weekend thing like so many couples.'

Erin was filled with the excitement of Luke actually asking her to move in with him, waking up to each other every morning and going to bed together every night. It was all so romantic, and a big stepping stone towards their relationship becoming far more permanent.

'Do you mean it?'

'Of course!' he said loudly. 'I want you to come and live with me.'

'Couldn't we live together in Dublin?'

'Look, this move to here would be great – not just for me, but probably also career-wise for you. You can see how well Lisa's doing and she seems very settled here.'

'I know. She was telling me there is plenty of design work around and lots of places are taking on staff.'

'There you go, Erin! Better for you and better for me.'

'I don't know. What about work and the apartment and the girls?'

He put on a mock offended look.

'Haven't I been listening to you go on and on about work, and how worried you are about Monika and Declan's business collapsing or you being let go?'

'I know, I know,' she said, squeezing his hand.

'And you can't live with your best friends for ever! You do know that.'

'I know,' she giggled. 'Nikki and I keep thinking that Claire and Donal are going to move in together.'

'Well there you go!' he laughed, reaching over and kissing her, killing any more protests she might have. 'Listen, later next week I'll be home and I'll talk to Gordon Leonard, the senior partner, and then arrange to meet with Tim Bennett over here and see what kind of package they will offer me.'

'Great.'

Luke was ambitious. She'd always known that. He was the kind of guy that would probably always expect his girlfriend or wife to pack up her tent and follow him, wherever he went in the world, to be his back-up and support. She loved Luke, wanted to be with him, probably even spend the rest of her life with him, but it meant giving up so much and putting all her trust in him. Was she ready for that . . . to make such a decision? She wasn't sure.

'Let's have another drink to celebrate us!' he said, calling the waiter over.

Erin sipped at a glass of Le Cave's sparkling wine as Luke excitedly talked about his potential move to London. She was just being stupid and pathetic. The most gorgeous, perfect guy she had ever met had just asked her to move in with him, for the two of them to become a pair, live together, build their careers together and become a proper couple, take that big step on the path towards marriage and a lifetime together.

'Erin, you are listening to what I was saying about you registering with some of the big recruitment agencies and coming over and setting up job interviews, and we can try and find an apartment to rent?'

'Of course. It's just that I wasn't expecting it and my mind is racing all over the place.'

'Everything will be fine,' he promised, kissing her. 'Being together – that's the important thing.'

Back at the hotel, as she curled up in his arms, she convinced herself that this was where she really wanted to be – here with Luke, planning their future, making a life together.

Chapter Eleven

ERIN WOKE TO THE SOUND OF THE POWER-SHOWER GOING IN the bathroom. Luke had beaten her to it. They had woken earlier, made love and must both have fallen back asleep. She was just stretching and getting out of bed when a waiter came to the door with breakfast and the *Sunday Times*. She was meeting Lisa in less than an hour, but a big glass of orange juice, a bit of toast and some fresh coffee from the pot was badly needed to help wake her up. Last night had been wonderful, but there had been far too much drink, she thought, as she sat on the bed and helped herself. They'd even hit the champagne in the mini-bar!

'Hey, leave some breakfast for me!' teased Luke, appearing wrapped in a towel.

'I'm just having a bite,' she laughed, nicking another piece of toast. 'I'll be eating with Lisa.'

She watched as he tucked into sausages, bacon and scrambled egg.

'What are you going to do?' she quizzed.

'Damien and I and some of the lads are meeting in Molloy's

Bar later to watch some football, if you want to join us.'

'I'd prefer to go shopping with Lisa, if that's okay.'

'Sure. What about I meet you back here, then, around half five? We can grab something quick to eat together downstairs before you head for the airport.'

'That sounds great,' she said, kissing him before taking over the bathroom.

Lisa was sitting in the midday sunshine at an outside table at Bonne Bouche, waiting for her. The place was packed.

'I booked a table,' laughed Lisa, as if reading her mind. 'You have to on Saturdays and Sundays over here.'

Erin hugged her. She missed Lisa and, if she did move over here, having Lisa around would be fantastic.

'Well, how's the romantic weekend going?'

'Great – really great,' Erin said, embarrassed. 'In fact, so great that Luke wants me to move in with him.'

'Yippee!' yelled Lisa, making heads turn in their direction. 'I can just see the two of you getting a really fancy place in Dublin.'

'Over here in London,' revealed Erin.

'What?'

'Luke wants to transfer to work in Hibernian's office in Canary Wharf and has asked me to move over here too.'

'Oh Erin, that's wonderful! The two of us being over here and being able to see each other and meet up, and Gavin and Luke get on great. You'd already have friends here.'

'I know.' Erin hugged her.

'I'll keep my ears open for jobs for you.'

'Will you?'

'I promise.'

Erin had been so busy chatting that she had barely studied the menu, but she ordered a tempting Croque Monsieur, which the people on the table beside them were devouring. A jug of chilled juice and a big pot of French coffee – she couldn't imagine a nicer way to enjoy Sunday.

Lisa was more excited about the prospect of her move to London than she was, but her enthusiasm was infectious as she reeled off possible places to apply for work, good places to live, and even the name of the gym that she had joined; and she told her all about the all-Irish girly book club that she had joined.

'It'll be such fun having you over here, Erin, I can't wait!'

'Well, there are a few major things to sort out first, like me getting a job . . . getting a job . . . and, of course, getting a job.'

'Okay, okay – we need to get you a job . . . But Luke's right. You do need to get in touch with some of the big recruitment agencies here – set things up. I'll email you a list and some names of people I used.'

Afterwards Lisa brought her shopping to a little area full of new young designers with just the kind of clothes Erin liked.

'The high street is great, but this little black dress is just wow. I can't wait to wear it.' She also hadn't been able to resist a jacket and skirt in Anastasia's. Then, realizing the time, Erin and Lisa said their goodbyes as she raced back to meet Luke.

Luke had had a few pints with the lads and was hungry. The hotel's plush restaurant wasn't too busy and the waitress promised to serve them quickly.

'Do you want me to come to the airport with you?' he offered.

'No, I'll be fine. I'll just get the Express.'

'Then I'll see you later this week. Hopefully I'll be home on Thursday or Friday.'

Erin realized as they said their goodbyes that she hated leaving him.

Sitting on the flight, she sighed as the plane took off. It was only when they were in mid-air that she realized that Luke, when he'd asked her to move in with him, had never once said the words 'I love you'.

Chapter Twelve

KATE CASSIDY AND HER BEST FRIEND TRISH HAD JOGGED THEIR regular circuit all the way up through their estate, through the local park and then taken the coast road on their way back home.

'Come in and have a coffee?' Kate urged as they both stood, sweaty and panting, outside her front door.

'No coffee – it'll only make me crave a biscuit or two,' Trish said determinedly. 'But a big pint of cold water would be great.'

Kate went into the kitchen and got two glasses of water but still put the kettle on to boil.

The two of them had taken up a keep-fit regime a few weeks ago with very definite goals. Trish was aiming to be at least a stone and a half down by the time her son Aongus got married in Croatia at the end of July, while Kate hadn't much weight to lose but wanted to get fit and firm up her flabby tummy and arms in time for her Silver Wedding anniversary in September.

Sitting down and relaxing as they got their breaths back, Trish filled her in on the on-off relationships of her twenty-four-year-old daughter Niamh.

'That girl has so many boyfriends that Alan and I can't keep up! God knows who she will bring to Aongus's wedding! We are all booking our flights to Dubrovnik and our accommodation and we haven't a clue what to do about her. Is she sharing a room with young Roisin or not?'

'Trish, I'm sure if she is bringing a boyfriend that he'll organize his own flight and they'll get their own place to stay,' Kate said soothingly as she put two mugs of coffee on the table in front of them.

'Black – well, almost black – for me,' insisted Trish, who usually loved her coffee creamy and sweet. Kate tried not to smile when she saw her grimace as she sipped it. She just pushed the milk jug towards her.

'What about you and the party?' asked Trish.

'Paddy is doing up a list.' Kate sighed. 'It's getting bigger and bigger! He won't listen to me about keeping it small.'

'I hope I'm on this list!' laughed Trish.

'Of course you and Alan are on it!' Kate took the pad of paper from the worktop and passed it to Trish.

'Holey Moley, where are you going to fit all these people?'

'I've no idea, but you know Paddy – he is so determined.'

'Maybe you should count yourself lucky that after twenty-five years Paddy still loves you so much that he wants to celebrate it in style!'

'I know,' said Kate. 'I do.'

'Hey Mum, hey Trish,' said Kevin, coming into the kitchen. 'The post has just come.' He dropped two letters for Kate on to the table.

'No bills, hopefully!' teased Trish as Kate began to open them.

Kate stopped the minute she had opened the large white

envelope. The address on the top of the letter inside it was immediately familiar to her. And it seemed to contain another letter.

'It's just a charity thing looking for another donation!' she pretended, as she closed the envelope and put it away on the counter, trying to disguise her total dismay as Kevin busied himself making a sandwich for college.

Her younger son was so like Paddy, easygoing and trusting and great fun. He was very popular and he loved the course on computers and business that he was doing in college. He lived in a uniform of jeans, T-shirt and hoodie, and with his unruly fair hair, blue eyes and broad face he was the spit of his dad.

'Hey, I'd better get going!' He leaned down and kissed her quickly as he grabbed his backpack. 'I'll be late home tonight, but will you keep me dinner, please, Mum?'

'Hey, I'd better get going too,' announced Trish, standing up. 'I've to collect something from the dry-cleaner's and go to the chemist. But I'll see you tomorrow, Kate.'

Kate waited till they were both gone, the house quiet and empty, before she picked up the envelope and opened it. It was a letter from the adoption agency to tell her that her daughter had been in contact with them and that she had a copy of her original birth certificate and had written a letter to Kate, which they enclosed. Her daughter wished to establish some kind of contact with her birth mother and was interested in meeting her. The letter had been sent by a social worker called Marian Kelly, and she had enclosed her daughter's letter to her.

Kate couldn't believe it. She felt a chill going through her as she looked at the words on the page. How had they managed to find her? How did they discover her current address? She opened the second letter. It had been handwritten on expensive white paper.

She read it over . . . and over again . . . It was almost like a voice talking to her.

'I am twenty-six years old, happy and healthy . . . living in Dublin . . . with my family . . .' Kate had to stop. She couldn't breathe. This was too much.

'I often think about you. I wonder what you are like and wonder if the two of us are any way alike?'

Kate read on.

'I would really like to talk to you, to see you, to meet you, even if it is only once in my life so that I know who you are and . . . I suppose, who I am.'

Kate read the letter over and over again. Touching the words, she traced them with her fingers. Her daughter had written them only a day or two ago . . . Suddenly there was a link between them.

She read both letters again. The agency shouldn't have contacted her. She had told them, years ago, that she didn't want any future contact with her child. Didn't they understand that? This is what all these reforming social workers and justice people were doing by saying people had rights to information. What about her rights to protect herself and her family?

She read the letter again

'With love from your daughter
Erin'

She must have sat in the kitchen for hours.

'You okay, Mum?' asked her sixteen-year-old daughter Aisling, coming in from school.

'I'm fine – just feeling a bit tired, love.' Kate quickly put the letters back in the envelope.

'I've got so much homework it's unbelievable!' complained Aisling as she grabbed a drink and a banana. 'We have a whole page of algebra to do and I haven't a clue.'

'Maybe Kevin can help you a bit when he comes in later?'

'Yeah – he's the maths genius!' she grinned.

'Listen, I think I'll go up and have a rest for an hour,' Kate said. 'I'll get the dinner later.'

Upstairs in her bedroom she hid the envelope.

Kate had never expected to hear about what happened to her first daughter. It was something that she had accepted would probably secretly gnaw at her and upset her all her life – and now this letter. She didn't know what to think. She couldn't think. What happened if somehow Paddy or the kids found out about this girl – found out that she had a daughter called Erin who wanted to meet her?

'Kate? Kate, are you okay?' Paddy was standing at the side of the bed.

'I've a bit of a headache,' she said stirring under the duvet. 'I thought I'd try to sleep it off. What time is it?'

'Seven p.m.'

'Why didn't someone wake me?'

'You looked exhausted and you were having a great sleep. It will do you no harm.'

Kate sat herself up in the bed. She felt terrible, like she had been in a car accident. She felt physically and emotionally drained.

'What about dinner? I'll get up and get it.'

'You will not!' warned Paddy. 'Kevin and Aisling are just cooking something downstairs. Leave them at it.'

Paddy went off downstairs and Kate lay back down, her eyes closed, disbelieving . . . What the hell was she going to do?

Chapter Thirteen

'THIS IS ALL YOUR FAULT, SALLY!' SCREAMED KATE ACCUSINGLY as she paced up and down on the tiled floor of the sun room of her sister's house in Rathfarnham. 'Why did you have to go and interfere and give them my address? Why couldn't you say you had no idea where I live or what I'm doing?'

'I'm your sister,' Sally reminded her. 'They obviously still have kept a record of all the details from when you were pregnant and in hospital. Remember you put me down as your next of kin? You gave them my address, my phone number and told them where I worked. The hospital and the adoption agency both knew you were staying with me.'

'Shit, you're right!' admitted Kate, collapsing down on to the blue armchair.

'The adoption agency phoned me at work,' continued Sally. 'What was I meant to do – change my job and give up working in St James' Hospital because of you? I love my job and I'm good at it. Anyone phoning the hospital switch would be told the ward and floor I work on. I have nothing to hide,' she said angrily, her blue eyes flashing. 'You need to calm down about this, Kate. Marian Kelly, the social worker, told me that everything they do is in total confidence. She promised me that they will not give your address or phone number to anyone and I believe her. She posted on the letter to you. Your daughter Erin has no idea where you are. No one has.'

'I'm sorry, Sally. I guess I'm paranoid about it,' Kate apologized. She had been a nervous wreck for the past week, ever since she had got the letter. Sally and Mike had been away in France for a few days and she had totally panicked about what to do. She couldn't tell anyone and she hadn't wanted to ruin her sister's holiday by phoning her.

'You *are* being paranoid!' said Sally, seriously. 'Nothing bad is going to happen and if you keep acting as if your world is falling in, Paddy is bound to notice.'

'I know, but I keep thinking about it. I can't sleep. I wake up at two or three in the morning in a sweat, thinking of what I did. It's so awful, Sally—'

'I know,' said Sally, slipping her arms around her. 'But surely, you must have thought sometimes that your daughter might when she was older try to find you?'

'No, I didn't. She was gone from me for ever – and I had got used to the idea. It was as if she was dead – as if I had lost my baby when she was born . . . You don't understand, Sally, but I had to think like that or otherwise I would have gone mad.'

Kate found even saying it out loud to her sister was releasing some of the immense stress and guilt that she'd been feeling since she'd got that letter.

'Kate, can't you be happy that Erin is well and has grown up into such a nice young woman – you can tell by her letter. She's not a drug addict or an alcoholic or some kind of dysfunctional needy person. She has a job and a boyfriend and a lovely family, who have raised her really well and who she is very close to. She's not looking for anything from you, so why are you so afraid?'

'I don't know.'

'She has written to you. Why won't you write back to her? She deserves to know something about herself, Kate, it's only fair.'

'What if Paddy finds out? What do you think that would do to our marriage?'

'I don't know,' Sally sighed, 'but Paddy is a very decent, fair man. I don't think his reaction would be half as bad as you think.'

'You don't know that. Can you imagine the kids' reaction? Imagine Aisling suddenly finding out she has an older half-sister! She'd be heartbroken.'

'You keep worrying yourself about what other people will feel,' said Sally. 'But this is about what you and Erin feel.'

Kate could feel herself calming down as she sat in her sister's sun room. Sally had always been able to make her feel better about things. Maybe that was why she was such a good nurse, because she could clearly put things in perspective.

'I think that you should write back to her,' Sally said firmly. 'She is your daughter, and Erin deserves to have you write a letter to her, to have a few words on the page from her mother. It would probably mean a huge amount to her. It is the least you can do, Kate.'

'I know,' said Kate, trying to control herself. 'I have to write back to her.'

'And I think you should give some consideration to meeting her too,' insisted her sister. 'She is your daughter and all she wants is an hour of your time. I don't think that is a lot for Erin to ask for.'

'No – I'm not meeting her!' cried Kate, flying off the handle again. 'I'll write back, but I don't want to see her, or for her to see me, and that's all there is to it!'

'Are you sure?'

'Yes, I'm sure. I'll do the letter, I promise, but I'm not taking things any further,' she insisted. 'You're right, it is good to know that she is okay and happy. I always only wanted the best for her – that was why I agreed to have her adopted. But now she is grown up I'm not a part of her life and I don't need to be. Erin has great parents by the sound of it, and I have my own family. My priority is to protect them.'

'If that is the way you see it, Kate, then just do the letter,' Sally urged quietly. 'Write to her this week.'

'I will,' she promised.

Driving home, Kate felt drained, her energy sapped from her. She had barely been able to think for the past few days, and had had a massive row with Kevin over something stupid, and had berated Aisling about the state of her school uniform, and had implied to Paddy she had some sort of virus so he wouldn't get too close to her . . . Her poor husband hadn't a clue what was going on. She had to sort this out.

She'd think about it and try to write to Erin, but she would make it very clear to her daughter that there would be absolutely no more contact except for that letter.

Chapter Fourteen

ERIN KEPT HERSELF BUSY AS THE WEEKS DRAGGED ON AND there seemed to be no response from her birth mother. She was deeply disappointed. She had written a good letter to her and was getting nothing back. What kind of person was this Kate woman to treat her like this?

Her mum and dad had asked a few times about it, and who could blame them? It was very obvious that once again this woman had let her down. Nikki and Claire said nothing, and even Luke was discreet and didn't ask her.

She wanted to shrug it off and say it didn't matter, but inside it did. It hurt, really hurt. She talked to Marian Kelly on the phone and Marian suggested she see Sheila Lennon, the agency's counsellor.

'We recommend anyone who is going through the process here has at least one meeting with Sheila. She's very good. I'd really advise it, Erin. Whether you get to meet or make contact with your birth mother or not, it is very important to talk through some of the issues with a good counsellor like Sheila.'

So Erin found herself meeting this Sheila woman. She

wasn't expecting much and was totally surprised at how well she got on with the large, blonde woman, whose warmth and sincerity immediately made her relax.

'I'm here to help, Erin – that's my job.'

Erin told her about the lack of response to her letter.

'Erin, put yourself in Kate's shoes. She's spent twenty-six years trying to forget about a child she gave up, put the guilt and the shame and the tragedy of it behind her and create a new life for herself. Can you imagine the turmoil such a letter creates? First the relief to discover that you are well and healthy and happy and have had the good life she wanted for you, and then the dismay and worry – especially if she has not told her husband and family – that the life she has created will be destroyed, and that she will be a disappointment to you and not what you expected.'

'I see.' Erin hadn't considered the implications for Kate of her initiating contact and the panic it would cause. 'Maybe I should never have written to her.'

'No, Erin, the letter you sent is important. Kate will realize that and get comfort from it, but it may take time for her to be able to respond to you. So try to be a bit more patient.'

Erin smiled. Her dad was always saying that she was in a rush about everything and needed to slow down a bit!

She found herself telling Sheila things she had never told anyone before. Erin had first learned when she was about five that she was adopted. She hadn't really understood about it until her mum and dad had sat her down and explained it more when she was nearly eight. There never had been any problems at home talking about it openly with her mum and dad and brother and the rest of the family. But so much of what she had felt about being adopted she had buried deep inside her, not wanting to hurt or upset them. The immense sense of rejection, of fear, of absolute terror that something would happen to her mum and dad; then the crazy belief when she was small that her real mother must secretly be a film star, an actress, a writer or somebody famous or special who had a very valid reason for not being able to keep her. Then when she became a teenager she had swung to the opposite end of the pendulum, suspecting every drunk, drug addict, tart or homeless woman she saw of being her mother. She searched their faces as she passed them on the street to see if there was any recognition. She had felt secretly worthless and ashamed, though she had done nothing; but gradually it had passed and she had developed her own sense of worth and strength and begun to feel really good about herself, which was unexpected. She was lucky to have wonderful parents, friends and family whom she loved, but she had finally learned to love herself too.

'Are you happy?'

'Yes,' she laughed, realizing that she was. She had an immense capacity for happiness, wherever it had come from.

'That's very good to hear,' smiled Sheila. 'The ability to be happy is a gift. Try to remember that, and whether you hear back from Kate or not you know that you have done your best at this stage to make contact with your birth mother. Be happy for the life you have!'

'I am,' said Erin, realizing how much she really meant it.

'You may never get a response from Kate,' cautioned Sheila, 'but I'm afraid you will have to respect her decision.'

'I will,' promised Erin, trying to accept the fact that there was every likelihood that her birth mother still wanted to forget she existed.

Chapter Fifteen

KATE TURNED AROUND IN FRONT OF THE MIRROR. THE NEW red dress she had bought in Zara looked great. She'd added a black wrap cardigan and black heels and was really pleased with the results.

'You look really well,' said Paddy approvingly, pulling her into his arms. 'I'm glad that you are over that old virus thing you caught.'

'So am I,' she smiled. 'I'm feeling much better and looking forward to dinner tonight.'

For the past few years Paddy and Kate had had a routine of going out on their own for a midweek dinner to one of the nearby restaurants. Running an off-licence business meant that Paddy often worked late at the weekends, with only every second Saturday off. So they had got accustomed to having a dinner together on a Wednesday night, away from kids and work and worries. The kids were older now, but they had kept up the routine and both enjoyed it.

'I booked us a table at The Kish,' said Paddy.

Kate loved the fish restaurant, which was literally perched

on the pier in Howth and served the fish of the day that had just come in off the boats. They had a table at the window overlooking the busy fishing harbour.

'What are you going to have?' Paddy asked as he buried himself in the wine list.

'Well, I'll go for what's up on the board for tonight,' she replied. 'The hake sounds good and they have that yummy chilli prawn thing to start.'

'I'll have the seafood pâté and the mussels. They have that new Sancerre I was telling you about – will we give it a try?'

Kate laughed every time they went to a restaurant. Paddy always went through the wine list and if he found something new and good, he might stock it in the shop. God knows how many wines she'd tested over all the years of their marriage . . . She watched as he chatted to the wine waiter, Hans, who had become a friend by this stage, the two of them discussing the merits of one new Bordeaux compared to another.

'I'll bring you and Kate a glass to try,' offered Hans.

Kate was feeling so relieved. She had sent a letter to Erin via the adoption agency and hopefully that was an end to the whole thing. She really did sincerely wish only good things for her daughter, but too much time had gone by for either of them to be a part of the other's life. The past was the past, and it was far better it stay that way. She had, however, at the last minute had a bit of a rethink and said that she might consider meeting her once, but only if their privacy and discretion could be maintained.

She looked across at Paddy. He was a good person. He had absolutely no idea of what had happened to her and she never intended telling him. She had known him for years, as he had gone to school with her brother John and had grown up on a farm less than eight miles from where she had grown up. She had met him at a Galway–Kilkenny hurling match in the old stadium at Croke Park, which Sally and Mike had dragged her along to. Poor Paddy had injured his foot playing hurling and was hobbling around on crutches with a sprained ankle, and the two of them sat down and talked for ages in a nearby pub afterwards.

He'd asked her out the following Sunday and she, lonely as hell, had agreed to go on a date with him. Paddy Cassidy was nothing like her former boyfriend, Johnny. He was old fashioned and dependable and kind and made her laugh. He was a good bit taller than her and sturdily built, his hair fair, and he had kind eyes that somehow seemed to calm her. His parents, Larry and Nance, were a lovely couple, and he came from a family even bigger than her own. Paddy worked in O'Hara's, a large city-centre pub.

As the months passed they had got closer; she had begun to rely on him more and more and look forward to being with him. Sally had worried that she was only going out with him on the rebound from Johnny, and maybe she was at first – Paddy the substitute, second best in the boyfriend stakes. But as the months passed that had changed; Paddy had become more and more important to her and she had realized that she loved and trusted him, and that he loved her too. His proposal had come out of the blue and Kate had surprised herself by accepting him. She had insisted on a smallish wedding in a Galway hotel with only sixty present, which included both families, a handful of friends and some of Paddy's hurling team. Her dad had given her away and on that day she had wished desperately that her mother was still alive to be with her.

They had gone to Italy on their honeymoon and she had

conceived straight away, their son Sean born the following June. Holding her newborn baby in the maternity hospital she had debated telling Paddy about Anna, but knew that it would break his heart as he boasted about their firstborn and what a wonderful mother she was. And so she had kept her secret – hidden it away, buried her feelings again as their second son Kevin and then finally Aisling were born.

Paddy had moved to managing a pub in Clontarf with a small off-licence business attached to it. Seeing the potential to develop a business of his own, four years later he had taken out a loan from the bank, bought an old hairdresser's premises on a busy crescent of shops and converted it to Cassidy's Off-Licence, selling wines and spirits and beer. He was a Trojan worker and passionate about sourcing good wines at competitive prices for his customers.

Between the business and raising three children, time just seemed to have slipped by – almost twenty-five years of it, and Kate had nearly managed to forget what she had done . . .

'What do you think of this Sancerre?' he asked her.

'It's lovely, far nicer than the one we had last time,' she said, taking another sip from her glass. She was no wine expert, but they did have fun as Paddy tried to develop her palate.

For their anniversary present she planned to surprise her husband and take him to Bordeaux for one night in beautiful St-Emilion, then two nights at the renowned Château Beychevelle in St-Julien. It was a trip she knew he'd really enjoy.

'Kate, did you have any more time to go through the list I gave you for the party?' Paddy asked as they were served their main courses.

'Yes, I was showing it to Trish and she was wondering how we will possibly fit everyone in the house!'

'I know it's a bit of a crowd, but we are both from big families and we cannot leave out our friends,' he said, serious. 'The alternative to having it at home is to go to one of the big local hotels or the golf club or somewhere like that.'

'I don't want a party in a big function room,' she said. 'In fact, I'm not sure that I want a party at all.'

'But we have to celebrate twenty-five years of a good marriage,' he said firmly. 'A marriage built on love and respect, honesty and truth, and friendship.'

Kate reddened. They had a good marriage, yes, but she hadn't been honest and she never would be able to tell him the truth about what had happened before she married him.

'What about if we put a gazebo thing up in the garden?' he continued. 'It might give us a bit more space.'

Kate laughed. Paddy was determined to have this party and there was no stopping him. Once her husband got a notion about something he rarely gave up.

'Get a gazebo if you want, Paddy!' she smiled. 'With it we might just be able to squash everyone in!'

Chapter Sixteen

DISAPPOINTED, ERIN HAD ALMOST GIVEN UP ANY HOPE OF hearing back from her birth mother when, almost four and half weeks later, a letter arrived from Kate. Erin shook from top to toe as she read it and burst into tears. Her birth mother was real, she existed – she had the proof in her hands – and she was finally acknowledging her. Erin read the letter over and over again, studying the handwriting, the paper, the language . . .

Kate Flanagan was married now with three children: two sons and a younger daughter. She hadn't told their names, but gave their ages – twenty-three, nineteen and sixteen. Kate worked part time in a family business. She had never told her husband about giving birth to a child and did not want this information revealed. She was happy to hear from Erin and comforted to know that she had grown up in such a good family, as it proved that she had made the right choice for her. She was proud of Erin's accomplishments in going to college and getting a degree. She herself had gone to a business college but unfortunately had been unable to finish her diploma. She liked music and cinema and fashion and had a cat called Cleo.

If she agreed to Erin's request to meet, Kate insisted that it be some place neutral and away from her own home and locality. She was adamant about protecting her privacy and family life.

Erin couldn't believe it. There was a possibility that she was going to meet Kate – see her face to face, be able to talk to her finally . . . It was unbelievable!

She phoned Marian Kelly, and rang Sheila too. Marian would act as a go-between, arranging the time and place Kate and Erin would meet. She refused to be drawn as to where Kate would be coming from, not wanting to reveal where she lived or even her married name.

'If she wants to tell you these things, it is up to Kate to tell you herself,' Marian reminded Erin. 'But remember, you also need to protect your own privacy.'

As Marian made the arrangements for them to meet in a neutral venue, Erin couldn't believe it. She was going to meet her birth mother next week in the centre of Dublin, in a little café just off Dawson Street at twelve o'clock on Saturday morning . . . It was nerve-wracking, but she couldn't wait!

Chapter Seventeen

ERIN STUDIED THE TEXT FROM HER UNCLE BILL INVITING HER to join him for lunch in his club. She smiled and texted him back immediately. She loved her uncle and being invited for lunch at the inner sanctum of the dining room of the St Stephen's Green Club was a treat.

Ever since she was a little girl, her uncle had played a big part in her life. He always used to bring Jack and herself on all kinds of outings, to the cinema, the Christmas pantomime at the Gaiety Theatre, concerts in the Concert Hall, and to play in the big playground in Herbert Park, which was only a few minutes' walk from the Donnybrook house where he and Charles lived. Now she was grown up there were visits to art galleries and theatre nights and jazz nights and meals together, which she really enjoyed.

The club was quiet and the waiter led her to where her uncle was sitting at a table in the window.

'Hello, Erin darling, how are you?' he asked, standing up to greet her. He really was such a sweetheart and one of the kindest people she knew. He had no children of his own, but was so good to all his nieces and nephews and had time for them all.

'I'm fine, Uncle Bill,' she said, kissing him.

He looked handsome as ever in his navy blazer, crisp white shirt and red–and–navy tie.

The waiter came over to take their order.

'Wine?' suggested her uncle.

'Not for me, thanks. I'm working on a new logo for someone this afternoon and wine and drawing, I've discovered, do not really work,' she laughed, ordering fizzy water instead while her uncle went for a glass of red wine.

She always enjoyed his company and listened as he told her about the trip to Bilbao, San Sebastián and Santander that he and Charles were planning. Her uncle and his partner Charles seemed to have been together for ever and were a great couple.

'Your dad and I were out sailing last week,' he said as the waiter served their main course. 'Tom told me that you are planning to meet your birth mother very soon – that it is all arranged.'

'Yes, the social worker for the adoption agency has set it all up,' she confirmed. 'I'm very nervous about it, Uncle Bill – I really am!'

'Of course you are,' he said soothingly. 'Heaven knows what the outcome might be! You and your birth mother might be very alike and get on splendidly, or you may realize that you have very little in common and that you are both just satisfying your curiosity.'

'Exactly,' Erin said, admitting her own fears. Trust Uncle Bill to put it so succinctly! No wonder he was such a successful barrister. He always had a way of getting straight to the crux of a matter.

'I'm not trying to influence your meeting with this woman,' he said gently, 'but I do feel I need to let you know how your parents are feeling about it.'

'Mum and Dad are fine,' she said defensively.

'Is that what you really believe?' he asked, putting down his knife and fork and looking her straight in the eye, which was always disconcerting.

Erin blushed. 'They're upset?'

'To put it mildly,' he said. 'Tom is distracted, worried for you that this person will let you down or, even worse, take you away from them.'

'That would never happen!' she protested. 'You know that, Uncle Bill!'

Her uncle shrugged. 'And apparently Nina is not sleeping . . . awake until all hours. She's convinced that you and your long-lost mother will fall into each other's arms, and then she will become redundant. That you will find your own new family and no longer be a part of ours.'

'God, how could they think that, Uncle Bill? They're my mum and dad and that will never, ever change. They're the ones I love and no one can take that away!'

'I know,' he said, 'but it is how they both feel and you need to be aware of it, Erin. You've probably been so caught up with tracing your past and arranging to meet your birth mother and focusing on that, that maybe Nina and Tom's feelings have escaped your notice.'

'Uncle Bill, thank you for telling me,' she said. 'I guess that I've been so obsessed about this that I haven't thought properly about Mum and Dad's reactions.'

'I remember a long time ago when I was about your age I was caught up in something too – pretty self-obsessed about it,' he said as the pudding was served. 'I decided the time had come to tell my parents about being gay. Your dad and my sister Caroline and a few close friends had already guessed, but I don't think they genuinely realized. My father – your grandfather Gerald – was a very old-fashioned type of man with very strong moral values. I still remember the absolute denial in his eyes when I told him. No son of his was going to be a homosexual! That's all he kept saying. My poor mum didn't say a word because she was too busy weeping. Nothing was the same after that – I had changed everything between us in my quest to come out and be honest with them. I was focusing so much on what my agenda was that, in hindsight, I had very little regard for their feelings.'

'And what happened then?' asked Erin.

'Well, I suppose they both tried to make the best of it. My dad and I were never really as close afterwards. I always felt that I had let him down as a son. We met, we were polite, but something had disappeared between us.'

'What about Granny?'

'Your granny was a marvellous woman. Once she got over the shock of it, I think she felt tremendously sad for me that I wasn't going to have the same as the rest of the family in terms of marriage and children.'

'But you had us!'

'Some people are destined to be uncles!' he laughed loudly. 'Though she did like Charles. She got very fond of him in those last few years before she died.'

Erin remembered her Granny Nancy, with her white hair and pretty face and beautiful singing voice, who used to come and mind them and play with them all the time. She'd died when Erin was twelve and she still missed her.

'I'm telling you all this just to remind you to have a little care for Nina and Tom, please,' he said gently. 'Your dad – he's under a lot of pressure at the moment, and this extra worry about you and this meeting with your mother can't be helping.'

'Uncle Bill, thanks for telling me,' she said, genuinely relieved that he had made her aware of the effect it was having on her parents. 'I promise I'll try to tread carefully. I wouldn't hurt Mum and Dad for the world!'

'I know,' he said, patting her hand.

She thanked him for the lunch and, after paying the bill, her uncle walked her down to the door of the club, he turning in one direction while Erin headed back to work.

Chapter Eighteen

KATE SHOOK HER HEAD. WHY HAD SHE EVER LET HERSELF BE persuaded by her sister and that social worker to agree to meet her daughter? She should have stuck to her guns and said *No! No! No!* Marian Kelly from the adoption agency had got in touch with her to say that her daughter really wanted to meet her. One meeting and nothing more. Sally had told her to stop being so bloody selfish and think of her daughter – a poor girl who had no idea what her mother was like.

'Erin's probably been imagining all kinds of things about you, so if you meet at least it would put her mind to rest once and for all, as she'd know what her biological mother was really like,' urged Sally.

Kate had thought about nothing else for two weeks and finally agreed, with Marian's help, to set up a meeting with her daughter in a restaurant off Dawson Street. She was dreading it and was in an utter quandary as to what to wear. Half her wardrobe of clothes was out on top of the bed so she could try things on. What would Erin expect her to be like? She had no idea. Should she go really casual, or would Erin expect her to be all dressed up? She slipped on a black jacket and trousers with a white top. She looked like she was going for a job interview! She pulled on her turquoise silk wrap dress, but it looked far too fancy for where they were meeting. The scoop-neck red wool over-dress and leggings with her boots . . . Maybe she was trying to look too young? She didn't know what to wear.

She was pulling on a grey shift dress with pearls when Aisling came in and perched on the corner of the bed, her long black hair falling forward, her eyes rimmed with kohl, taking in the mess of the bedroom.

'What are you doing, Mum?'

'I'm trying to decide what to wear when I meet a friend tomorrow for lunch.'

'What?' Aisling looked puzzled as she took in the clothes strewn everywhere. Kate was usually a real neat freak and liked everything put away in its proper place.

'It's just this friend is a very old friend and we haven't seen each other since we were very young,' Kate explained, 'so I want to look well but not mutton dressed as lamb.'

'Mmmm.' Her daughter was giving it some thought. Sixteen-year-old Aisling had her own sense of style. Black boots, black leggings and some kind of sixties-style geometric print top worn under a half jacket, which seemed to accentuate her slim frame.

'That grey shift is good on you but a bit oldie really. What about this one?' Aisling picked out a simple but very expensive black dress and a white top to go under it. 'Wear it with your good black suede boots and maybe put a splash of colour with some jewellery too. You know that silver and purple neck thing Dad gave you? That might work.'

Putting on everything that Aisling suggested, Kate had to admit it was the exact look she wanted to achieve.

'Thanks for the help. You should be a fashion stylist!' she said.

'Nah, I'm more interested in biology! We're doing about genetics at the moment.' Aisling disappeared off to her own room as Kate re-hung and re-folded everything. She was so nervous about this meeting tomorrow, but at least thank heaven she had what she was going to wear sorted.

Chapter Nineteen

ERIN WAS IN BITS. IN ALL HER TWENTY-SIX YEARS SHE HAD never been so nervous and tense and anxious about anything. She kept taking deep breaths as she walked along Dawson Street, trying to calm herself. Her heart was racing so fast it felt like it could fly out of her chest.

'Do you want me to come with you?' her mum had offered. 'I can sit somewhere down the back of the restaurant, or go off and leave the two of you alone . . . Erin, I'll be there, nearby just in case you need me.'

Erin laughed, remembering how her mum had sat outside her primary school the day she started, waiting in the car for nearly an hour just in case she was needed, and had then gone home and sat by the phone in case Erin's class teacher sent for her.

'Mum, thanks for offering, but I'll be fine, honest. I have to do this by myself. I think that the first time we meet it's important it's just the two of us.' She could see her mum was wounded and she hugged her. 'But I promise the minute our meeting is over I'll phone you and tell you all about it.'

She smiled, thinking of Nina with her mobile phone at the ready.

Claire and Nikki had offered to come too.

'No one's going to notice two girls in a restaurant, sitting at a table over in the corner, eating and chatting,' they reasoned.

'I'd bloody notice!' she laughed. 'The two of you are no secret agents and I'd feel you were watching my every move. I promise I'll fill you in on everything when I get home, okay?'

'Okay,' they agreed, wishing her luck before she left.

Even Jack had offered to mosey along and sit and read nearby if she needed him.

'Jack, I am not going to have half my family and friends there the first time I meet my biological mother! Thanks, but no thanks!' He looked sort of relieved and she guessed her dad had put him up to it.

She had told Luke and even he had said he was just a call away if she needed him. 'But I'm sure that the two of you will get on fine. If she's even a patch on you, you will probably immediately bond with her.'

Erin wasn't half so confident about it and wished people wouldn't assume that this amazing mother–daughter bonding would happen. She had heard some pretty awful stories of people meeting their birth mothers, and even Marian had warned that often things just did not work out. But she really wanted to give it a try.

She had spent hours trying to decide what to wear, trying on outfits secretly in her bedroom. She wanted to make a good impression but didn't want to appear a fashion slave or to be dressed too casual. It was so difficult. She narrowed her selection down to two outfits – her grey-and-black-striped wool dress with leggings and her black suede boots, or her favourite jeans with a cute little blue knitted cardigan wrap and a white lace shirt that she had bought at a vintage stall in Galway. She opted for the latter and, twirling around in the mirror, hoped that the woman she was meeting would like it too.

Café Paradiso was in a laneway just off Dawson Street and was one of her favourite places. Meeting for Saturday lunch was ideal, as during the week the restaurant was busy with workers from all the nearby offices; but at the weekend it became a much more relaxed spot, the waiters happy to let everyone take their time, to sip their wine and drink their coffees and mull over the dishes of the day.

She got a good table, positioned where she could see the door yet away from other people, so no one was able to sit too close to them and overhear their conversation. This was perfect, she thought, allowing herself to relax as she ordered a coffee.

Every time the door opened her eyes flashed to the incoming female figures. Was that her? That must be her, definitely! That woman with the funky haircut and fur jacket on her own looked around the right age. Erin smiled at her, disappointed when the woman made for a table at the back to join a friend.

God, it was nerve-wracking waiting. She ordered another coffee. The tables around her were beginning to fill up – friends meeting each other, couples ordering lunch, tourists trying to translate the menu, but still there was no sign of her. The waiter hovered around her and she reassured him she was waiting for a friend who must have got delayed.

She noticed the older man near the window reading

Saturday's paper, and the guy with the glasses sitting right at the back, working on his laptop. She had read and re-read the menu several times and wished that she had brought a book or a magazine with her in her handbag. As if guessing her thoughts, the manageress handed her the glossy weekend colour magazine from the *Irish Times* to peruse.

'Thanks,' she said, disappearing behind its cover and glancing again at the time. What could have delayed Kate? Was it traffic, or trying to park? Where could she be? Surely she had allowed herself enough time on a day like this to get to their meeting.

Forty minutes later, she watched as the young couple beside her finished their meal and left. She was tempted to do the same, but what if there was a good reason for her mother's delay and she arrived to find Erin gone? It was too important. She'd waited a lifetime for this meeting – she would wait as long as it took.

She ordered the chicken Provençal, which was a house special. She was tempted to order a glass of wine but didn't want to be drunk when her mother arrived, so opted instead for sparkling water.

Still watching the door, relief washed over her when a glamorous-looking woman in an expensive black jacket came towards her. However, this lady was intent on grabbing a table of her own close by and was joined a few seconds later by her husband. Disappointment engulfed Erin. Her mother wasn't coming. She had stood her up, changed her mind about meeting her. She was silly to have believed that this meeting would happen. Her mother hadn't wanted her years ago and nothing had changed.

She wanted to pay her bill and go, but instead she stayed.

She had to give in to that glimmer of hope, the possibility that her mother might still turn up. No matter how late she arrived, Erin would be waiting for her.

'Would you like anything else?' the waiter asked kindly, clearing her plate away. She was so upset that she couldn't face the thought of dessert and instead ordered a creamy cappuccino. She could feel the sympathy from the staff in the restaurant, who were probably used to girls being stood up by bastards of guys who simply couldn't be bothered to be decent. But this was a much worse scenario, and she had to fight to control her tears as her gut instinct told her just run and get out of this fecking place and put the whole bloody fiasco behind you. Even the guy with the long black hair over on his laptop was looking at her.

The tables around her were emptying, the staff clearing up, resetting tables and trying to get a breather between the lunch crowd and the arrival of the early-bird diners. Shit – already she was getting text messages on her phone. Her family probably thought she was having a wonderful heart-to-heart, mother–daughter conversation instead of sitting here all alone.

She held her head in her hands as emotion wracked her. Kate Flanagan was doing it to her all over again – dumping her, getting rid of her as if she was a nothing, an unwanted piece of garbage she couldn't be bothered about. At this moment she actually hated her . . .

There were only the two customers left now, and even the guy with the laptop had gone to the bathroom, leaving his laptop on – he must know and trust the staff here. She was dying to go to the bathroom herself but didn't dare leave her seat as, knowing her rotten luck, it would be the very time her mother would arrive, look around for her and then leave. She really didn't know what to do.

Suddenly the laptop guy, walking back, stopped at her table.

'Are you okay?' he asked kindly. He was kind of scruffy, with thick black jeans and a jumper and thick black-rimmed glasses. He was about her age.

'I was supposed to meet someone . . . a friend.' Shit, he probably thought she was a right saddo and had been stood up by a boyfriend or some internet date. 'A woman friend, but she hasn't bothered to show, I think . . . unless something utterly disastrous has happened to her . . . I don't know what to do.'

'Maybe you could text or phone her, or you can email if you want. I have my laptop,' he offered.

'Thanks . . . I don't really know her and this was a kind of first meeting.'

'Like an interview?'

'Yeah . . . I guess.'

He hovered beside her.

'I'd better stay another while,' she sighed, 'just in case she comes.'

Two minutes later he had moved to the table next to hers and had opened his laptop.

'I had to get out of my place,' he explained. 'My flatmate's girlfriend is over from Amsterdam for the weekend, so I had to give them a bit of space. I said I'd come here to have some coffee and pasta and pass the time. I've a load of work to do on this new project I'm working on and if it's not too busy this place is fine to try to do some work.'

'I see.' She smiled, not really interested. But it was a relief to have someone sitting at the table beside her; at least she didn't look quite so awkward.

'They'll chuck us out of here in another forty minutes,' he said matter-of-factly.

Erin nodded. The matter at least would be taken out of her hands, and if Kate missed the deadline that was most definitely it . . .

She watched as he worked away, intent on what he was doing, going between print on his screen and lots of images. It looked like film.

After all the coffee and water she had drunk, Erin was really dying to visit the bathroom. 'I hope I'm not interrupting you, but I wonder if you could do me a favour?' she asked the stranger.

He looked up from what he was doing. It was so embarrassing . . .

'I really need to go to the loo,' she said, blushing. 'And I was wondering if by any chance the woman I am meant to meet turns up, could you tell her I'll be back in a minute? Even if you see a woman on her own coming in the door, or looking around the place, can you try and talk to her, please – it's very important. She'd be around mid-fortyish, I think. My name is Erin, by the way.'

It was only as she said it that she realized how bizarre the whole thing sounded. He must have thought she was mad.

'Sure,' he nodded, taking a slow sip of his coffee.

Erin raced to the bathroom. Tears overwhelmed her as she sat in the cubicle. Glancing in the mirror, she looked awful and she threw water quickly on her eyes to disguise the fact that she had been crying. Then, brushing her hair and putting another layer of lip-gloss on to her lips, she went back outside. The chefs and waiting staff were sitting down having their own meal. It was so embarrassing. She would have to leave soon.

'No one came,' he said, barely looking up at her as she slipped back into her seat.

Erin blinked hard, trying not to cry again. She sniffed and reached for a hankie.

'You okay?' he asked, worried.

'No,' she admitted, the word coming out like a gulping sound as she tried not to break down.

He left his laptop and came and sat beside her.

'It's a guy, isn't it? A right shit!'

'No, it's not.' Erin took a deep breath. She didn't know him at all, but she couldn't keep it up any longer. 'I was meant to meet someone very important in my life today – my mother.'

'Your mother?'

'Yes – my biological mother. We've never met. She gave me up for adoption when I was a baby. There's never been any sort of contact, but today was meant to be the big day. My social worker helped to set it up so that we would meet on neutral ground and in a public place like they advise . . . But what a fecking disaster. I guess she just chickened out – didn't want to meet me at all.'

'Don't be so hard on yourself and on her.'

'What?'

'It must be a very difficult situation – for both of you.'

Erin couldn't believe it. This stranger was actually taking her mother's part.

'You could say that!' she laughed. 'Talk about understatement.'

'I think they are closing up now,' he nodded in the direction of the restaurant manager, who was coming towards them. 'We'd better go.'

'I suppose.'

Erin grabbed her bill from the table and paid.

It was four thirty p.m. and she just couldn't face going home to the apartment or to her parents and the barrage of questions she would get. God knows how many missed calls and texts she'd logged; everyone would be dying to find out how things went with Kate. But she wasn't up to facing them yet.

'Will you go home?' he asked, standing beside her at the door.

'I couldn't face it yet,' she admitted candidly, trying not to cry.

'My place is still in use,' he explained, 'but if you fancy a drink, there's a nice bar around the corner . . . Not too loud or noisy, a good place to chill.'

Erin found herself nodding and falling into step with him as they made for O'Reilly's.

The place was dead – just two old codgers nursing pints of Guinness up at the bar and a few Italians sitting at a table near the door. They'd obviously been shopping and were having a reviving drink.

'What will you have?' he asked.

She was dying for a drink and he got her a glass of wine.

'Thanks.' Erin realized that she didn't even know his name.

'I'm Matt,' he said, introducing himself as he took a sip from his pint.

'I'm Erin – Erin Harris,' she said formally, shaking his hand. 'I'm sorry that I've interrupted whatever you were working on.'

'Just doing a few script changes for a documentary I'm making,' he said, looking at her. He had the darkest eyes she had ever seen – liquid, almost like a deer or a dog.

'You work in film?'

'Yes, for my sins. I go from project to project, on commissions we get from RTE or TV3, or Channel 4 or BBC. It's always a hassle trying to get projects off the ground and up and running. Budgets are being slashed all over the place, so it's tough out there!'

'Tell me about it!' she laughed. 'I work in graphic design.'

'Which company?'

'De Berg O'Leary.'

'They're good. I've met that guy Declan a few times. He did the design for us on a big documentary we made for BBC about Cromwell a few years back.'

'I remember that,' she said, impressed. 'He has a poster of it in his office. Maybe you want to work?' she added, gesturing towards his laptop case.

'Nah, I've done enough for today. I've a bit of editing on a piece we filmed a few weeks ago, but it can wait.'

Erin felt relieved. Half an hour later she was buying him another pint and trying to drown her sorrows in a lovely glass of Merlot.

'You okay?'

'Not really,' she admitted, 'but I'd prefer to be sitting here than facing a hundred questions from everyone.'

'They're just curious,' he said. 'Everyone's probably worried about you.'

Erin soon found herself confiding in this stranger, telling him all about herself, her family, and about Kate, the woman she was meant to meet.

'That's probably the end of it,' she trailed off. 'It's better to forget her, not try to see her again.'

'Do you usually give up so easy?'

'No, I don't,' she protested, 'but—'

'Then don't this time. You might regret it.'

'But Kate's made her intentions clear – she doesn't want to meet me.'

'Don't take *no* for an answer unless it suits you too,' he persisted, serious.

'I don't know what I should do . . . I can't even think straight . . .'

'Think logically. Go on, Erin – even I know something about the woman from what you've told me.'

'What do you mean?'

'You have her single name, Kate Flanagan, and you have her age; and the social worker as good as told you that she got married within two years of your birth . . . so it's quite a narrow window you have to search.'

'Search?'

'Yes, for her married name, the name on her marriage cert, presuming she married in Ireland. It should be fairly easy to find – then you will have an address at least and can start tracking more information.'

'Have you done this before?'

'I told you – I make documentaries. It's what I do,' smiled Matt. 'You get to be good at searching for and finding out things.'

'Thanks, Matt.'

'No problem.'

They had two more drinks and then Erin realized she really had to go home. She had about five missed calls from her mum and two from her dad, and even three messages from Luke.

'Look!' She passed her phone to Matt. 'What do I tell them?'

'The truth.'

'They'll be so upset for me.'

'Fair enough, but if you do try to meet Kate, maybe next time don't tell them . . .'

She watched as he started to use her phone.

'I'm putting in my number, just in case . . .'

He really was a nice guy – a bit nerdy, but in a nice, old-fashioned way.

'Hey, I'd better get going too,' he said, getting up and grabbing his things. 'I'm meeting someone later and I want to get rid of this stuff and check in with Ritchie and his Dutch lady.'

'Matt, thanks for everything.'

'I didn't do much.'

'You listened.' Erin hugged him.

O'Reilly's had started to fill up and some musicians were beginning to set up at the back of the bar. It was raining outside. They were going different directions, so Erin headed up towards the nearby line of waiting taxis as Matt pulled up his hood and disappeared into the wet night.

She checked her phone, reading her numerous messages. It was so embarrassing. Her mum, her dad, her friends, even Uncle Bill had texted her. What the hell was she going to say to everyone?

Chapter Twenty

KATE STOOD IN THE LIVING ROOM, FROZEN LIKE A STATUE, THE keys of her car in her hands. She couldn't do it. She couldn't move, leave here and drive in to meet her daughter. She wasn't in a fit state to get behind the wheel of a car, she was so anxious. Maybe she should order a taxi to collect her and bring her into the city centre? But she just couldn't do it. She stayed rooted to the spot, conscious of time ticking by and a girl sitting in a Dublin restaurant waiting for her to arrive . . .

Time passing . . . the moments slipping . . . away . . .

She went upstairs and searched in the bottom of her section of the wardrobe. She found what she was looking for, then sat down on the bed and opened the old cardboard memory box that she kept hidden. It was all that she had of her baby: a tiny clipping of hair, two photos, her plastic name-bracelet, and a copy of the birth certificate and the letter of permission that she had signed with the adoption agency. A pink and a white Mothercare baby-grow and a pink knitted hat. She felt the softness of the wool. Sometimes it seemed like she only dreamed about giving birth to a child, imagined it. But touching each of these items reminded her of the truth, and of her actions.

It was so long ago, but sometimes it seemed like only yesterday that she and Johnny had been together. Madly in love, obsessed with each other, two young fools who had no idea what the future would bring. Jonathan Devlin was everything she ever wanted in a boyfriend: tall and good looking, self-confident and sure of what he wanted – what they both wanted. Being with him was exciting and crazy, and made Kate feel happier than she had ever felt before. They were mad about each other, spending every spare minute they had together.

She was only eighteen when they first met, a Galway girl sharing a crowded student digs in Dublin with three other country girls. Johnny was from Wicklow, and, like Kate, was studying at the College of Commerce in Rathmines. Somehow they had found each other. She'd got a flat tyre on her bicycle and Johnny had fixed it and asked her out for a drink in McGraths Bar that night. So they began to go out. They became inseparable, always together, both full of plans for the future, travel, music, jobs, money, and having lots of fun and laughs together. She presumed that Johnny loved her just as much as she loved him.

When she found out she was pregnant she'd been scared at first, but she knew that Johnny would stand by her. They loved each other and that was all that mattered. A baby might not have been part of the plan so soon, but she knew Johnny would accept it, be happy.

Well that's what she had stupidly thought, but she had been wrong. Getting pregnant had been utterly disastrous. Johnny was young, scared just like her, and soon made it very clear that having a baby together was most definitely not part of his plan. If she wanted to keep this baby, she was doing it on her own.

Devastated, she'd hidden her pregnancy. She stopped going to lectures and stopped visits home to Glenalley as her pregnancy began to be very obvious. She was too scared to tell anyone about the baby, especially her dad, knowing his reaction. Dermot Flanagan was an old-fashioned type of man, strict but fair, often dictating what his kids could and could not do. He'd done his very best to raise them since her mum's death and Kate knew that he would be absolutely devastated to discover that his youngest daughter was pregnant. So she'd kept it a secret from him and everyone else who might have helped or supported her.

She went to stay with her sister Sally and Sally's husband Mike in Rathfarnham. They were wonderful to her – Sally even came to the hospital with her when she went into labour and baby Anna was born.

She had phoned and left messages for Johnny, but he hadn't even bothered to come and see their baby until the night before she was due to leave the hospital, and then he had barely bothered to speak to her, though he admitted how beautiful their daughter was. There was no offer of him helping or being in any way involved in their child's life.

Heartbroken, Kate had realized that it was finally over with Johnny. He was not going to change his mind. He did not want a baby and that's all there was to it. He was a student and had no intention of settling down with her. She was alone and she felt trapped. How could she manage raising a baby?

She had panicked. She had talked to the social worker a few times about the possibility of adoption, but now, faced with life in a bedsit living on social welfare with her small daughter, she realized that she wanted more – more for herself and certainly more for her daughter. So the process she had explored about giving up her child for adoption suddenly became real, and she signed the necessary papers and the adoption agency took over.

Sally kept asking if she was sure this was what she wanted, urging her to consider what she was doing, not to rush into it; but Kate was determined. She had done the right thing, gone through with the pregnancy, had her baby, but, like Johnny, she too was young and scared and just wanted to run away and forget about it. In hindsight, she knew she was in some sort of shock and didn't realize the consequences of what she was doing in giving up her daughter.

So her baby, Anna, had been adopted by a married couple who were desperate to have a child of their own. The final adoption order was granted almost twelve weeks after Anna's birth.

Kate had never returned to the college in Rathmines. Johnny had come back into her life briefly, some of the old magic rekindled, both of them crying for their baby – but she knew that the decision that had been made was something that would always eat away at any relationship between them. He was moving to London and asked her to come over, see how things went between them, give it another go; but there was no real commitment, and one of her friends hinted that he might even have started seeing someone else.

Johnny was gone, the baby was gone, and there wasn't a day that Kate didn't think about her impetuous decision.

*   *   *

117

She stopped suddenly. She heard someone's key in the front door and recognized Paddy's footstep immediately. What was he doing home?

'Kate, are you there?' he called from the kitchen.

She quickly pushed the box back into its hiding place and gathered herself. He was coming upstairs.

'I forgot my wallet,' Paddy said, making straight for the shelf in the wardrobe where he kept his keys and cufflinks and things.

'Why didn't you phone me?' she asked, watching as he rooted around.

'There it is!' he said, relieved, grabbing the brown leather wallet and sliding it into his trouser pocket. 'I was hoping I hadn't dropped it somewhere.'

'Do you have time for a coffee?' she asked.

'Sorry, love, I don't have time. I'm meeting someone from a New Zealand wine company to see what lines they're importing. Hey, you're all dressed up!' He suddenly noticed what she was wearing. 'Are you going out somewhere?'

'I was meant to go to a lunch thing with Sally, but she's come down with some kind of tummy bug so she cancelled it. I'd better change out of this.'

'Listen, I'll talk to you tonight.'

She kissed him briefly and watched from the window as the large, solid figure of her husband returned to the silver Toyota parked in the driveway.

Glimpsing herself in the mirror, she began to tear off her clothes, flinging them all over the bedroom floor. She thought of the girl sitting in the restaurant . . . She was a stranger to her. She must have been mad even to have considered going and meeting her. Heaven knows what that girl wanted from her. What good could come of meeting her? The past was the past, nothing could change or rewrite it. Her baby . . . Anna . . . was gone. Johnny was gone. Both hidden away like the old memory box deep in her mind.

She was not prepared after all these years for someone to come along and destroy her family and the good life she had built with Paddy.

The time had passed. The moment was gone. The choice was made.

Chapter Twenty-one

THE APARTMENT WAS EMPTY. ERIN WAS SO RELIEVED THAT Nikki and Claire were already gone out. She'd talk to them tomorrow. Even though they were her best friends she couldn't face letting them see how devastated she really was by Kate's actions. She needed to think, to sleep, and to forget that Kate Flanagan was ever a part of her life. She should never have gone searching and trying to find out who she really was. What a disaster! She should have let it lie and been happy with the nice life she had. Why had she done it? Why had she wanted to open the whole Pandora's Box? Upset her parents? Dig up the past? She had stirred up feelings she had never experienced before – and pain she hadn't believed possible.

She needed another drink and, grabbing a bottle of red wine from their wine rack and a glass from the kitchen, she flung off her shoes and jeans and cardigan and crawled into bed.

The phone rang again. It was her mum.

She couldn't put off talking to her any more. She had to tell her what had happened – or, more precisely, what didn't happen.

'Erin, is everything okay? I've phoned you so many times. I know that you and Kate were probably far too busy talking and getting to know each other, but I—'

'Mum, Kate didn't bother to even bloody turn up.'

'What?'

'I waited in the café for hours for her but she never came. She stood me up, Mum! It was awful.'

'Oh Erin, I'm so sorry, really sorry this has happened to you.' Erin could feel the genuine concern and upset in her mother's voice. 'I never expected something like this to happen . . . for her to do that. You poor pet. Where are you?'

'I'm here in Sandymount.' Erin struggled to control herself.

'Do you want to come home? Your dad and I are in tonight. Maybe you'd be better here with us.'

'Mum, I don't really feel like talking or anything. I just want to stay here on my own, sleep a bit. I've been so wound up about this all week and now I just need to crash.'

'You could crash here in your old bed at home,' her mother continued. 'I'll come and collect you.'

'Thanks, Mum, but not tonight. I just want to be on my own.'

'Are you sure that's wise? We could talk about it—'

'Mum, I don't want to talk about it.'

'Of course, love. I understand.'

Erin knew well that her mother didn't understand. Nina Harris was one of the most protective mothers ever and spent her whole life looking out for Erin and Jack, looking after them, catering for their needs, often putting her own life and interests on hold for the sake of her children. She was a good mother – the best ever.

'Erin, will you come over tomorrow then? We could go for a walk . . . '

Her mother believed half the troubles of the world could be solved by going on a walk, that the fresh air and exercise and rhythm of walking were a salve for the soul.

'Okay. Okay,' she agreed.

'Try to sleep, Erin,' finished Nina. 'You've had a shock.'

'Goodnight, Mum.'

Erin sipped her wine. She *was* shocked. She felt sort of sick and shaky and cold, and she pulled on her pyjamas and a fleece as she gathered the duvet around her.

The phone went. No doubt her mum again. But this time it was Luke.

'Hey, Erin, what's been going on with you and that new mother of yours? Why haven't you answered my calls?' he asked.

'Luke, it was awful, really awful.' She began to cry; she couldn't help herself.

'Don't tell me she's an absolute bitch!'

'I wouldn't know, as she never even bothered to turn up . . . I mean so little to her that she couldn't even be bothered to give me an hour of her busy bloody life after twenty-six years.'

'Shit!'

'Exactly,' said Erin vehemently. 'That is exactly how I feel right now.'

'Erin, baby, I'm really sorry about her. Where are you?'

'I'm back in the flat. The girls have gone out.'

'Do you want me to come over?' he offered. She could hear noise and laughter and music in the background.

'Where are you?'

'I'm in Doheny and Nesbitt's with a few lads. I've had a few

Three Women

pints but I'll get a taxi to yours, or otherwise you could come into town and join us. Davy's girlfriend Astrid is here. A few drinks might do you good!'

Erin had absolutely no intention of joining Luke and his drinking buddies for their usual Saturday-night session before heading off to a night club.

'Luke, I'm not really in the mood for a night out after today.'

'Then we can stay in together – talk about it.'

She certainly didn't feel like going back over it all again with Luke, which would no doubt end as usual with them going to bed and having sex, which was Luke's answer to everything.

'That's just it. I'm knackered and upset and I just need to sleep.'

'Exactly,' he murmured softly.

'No – I mean on my own, conked out with the duvet over my head.'

'Oh! Are you sure you don't need me there to help you un-wind and relax a bit?'

'No!' Erin insisted, sensing his disappointment.

'I feel like I'm letting you down, Erin.'

'You're not, honestly you're not.'

'Are you sure?'

'Yes. Listen, I'll talk to you tomorrow about it, Luke, okay?'

Putting down the phone, she felt so alone. But what she was going through was not something she could share with anyone. She was so disappointed and upset that she felt awful. She hadn't known what to expect when Marian set up the meeting. Maybe she had hoped that she and her birth mother could have some kind of relationship, or a type of friendship, but she hadn't been expecting Kate to become a big part of her life. She already had a mother she adored and was close to, so

123

she didn't need that from Kate, but she was expecting her to be decent and that the two of them would have some kind of connection. How wrong she had been!

Kate Flanagan must be a cold fish, uncaring and distant, glad to have got rid of her unwanted child and now unwilling to admit that Erin even existed. Luke was right – her natural mother must be a bitch to have done what she did to her today and put her through such turmoil. She would never forgive her.

Chapter Twenty-two

NINA COULDN'T BELIEVE WHAT THAT KATE WOMAN HAD DONE! Standing Erin up in a busy restaurant, leaving her to sit there for hours waiting for her to appear was cruel. Erin had built up the meeting with her natural mother and was hoping that some kind of relationship or friendship would develop between them and now this . . . It was heartbreaking and humiliating for her daughter to have to go through being let down by her so-called mother. Nina was fuming, and if she ever met that woman, birth mother or not, she would give her a right piece of her mind!

'Nina, for heaven's sake stop,' urged Tom, who'd been listening to her continuous rant since she got off the phone with Erin. 'Nothing you or I can do can change what has happened. Erin is an adult and no matter how much we try to protect her, she is going to have to deal with disappointments and heartaches like we all do. It's what grown-ups do, and she's a grown-up now even though you seem to think she's still a little girl.'

'She will always be our little girl and I'll do everything in my power to protect her for as long as I'm alive and even afterwards if that's possible!'

'Knowing you, that will happen,' he retorted.

'We waited so long to be parents, Tom – don't you remember it?' she demanded fiercely. 'All those tests and fertility charts and doctors and hospitals, and then getting pregnant, thinking we might have a chance . . . ten weeks . . . twelve weeks, and then miscarriages . . . losing another baby . . .'

Tom nodded slowly, his head in his hands.

'Then there were waiting lists, and interviews and inspections and assessments, and us jumping through hoops to see if we were suitable people to adopt . . . Imagine trying to see if we were suitable to even be parents! I fought so hard for motherhood that I can't help myself. That's why you and Erin and Jack are the most important people in my life.'

'Kids grow up, Nina,' he smiled, cupping her face in his hands and tracing the outline of her jaw with his finger. 'Then it will just be the two of us again. Will you mind being stuck with an old fogey like me?'

'Less of the old, please!' she hushed him. 'We still have lots of good years ahead of us, Tom, lots of things to do and places to go.'

'Nothing stays the same,' he said gently.

'I know that,' she said. 'But we have each other and the kids, and that's what matters.'

Tom opened a bottle of wine as they sat down to eat together. Usually they went out on a Saturday or entertained friends at home, but Nina herself had been so worked up about Erin meeting her birth mother that she'd told Tom that tonight she just wanted a quiet night in. Tom had been away on business so much lately and working so hard, that a night in relaxing would do neither of them any harm. He should be winding down now, work-wise, and beginning to think of retirement instead of always trying to meet clients and being so caught up in work. The business, Harris Engineering, was a medium-sized company that Tom had set up over twenty years ago, supplying heat and water and ventilation systems to many of the big building projects around the country: offices, hospitals, shopping centres and schools. But now, with government cutbacks and lack of investment funds, the company was taking on more and more projects overseas. Sometimes Tom seemed so preoccupied that it worried her. He was pushing himself far too hard.

'Oh, by the way, I'm over in Manchester next week,' he said, topping up her glass.

'You'll be home that night?'

'No, I'm staying over for two nights. Bit of business there.'

Nina sighed. At the moment Tom seemed always to be away or out somewhere trying to get business.

'And I'll probably play golf on Saturday with Frank. He's organized for a few of us to play down in Mount Juliet, so we'll stay over and have dinner afterwards. Do you mind?'

'Of course not. I'll organize to do something with Lizzie or one of my friends.'

The one thing Nina had learned about marriage over the years was to give each other space. Couples needed that if they were to survive years together and stay interested in each other. She and Tom had what she considered a good marriage, but they definitely had each developed interests of their own.

'Is there any dessert?' he asked.

'Eclairs!' she laughed. Tom had such a sweet tooth. 'And I'll make us some of that French filtered coffee you like before we put something on the TV.'

As she relaxed in front of the fire, Nina thought of Erin all alone in the apartment tonight. She should have insisted that she come home. As she sipped her wine she slipped off her shoes and pulled her feet up on the couch. Even though she was angry about the way Kate had treated her daughter, Nina had to admit that she was secretly relieved that the actual meeting between her daughter and her birth mother hadn't even taken place . . . and she hoped it never would.

Chapter Twenty-three

IT HAD BEEN SUCH A SHIT WEEKEND THAT ERIN WAS ACTUALLY glad to be back in the office on Monday with plenty of work to keep her busy. She'd been handed a design brief that had just come in for a new Italian children's shop that was opening off Grafton Street, and she had also been asked to create an album cover for Lia, a young Irish folk singer. She had listened to her songs and they were amazing! And to top it all, Monika had asked her to take over working on Declan's project, developing an overall concept for the online marketing package for a new brand of Irish foot lotions that were based on all-natural seaweed ingredients and were selling all over the world.

'Why they all come at the same time I don't know, but that's the way it goes,' shrugged Monika. 'We sit around twiddling our thumbs for months with little or no work and then everyone wants us. Declan has got that big contract for Nua, the new green energy company, so we have to try to keep a balance with the rest of the work. Clients are like gold dust, so it's important that we perform and keep everyone happy.'

Erin nodded. She really liked working here and would love to see the company prosper again. Declan and Monika gave their staff immense creative freedom in terms of ideas and design concepts compared to some of the other companies, and there was a huge camaraderie among the staff working for them, with none of the bitter rivalry about projects that she knew existed elsewhere. Her friend Lisa had hated the work atmosphere and constant backstabbing in her old office before she eventually quit and moved to London.

Turning on her Apple Mac, she began to play around with the shop name. She yawned, still tired and shell-shocked from what had happened.

Yesterday, despite almost a gale blowing, she'd walked the West Pier in Dun Laoghaire with her mother, Nina barely able to disguise the anger she felt about Kate while trying at the same time to be sympathetic.

'Put it behind you now, Erin. You have made the contact. You have written to each other. She knows about you and you know about her. You are both alive and well and have very separate lives. Let that be an end to it.' Perhaps her mum was right, she thought, as they enjoyed a bagel and coffee afterwards.

Nikki and Claire, she knew, were embarrassed and hurt for her and the way she had been treated. They had a very low opinion of Kate Flanagan now and didn't bother trying to hide it.

'She doesn't deserve to be your mother, Erin, honestly she doesn't. Forget her!'

Luke had arrived on Sunday evening with flowers, a consoling bottle of wine and a takeaway and there were none of the 'I told you so . . .' recriminations from him that she was expecting. It had been nearly midnight when he'd reluctantly finally left the apartment and gone home.

Luke had talked to his boss and it looked like the move to the London office was almost definite now.

'Erin, this is such an opportunity for me to transfer over there. You do realize what it will mean in career terms?'

'Of course,' she said, not wanting to admit she had no idea of the inner workings of the company he was always talking about.

'I'll be at the heart of everything in Hibernian – the London office is where all the major transactions happen. My bonus will be bigger, I'll get a much broader experience and with any luck there'll be far more chance of promotion, not like here where everything is on hold.'

He was excited and happy – the total opposite of what she was feeling.

'It'll take about six weeks or so to organize the total transfer, but I'll be working full time in London by then.'

'Luke, I'm so happy for you. I know that's what you want,' she said, kissing him.

'Yes, but I want you there with me too, Erin. Have you heard any more about the interviews?'

'Nothing yet,' she replied. 'But I'll chase them up.'

She wasn't going to tell him that she'd been asked to go over last Thursday for a first-round interview with a really good design company in Battersea and she had turned it down.

'I'll go and look at some apartments next week when I am over, try to get an idea on rents and locations. We want to be pretty central, so it's probably going to cost a fair bit,' he warned as he kissed her goodnight.

Erin was stunned. She didn't want to be rushed into things; she needed time to think.

'Couldn't you share with some of the other guys for a bit until I know what's happening?'

'What do you mean?'

'Well, with my career . . . Getting a new job might not be that easy and I have a lot of projects here that I need to finish.'

'Okay, maybe you're right,' he grinned, kissing her again, 'but that's only temporarily, until you and I get a really nice place of our own.'

Erin couldn't even think about London now – she was much too busy. Luke was thinking about his career and she had to think about hers . . .

Chapter Twenty-four

NINA HAD BOOKED THE CINEMA AND ORGANIZED TO MEET HER old friend Vonnie for an early-bird meal in Bruno's Bistro in Dun Laoghaire before heading to the cinema to see the screen version of *The Dressmaker*, a French book they'd both really enjoyed reading.

'My book club loved it too, but I'm just nervous that they'll destroy the book,' admitted Vonnie, 'and then no one will want to read it again.'

'Sometimes the film works really well and brings the book to an even bigger audience,' said Nina, who was always struck by the visual elements of everything she read. 'Remember *The Help*, and *The Boy in the Striped Pyjamas* and *Chocolat*. They all were brilliant!'

They ordered quickly, both opting for the red wine, as the restaurant filled up with Saturday diners.

'Thanks for asking me,' said Vonnie. 'It beats sitting in on my own!'

'I'm on my own tonight too,' laughed Nina. 'Tom's in Kilkenny having dinner with some friends after a golf outing.'

Nina knew how hard it was for Vonnie ever since she and her husband, Simon, had separated. It was no fun being single again at their age and trying to manage on your own. Vonnie's life had literally fallen to pieces eighteen months ago when Simon had left her for a twenty-eight-year-old who worked in the bank with him. Vonnie was doing her best to keep things normal at home, but she was under enormous financial and emotional pressure.

Nina found herself confiding in Vonnie about Erin's birth mother's failure to turn up to meet her last week.

'What kind of woman would do that to her daughter? She sounds like a right b—, if you ask me. Erin must be so upset!'

'She is, but you know something? I'm happy that that woman is not coming back into our lives. It's something I've been dreading for years,' Nina admitted, 'that Erin and this birth mother of hers would meet and just click and be so alike and in tune with each other that suddenly I'd become obsolete.'

'Don't be so stupid, Nina! You're her mum. Nothing will change that!' insisted Vonnie. 'How could you even think that?'

'I know it's pathetic, but it's what I was worried about and now, thank heaven, it's not an issue any more,' Nina said, relieved, as Vonnie filled her in on her week.

'Simon's so enthralled with bloody Louisa that it's as if our three boys never existed. He suddenly wants to be young and carefree with no dependants,' she confided. 'He's complaining about paying their school and college fees and the cost of keeping them. Honestly, does he think the boys are going to stop eating and growing just because he's not around? I have to find some kind of job, Nina, I badly need the money.'

Nina felt so sorry for Vonnie. Her friend had been a stalwart over the years, generous and kind to all who knew her, and with her blonde hair and curvy figure she was absolutely gorgeous. Simon O'Neill must need his head examined to have left her for another woman.

'Jobs are really scarce,' said Nina, knowing well that if twenty-three-year-old college graduates couldn't find work with all their degrees and energy and computer savvy, with the best will in the world it was going to be almost impossible for someone like Vonnie to find a job.

'Trust Simon to go and pick the worst time in the bloody world to dump me!'

Nina burst out laughing.

'I'm serious, Nina. I have to do something. I saw a computer course advertised in the local employment office to help people get back to work and I put my name down for it.'

'You and computers!'

'I know – but I just have to master all the stuff employers want nowadays. Excel and PowerPoint and CAD or whatever it is I need. The boys said they'd help me. Anyway, I'm bored sitting at home. It'll be good for me to have to go to a class every day and meet new people.'

'That's wonderful, Vonnie – you'll do great. How long does the course last?'

'Six months, but then you can do an advanced course if you want.'

Nina was full of admiration for her. Vonnie had courage and was picking herself up and starting over again instead of feeling sorry for herself.

They both had ordered the seafood bake for their main course and shared a dessert of warm, gooey chocolate pudding and home-made ice cream afterwards, keeping an eye on the time, conscious of people waiting at the bar to get a table.

As she paid the bill and they grabbed their coats and passed along by the other tables, Nina stopped suddenly, spotting friends of theirs.

'Hey, Nina, how are you?'

It was Frank Hennessy and his wife Brenda with their son Richard and his wife. Frank, with his bald head and big build in a tight-fitting blue-striped shirt, stood up to say hello. She introduced them to Vonnie.

'Frank, I thought you and Tom were playing golf today,' she said, kissing him.

'No, Richard and I played this afternoon – he wiped the floor with his old man!'

'Were you playing down in Kilkenny?'

'No, not today. We stuck close to home. The two of us played out in Woodbrook. Why?'

'Oh, I must have got mixed up. I thought Tom mentioned that he was playing with you today in Mount Juliet . . . My mistake – it must be someone else he was playing with,' she said, suddenly embarrassed.

'The cinema,' mouthed Vonnie silently.

'Look, we've got to go – we're rushing to see a film,' she explained as they grabbed their coats and headed outside.

Nina wondered if maybe Tom was at home and checked her phone. Nothing, no messages.

'What's up?' asked Vonnie as they walked together towards the large Omniplex cinema.

'Nothing – just me getting a bit mixed up about what Tom was doing today.'

'You're lucky you don't have to worry about Tom, not like

the way I was about Simon. He told me so many lies – working late, stuck at work things, weekends away with work colleagues on so-called conferences and business things. It was just one lie after another, and I never even suspected. Imagine – new suits, new shirts, new clothes, new flipping boxers and socks and aftershave, and I still didn't twig it . . . I was such a fool. Alarm bells should have been ringing.'

Nina said nothing. Tom had invested in a new business suit and shirts a few months ago and dumped most of his comfy old underwear too. He was nothing like that bastard Simon, but what the hell was going on?

The cinema was packed and even though she tried to lose herself in the film, her mind was racing. Where was Tom tonight, and who was he with?

She could see Vonnie was engrossed in the story, but she was finding it hard to concentrate. She was being silly, imagining something when there was absolutely nothing going on, only that she hadn't been listening properly to what Tom was saying . . . She turned her attention to the screen.

Coming home in the car, Vonnie rambled on about the film. Nina said little. Truth to tell, she had barely seen it. Vonnie asked her in for a cup of coffee. She couldn't face going home on her own in the state she was in and was glad to sit in the cosy kitchen as her friend made her a cup of caffeine-free coffee and produced a packet of her favourite Jaffa cakes and they tried to concoct a hundred crazy ways for Vonnie O'Neill to make money quickly . . .

Chapter Twenty-five

NINA HAD BARELY SLEPT A WINK ALL NIGHT. THERE HAD BEEN no message from Tom and even though she had been tempted to phone him and demand to know where he was, she had somehow retained her composure and done nothing. Something was going on; she had no idea what it was, but one thing she was sure of was that her husband was absolutely nothing like Simon O'Neill, who had always been a womanizer. Poor Vonnie had put up with a lot with that Romeo, and even though it was hard on her she was probably better off without him.

After getting showered and dressed, she walked down to Dalkey village, went to mass and bought the Sunday papers. There was probably a very innocent reason for her thinking Tom was in Kilkenny.

It started to lash rain around lunchtime and all plans to bring the dog for a walk were abandoned, as Bailey had developed an aversion to rain in his older years and would almost have to be dragged out the door if he felt a raindrop. Wanting to keep herself busy, she decided to work and sought the refuge of her study.

She had been commissioned by one of her publishers to do ten illustrations for a beautiful new collection of Oscar Wilde stories. He was one of her favourite Irish authors and she was very excited about it. Drawing and painting had always been a big part of her life and she was lucky to have had the opportunity to go and study art when she left school. Work had been hard to come by when she graduated and she had done bits of everything: illustrations for magazines and newspapers; selling her prints and paintings at various exhibitions and shows; and over time she had built up a body of work. Even when the children had come along, Tom had encouraged her to keep her own career going – he knew how much it meant to her. Once she sat at her drawing board or easel, time and worries and cares seemed to disappear. The room was a mess – organized chaos, she called it – but she knew where everything was. Sitting down, Nina concentrated and began to work.

It was just starting to get late when she realized the time and switched on the lights. She never pulled the curtains, as she liked to see the garden. Daylight brought the birds and the cheeky squirrel, and dusk the fox and the hedgehog and the small creatures that preferred the dark.

Bailey was asleep at her feet in his basket. She'd better feed him and, now the rain had finally stopped, let him out into the garden. She went downstairs to the kitchen, surprised to see that Tom was home and reading the papers.

'When did you get back?'

'About an hour and a half ago.'

'How was the golf?'

'The golf was great yesterday and I stayed on and had lunch with Frank today. The rain was so bad I decided there was no point rushing back.'

Nina didn't know what to say or do. Should she say about meeting Frank last night – confront him and have a massive row? Why would Tom lie to her? What reason could he possibly have to try and pretend he was somewhere he was obviously not?

'How's Brenda?'

'Well I didn't see her, but she's fine,' he said before burying himself in the business section of the *Sunday Times*. She felt like snatching it out of his hands and smacking him round the head with it.

There was definitely something up, and she had no idea what it was. Tom was normally as honest and straightforward as they come; there never had been deceits and lies in their relationship over all the years.

'Tom, is everything okay?' she asked, hovering over the table opposite him.

'It was an awful drive back,' he said, putting the paper down for a second, 'so a nice cup of coffee wouldn't go amiss.'

Honestly, she'd strangle him, she thought, as she put on the kettle. If something was going on with her husband she was determined to find it out.

Chapter Twenty-six

ERIN WANTED TO PUT KATE FLANAGAN OUT OF HER MIND, forget about her, just the way Kate had blanked her from her mind. But she just couldn't forget about her, however much she tried. It was eating away at her no matter what she did.

She had talked to Marian and to Sheila about it. Marian had made it very clear that, while Kate regretted what she had done in standing her up, she was adamant that she didn't want to meet her or have any further contact with her.

'Can't you get her to change her mind?' Erin pleaded.

'I'm sorry, but we have to respect your birth mother's wishes,' Marian had said firmly, closing the door to any further discussion about the matter.

'It's very hard for you to listen to what she is saying, but you have to learn to accept it,' advised Sheila when Erin met with her.

To Erin it seemed like her natural mother had given her away for a second time, deliberately walked away from her again. Maybe she should take everyone's advice and just forget about her and be satisfied with the information she had. But somehow she couldn't accept it. She wasn't a three-week-old baby, a child, any more and she wasn't going to give up.

'How are things? Hope you haven't given up!'

Erin smiled at the text from Matt, the guy she had met in the restaurant. She texted him back, telling him she seemed to have hit a brick wall.

'Brick walls are for breaking or kicking down,' he texted back. *'And I'm available!'*

Erin remembered that Matt had advised her not to give up and to use the information she already had. She had to sort out what she knew about Kate and what she needed to find out. There wasn't a huge amount to go on, as all she had was her own birth certificate and Kate's letter to her, but she phoned Matt and agreed to meet him for a sandwich at lunchtime at a pub round the corner from work.

'Are you sure what I'm doing isn't illegal, Matt? I don't want to be arrested,' Erin fretted.

'If that was the case, almost every journalist and researcher and person trying to make a family tree would be in prison,' he said firmly. 'You are only looking at documents that are public records. And I presume if you do manage to trace this woman you have no plans to assassinate her?'

'No, I just want to find out for myself . . . maybe see her – I don't know . . .'

She listened as Matt, dark eyes serious, briefly outlined what she should do and where she should go, and told her to detail every name as a process of elimination would be needed.

'You will probably find there are about a million Kate Flanagans and you are trying to discover which one is yours.'

Erin thanked him when they finished. Matt was such a nice guy – one of those long-haired arty types that had packed her college and spent their time trying to change the world with their films and music and art, and always seemed to be just scraping by.

Okay, she knew Kate was married, but she had absolutely no idea of her married name or who she had married or where she lived. But Kate had said that she had a son of twenty-three. That probably meant that Kate Flanagan must have been married by then to have him. If she was born in March 1985 and if her half-brother was twenty-three, then he was born between 1987 and 1988, so Kate must have got married some time between those dates. There was a three-year window of 1985 to 1988 – but would someone get married within a few months of having a baby and giving it up to be adopted? No, it was more likely Kate got married in 1986 at the earliest. She needed to check the official Registry of Marriages to see if she could find out.

Erin had to take a holiday day off work to go to the Central Office for Registering Births, Marriages and Deaths in the city centre. It was already warm outside, with the weather forecasters saying the day would be a scorcher. She was tempted to grab a towel and a book and her sun lotions and head to Sandymount Strand for a few hours and forget about ever trying to track Kate down, but something inside her said, 'Focus. Do the proper research and get the information you need about your birth mother.'

Going into the office, she joined the queue and took a ticket. It was only 9.30 in the morning but already it was busy. She could see there were a lot of Americans researching their ancestry, and others trying to get information for their family trees. If anyone asked, that's what she would say she was doing. She was nervous as hell and wasn't sure what way the information she required was logged. Was it done alphabetically, or by year, or even place? She had no idea.

She went up to the help desk and asked about trying to trace the marriage of a relation.

'What year?' the girl at the counter asked.

'Maybe 1986, or perhaps it was 1987,' Erin replied. 'I'm not quite sure.'

'Do you know what month?'

'No.'

'Well then, you will have to start off with the first quarter, January to March, and I can let you have the second quarter too. Once you have finished with them, I can issue you with the two for the other half of that year,' she explained. 'If you take a seat at one of the desks, someone will bring it over to you.'

Erin sat down and waited. A man appeared with two massive books and placed them in front of her. Leather-bound, they were like giant ledgers and Erin felt immediately overwhelmed. This was like trying to find a needle in a flipping haystack. She opened the first page, 1 January 1986. The names of all the couples who got married on that day were listed alphabetically, line after line, giving the name of the groom, the name of the bride, their ages, where they were married, who married them, etc. She had no idea of the groom's name, so she was going to have to trawl through every name until she spotted a Kate Flanagan getting married.

A Kate Flanagan got married on 8 January and another one on 12 January. Shit! This was going to be impossible!

She wrote down the details on her notepad, but then when she figured out the ages of each she realized that they were both too old to be her mother.

This was going to take hours . . .

It was methodical and exhausting. She couldn't believe quite how many Kate Flanagans there were and how many of them had got married during that time frame and were approximately the same age. As she worked through the registers, she soon had thirteen Kates on her list! She was on the third quarter of 1986 when she found the details of a fourteenth: a Kate Anne Flanagan who had got married on 23 September 1986.

Erin couldn't believe it. This Kate had given a familiar address: the same Rathfarnham address as on Erin's birth certificate. This must be the Kate she was looking for. It had to be. She had married a Patrick Cassidy from Galway and her birth date, 15 June, made her twenty-two years old – the right age – when she got married.

Erin was so excited. Carrying the book up to the desk, she gave the reference number for their marriage and paid, then waited as the girl printed out a copy of the marriage certificate for her.

Kate's married name was Cassidy – Kate Cassidy. She now knew her mother's full name . . . But how was she going to find out where she lived? The phone book was probably full of Cassidys, and what if their number was ex-directory or they didn't use a landline?

Her half-brother's birth had got her this far; maybe if she could find his birth certificate it would give her even more information.

She went back up to the central desk and this time requested the Register for Births for the first quarter of the year 1987. Two Kate Cassidys had given birth to baby daughters, and an Anna May Cassidy had given birth to twins, a boy and a girl . . . She went back up and got the massive book for the second quarter. She went through each day alphabetically, glad that at least the surname began with a C.

Then she stopped. She'd definitely found it. Kate Anne Cassidy, *née* Flanagan, had given birth to a baby boy, Sean, on 16 June 1987. Father: Patrick Cassidy, with an address in Dublin – 125 Bayview Park, Sutton. She had found her mother and where she lived – she had her address!

Kate wasn't living down the country or miles away; she was living the other side of the city from her, probably only about eight or ten miles away at most.

Elated, Erin took out her iPhone, googled Directory En-quiries and put in the name Patrick Cassidy. She searched through the Dublin directory list and was amazed when she found a Patrick Cassidy living at 125 Bayview Park, Sutton. He and Kate and their family had never moved – she had found them!

Going home on the DART, she still couldn't believe it. She had uncovered the information the adoption agency wouldn't give her.

The girls were sitting out sunning themselves on the balcony by the time she got home.

'Where were you all day?' asked Nikki. 'What were you doing?'

'Researching,' she grinned, helping herself to a chilled Corona from the fridge.

'Boring . . .'

'Actually it was fascinating, because I'm almost a hundred per cent sure that I've located my birth mother Kate's home address!'

'Wow . . . I thought that it was top secret and kept under lock and key!' Claire said, looking up at her through her expensive Ray-Ban sunglasses.

'Yes, but I've got it!'

'Erin, that's great,' Nikki said, sipping a fizzy orange drink with ice. 'Now you can find her if you want to.'

'Yes.' The decision was hers now.

Chapter Twenty-seven

ERIN SAT OUTSIDE THE HOUSE IN BAYVIEW ESTATE IN HER CAR, watching.

It seemed a nice house, in a good middle-class area, semi-detached, double-glazed windows, well maintained, with four bedrooms she guessed, a neat front garden with space for parking two cars, and a climber creeping over the front door and around the living-room window. Nothing special, but it probably had a fairly big back garden where the kids in the family had grown up and played and barbecued and done all the usual family stuff that nice ordinary families did.

She would sit out here in the car for a while and keep watching. There was nobody home yet – the house still empty, but she could wait.

Listening to the radio, Erin ate a bar of chocolate she'd bought in the petrol station down the road and sipped a bottle of chilled water. She had told Declan that she needed some time off and had left the office early.

She felt uncomfortable, like a voyeur, a stalker, hiding, trying to see into someone else's life – a life she had absolutely no idea about.

It was about 4.45 when she spotted the silver Golf drive up the road, indicating as it turned into the driveway of number 125; a dark-haired woman getting out, a tall skinny teenage girl in a school uniform slamming the passenger door and running ahead to open the front door as the woman lifted what looked like a bag of groceries from the boot and locked the car.

'Turn around,' Erin wished silently. 'Let me see you.' But all she got was a glimpse of the woman's grey cardigan and jeans as she disappeared inside.

She sat there, hoping that her mother would come back out again. She waited and waited but Kate didn't appear.

An hour later she saw the tall, loping figure of a guy of about twenty with a heavy backpack, engrossed in texting on his phone as he turned into the house. He must be one of her sons. Well built and rugged, with wild fair hair, he looked kind of fun and reminded her a bit of Jack, who always looked like he should be on some sort of sports ground rather than doing mundane normal stuff like studying or working.

Kate was probably inside starting to make dinner for her family. She wondered if she was a good cook. Did they all eat together and chat around the table? What kind of family were they? Twenty minutes later another car turned into the drive-way – a black jeep – and she held her breath as a man got out of it, lifting some folders and a laptop case. He was average height, she guessed; the same unruly hair as the son, but his was grey and shorter, his blue-and-white shirt highlighting his large stomach and chest. He looked kind of handsome in a stocky sort of way.

As he shut the door, Erin felt herself shut out, excluded from the life these people had built and created for themselves. She had no connection with them – not really.

Had Kate thought about her over the years, worried about her, wondered if she was happy or sad, and if the adoption had worked out? Tried to imagine what she was doing with her life? Or had Kate simply put it all behind her and blocked out the fact that she'd ever had a child and given her away? Did Kate guess she was so close by now, so near her?

In a minute or two she could be at their front door, introducing herself, interrupting their family meal like some mad suicide bomber with her explosive strapped to her chest, coming among them ready to blow their safe family life apart.

Had Kate ever told her husband she'd had a baby? Told her daughter she had a sister? Confided in her sons?

Erin considered it, wanting just to get it over – talk to the woman, meet her, look into her eyes and see the truth of it. But she thought of the kid in her school uniform. She was only sixteen – a bad age for a girl to find out she had an illegitimate half-sister. The girl didn't deserve that.

Erin's heart was pounding in her chest, her adrenalin high, but not high enough for her to cross that driveway and invade their space. It was Kate she wanted to talk to, to meet and confront. She didn't want to hurt or embarrass anyone else. God knows what kind of lies her natural mother had told to protect her secret. She'd wait. Come back tomorrow, try to get Kate Flanagan on her own. This was between the two of them – that is, if there was any kind of connection between them other than just blood.

For years she had played the scene in her head, a continuous loop of the various scenarios that might be acted out the day she met her birth mother. What would they say to each other? Would there be an instant rapport? Would they fall into each other's arms? Or would Kate simply say that she had no interest in a relationship with her?

Erin had absolutely no idea what the outcome would be, but she had come too far and waited too long to be deterred, and tomorrow she would definitely go and meet Kate. She was determined to find out the truth about her birth and discover who she really was.

Inside, someone drew the curtains, the warm glow of yellow light the only thing visible from the window.

Turning her ignition, she started the engine and drove back out of the estate and headed for home. She'd waited so long for this, the day she would see her birth mother. Another day would make no difference.

Chapter Twenty-eight

ERIN DROVE ACROSS THE EAST LINK BRIDGE AND OVER TO THE Cassidys' house again the next day. She parked her little silver Polo a bit down the road. Kate's car was in the driveway and the windows were open upstairs, so she presumed that Kate was at home.

As she walked up the driveway towards the blue front door she noticed through the sitting-room window a marmalade-coloured cat sitting on a chair staring out at her. She was definitely in the right place.

Taking a breath, psyching herself up not to be afraid and to keep her resolve, she rang the door bell . . . She rang it again . . .

It seemed to take ages. Her heart was hammering in her chest . . . and then the front door swung open.

'Yes?'

The woman in front of her had shoulder-length dark hair and was wearing a pair of cord trousers and a fitted cream knitted sweater. She looked younger than Erin expected.

'Are you Mrs Cassidy?' she asked, almost in a whisper.

'Yes?' She was obviously presuming that Erin was one of

those young women who regularly called to the door trying to get customers to swap over from their current phone or TV or energy provider, and was waiting politely for her to begin her sales speech.

'I'm Erin . . .'

'Erin?' Kate looked totally confused.

'Erin. Your daughter . . . I wrote to you . . .'

'Oh my God!' Kate's hands flew to her face and Erin could see the shock in her eyes, her face paling, disbelieving.

'How did you find me?' she asked accusingly. 'Did someone in the agency give you this address?'

'No, I found it myself.' Erin could feel waves of utter disappointment washing over her. She felt sick, shaky . . . She should never have done this. The woman in front of her really didn't want anything to do with her. She should have believed Marian Kelly. She'd made a huge mistake coming here. Like a little kid, she felt like turning tail, running and getting the hell out of here.

There was utter silence. Neither of them knew what to say.

'I have to go out soon,' Kate suddenly offered. 'But if you want you can come in for a few minutes.'

She opened the door wider and Erin followed her through the hall and into a bright, square kitchen overlooking the back garden. They stood staring at each other. Funny – she was taller than her birth mother and probably at least a size smaller.

'I'll make us tea or coffee – which do your prefer?'

'I'll have coffee.' Erin watched as Kate busied herself in the kitchen. The room was immaculately clean and tidy, the dishwasher on, with only today's newspaper on the table, everything neat and tidy and organized – a complete contrast to the clutter of their big kitchen at home. A framed family photo of Kate with her husband and three children, obviously taken on an overseas sunshine holiday, hung on one wall. Curious, Erin secretly studied it.

'It was taken five years ago in Spain,' Kate said, catching her looking at it. 'It's my husband Paddy with Sean and Kevin and Aisling. It was a great holiday!'

Erin's eyes began to well with tears. Kate playing happy families, with no part for her. She turned away, looking out towards the garden as she struggled to compose herself.

'Why did you come?' Kate asked.

'I just wanted to meet you . . . to see you . . . for us to talk.'

'I'm not sure what you want me to talk about . . . to tell you.' Kate sat down at the table after passing her a mug and putting milk and sugar on the table.

'I need to know about me,' pleaded Erin. 'I'm twenty-six years old and I still don't know a lot about me and who I am . . .'

'I wasn't expecting this,' admitted Kate. 'I've kept having you a secret all these years. No one knows about you and I want it to stay that way.'

'If that's what you want, Kate,' Erin sighed, feeling strangely old, 'I'm not going to tell your secret. And in case you're worried, I don't need a mother because I already have a really great one that I love to bits. But I do want to find out about the past, what happened, why I was adopted . . . I don't know if you can understand that, but that's all I want from you.'

'That's all?' She could see the relief in Kate's eyes – funny, but they were just like hers, with the same kind of weird way of changing colour.

'Yes. You have your family and I have mine.'

'Okay,' said Kate, taking a deep breath, even more nervous

than Erin was. 'I'll tell you. But let's get some more coffee. I need it.'

Erin could see that she was shaking. So tense and stressed. Erin wanted to touch her, say to relax, it was okay. She didn't mean her any harm.

'When I had you I was very young,' explained Kate, sitting down with a big mug of coffee cradled in her hands. 'After I finished my Leaving Cert I was mad to go to Dublin. I got a place in the College of Commerce in Rathmines doing a business and accounting course. I always liked numbers. Like lots of other country kids I couldn't wait to get out of the place I grew up in, a little town outside Galway called Glenalley. My dad ran the local pub there. Mum died when I was fourteen, so it was left to Daddy to raise us and try to run the business. Coming to Dublin was strange and exciting, but I loved feeling all grown up and going to college. You know, I didn't miss home at all – not a bit, and I joined every club and society in college.'

'I did the same,' said Erin.

'I just wanted to try everything out – meet new people, have fun. I dated a few guys – nothing really special – then I met Johnny. I got a puncture on my bike one day and he fixed it for me. He was nice, really nice. He was studying journalism back then! We got on really well and began to go out. We were mad about each other. Both liked the same things – music, going to gigs and parties, staying up nearly all night talking about stupid things. Johnny was a big talker – he could talk for Ireland!'

'Did you love him?'

'Yes, I was mad about him. Then I got pregnant. I couldn't believe it. I checked the result three times but the doctor confirmed it. I had my second-year exams in May and you were due in March. It was a nightmare, but I knew that Johnny and I were okay and was sure we would somehow manage. He had a part-time bar job and I worked two evenings a week in Captain America's, the famous burger place.

'Then when I told him he freaked out. He said that we were too young to be parents and he was not giving up college to support me. I didn't know what to do, but I was sure he'd come around when he got used to the idea, and that we would be fine. We loved each other. Anyway, it wasn't fine.'

Kate struggled not to cry as she continued. 'I went and stayed with my sister. She's a nurse and she was so good to me. When you were born, Sally phoned Johnny to tell him. I was sure that once he saw you – you were such a beautiful little thing – that he would come around and that it would all work out. But Johnny didn't come to see you until the day I was ready to go home. He said he was too busy. Then when he came he told me that after his exams he had a summer job lined up in England and that he'd be gone for months. I remember I cried so much that the nurses had to give me something to calm me down. Anyway, I was on my own with you – no money, no job, nothing.'

'What about your dad or family?'

'My dad is a good man, but he was a bit of a religious nut. He was very strict with us. If he found out I was going to have a baby he would literally have killed or disowned me. My sister Sally was great, but she and her husband had only a small house and had their own kids. I stayed with her for a few weeks before you were born.

'I felt awful. I couldn't cope with having a baby and didn't see any way out of it all. When I was pregnant someone had said to me about adoption and I had talked to a person from the adoption agency about it. Johnny was totally out of the picture, so I began to think about it again – to see it as an option not just for me but for you too. Sally tried to persuade me not to go ahead with it, but I was in such a state and couldn't cope at all. I decided it would be better for you to be adopted by a good family, and better for me to be able to put the whole mess of what happened with Johnny behind me and get on with my life.'

'I see.' Erin's eyes welled with tears.

'Erin, I'm sorry . . . but I was so young, I hadn't a clue. You were my baby, my first baby, and I really thought that I could manage bringing you up on my own . . . but I couldn't. Giving you up was so hard. I never stopped thinking about you. I kept thinking of my baby, my toddler, my little girl, imagining what you would be like at each stage. Walking, talking, starting school . . . I suppose in my mind I kept you frozen that way, never really growing up.'

Erin took out a hankie and blew her nose.

'So you gave me up for adoption?'

'Yes. The social workers organized it all. I think I was so messed up and upset that I hadn't a clue what I was doing. They told me that they had found a really lovely couple to adopt you who couldn't have children of their own. I took some comfort from that and pictured you with them, a proper mummy and daddy who could give you a home and things that I just couldn't.'

'I have a lovely family,' Erin said. 'We are all very close and my brother is adopted too.'

'You told me in your letter . . . You know, getting your letter was such a shock. I had a grown-up daughter now who suddenly wanted to find me. I was scared, Anna – I mean Erin. I'm still trying to get used to the name . . . I should never have agreed with the social worker that I would meet you. And the day we arranged to meet, I just couldn't go through with it. I panicked. I'm so sorry about that. I didn't mean to hurt and upset you.' Kate's eyes welled with tears as she continued. 'I'm so ashamed of what I did, not turning up to meet you, but I was just terrified. Paddy has no idea I had a baby. It would kill him if he found out.'

'What about Johnny, my father – did you ever see him again?' Erin asked, curious.

'He came home later that summer. We went out a few times. I think he was ashamed of how he behaved towards me. We tried to make it work again. But it just was never the same, though we both really tried. How could we get over what I had done?'

Erin didn't know what to say or think. Kate and her boyfriend had been so young when she was born. There was Nikki freaking out about being pregnant and she had a good job and masses of support, and even a bloody crèche in her office!

Kate sat back in the chair. She looked older, exhausted, and she began to cry softly. 'I did a terrible thing – don't you think I know that? That it has haunted me for years? When I look at my three kids, I say secretly, "I have four kids". I think about it constantly – what I did never goes away.'

Erin didn't know what to say to her.

'It's like I have this void inside me – a secret place that is so empty and dark and lonely that I can never get rid of it,' Kate finished.

They sat there for a while saying nothing.

'You are very beautiful,' Kate said, looking at her. 'Tall, like my sister, but you've got my freckled skin and my eyes!'

Erin laughed. 'My mum calls them "witchy eyes"!'

'Tell me a bit more about yourself,' said Kate softly. 'About your life and growing up, and all the things I've missed.'

Erin couldn't believe it. Kate was actually interested in her.

An hour later she was still talking, telling Kate about Nikki being pregnant; about Bailey her lovely Labrador getting old; and how she was allergic to penicillin and had always to wear a medic alert bracelet . . .

'Snap!' said Kate, dangling her wrist and showing her own gold medic alert band. 'Listen Erin, I'm really sorry, but I have to go. I'm collecting Aisling from school today as she has to go to the dentist – even though she's sixteen she won't go on her own!'

'Sure.' Erin felt suddenly awkward. Kate wanted her gone, obviously. She stood up. 'I've kept you too long anyway, but Kate, I am glad that I came and that I met you.'

'I'm glad too.' Kate stood beside her. 'Erin, let me give you a hug.'

The hug seemed to go on for ever, both of them trying to control their emotions as they held on to each other. So many years of feelings and loss, all in a hug . . .

Kate's mobile rang on the kitchen table.

'That's Aisling looking for me,' she said, breaking apart. 'I'm sorry, but I have to go – I really do. And you have to go too – Kevin could come home any time. You have to go, Erin!'

Erin waited to see if Kate would suggest meeting again, talking again, or even staying in contact. Kate grabbed her car keys and phone and handbag as they walked to the door, but she said nothing. Erin grabbed a card from the side pocket of her own bag.

'This has all my contact details, my work number, my mobile number, and I've written my home address on the back just in case you ever need it.'

'Thanks.' Absentmindedly, Kate took it as she opened the door.

Erin decided she was the one who had made the big step today, done all the work tracking and finding Kate Cassidy. If her birth mother wanted to see or speak or be in touch with her again, it was up to her to do it.

She drove home across the East Link and pulled into the car park of her apartment building. She felt elated, emotional – what an adrenalin rush. All the years of thinking about her mother and wondering what she would be like; then today. She'd finally met Kate. She was happy . . . so happy.

She got her phone. *'Matt everything went great. She's lovely. Angry first but she got over it. I'm so glad I kicked down that wall! Thanks for everything. Erin'*

Chapter Twenty-nine

KATE HAD ABSOLUTELY NO IDEA HOW SHE HAD MANAGED TO drive from home to the school. Her hands were trembling so much on the steering wheel. She couldn't believe it: she had finally met her daughter. So many times she had tried to imagine what she would look like, but had always stopped somewhere around the age of six or seven, never able to take the image beyond that. And then today . . .

Erin was lovely, so lovely – intelligent and bright and kind, and yet with a strong will and a very impetuous streak. A bit like what she had been once. A graphic designer – where had she got that from? She herself was hopeless at art and could barely draw a stick figure. Erin was her daughter, her own flesh and blood! She was Erin's mother, she was the one who had given birth to her. Seeing Erin and hearing about her family and her life had hurt her, made her feel such regret, but talking had at least proved that she had made the right decision twenty-six years ago. Erin's parents had given her so much, things she as a single parent never could have given.

Aisling came out to the car, flinging her bag of books on the floor, rude and distant, already on her phone. Kate pulled her into her arms and held her a minute.

'You know I love you, Ash, don't you?'

She could see the confusion on her younger daughter's face. Their relationship was a bit tumultuous, to say the least. Having a moody teenage daughter who wanted to be left alone and veered between being melancholic and aloof and crazy-happy was challenging to say the least. Aisling was totally different to both of her brothers, who might wreck and mess the house but never wrecked her head the way her daughter did.

'You okay, Mum?'

'I'm fine,' she said, 'fine . . . Can't I hug you if I feel like it?'

Ash looked perplexed. 'You are still coming into Mr Costello's with me, Mum, aren't you?'

'Yes.' She knew Aisling hated the orthodontist who had fitted her braces, which at this stage needed adjusting every three months, and who always seemed to be fiddling with her mouth.

'You won't let him torture me?'

'I won't, promise.'

Driving along the Malahide Road, Kate realized that something had changed. The strange feeling of constant fear and dread she always carried seemed to have lightened, almost melted away. Her head felt clearer – it was almost exhilarating.

She had expected something awful, catastrophic to happen if she ever met Erin, but it had been totally different from what she had anticipated. Emotional and challenging, but not in a bad way. Despite totally ignoring her wishes and her request to the adoption agency, Erin had no agenda. She hadn't come to wreak revenge on Kate, to try to make her feel even more guilty than she already felt. Her daughter had simply wanted to meet her – and she was so glad that it had happened.

Today she had been given a gift she had never expected.

After dinner she left Paddy and the kids to pack up the dishwasher and tidy up.

'I have to go over to Sally's for a while,' she announced. 'I'll be home later.'

Paddy was working tonight, but she just wanted to get out of the house away from everyone before she blurted it all out. She had texted Sally briefly to say she had some very big news and would come over to tell her. She knew her sister would be bursting with curiosity and just couldn't wait to tell her that somehow or other a miracle had happened and Erin had come back into her life.

Chapter Thirty

'*MUM I MET KATE TODAY. SHE'S LOVELY. TALK TO YOU LATER!*'

Nina read Erin's text message over and over again. So a meeting had obviously finally happened. She wondered which of them had instigated it this time. Wherever it was, it had obviously gone well. So much for hoping that it would never happen! It sounded mean, but she'd been certain that there would never be a possibility of Erin wanting ever to see this Kate woman again after what she had done. But there it was on her phone: Erin thought the woman was lovely . . . She couldn't deny the pang of extreme jealousy she felt.

Tom was away in Sheffield on business, so unfortunately she was on her own. She couldn't sit staring at the four walls feeling like this; she had to get out of the house, go for a walk, get the absurd feeling of absolute betrayal she felt out of her system. Fresh air and exercise always made her feel better.

She put on her trainers and her light fleece jacket. Bailey was lolling somewhere around the place and she grabbed his lead from the hook in the kitchen and called his name. The old dog was getting a bit deaf and she found him sitting in his bed inside the cluttered TV den, snoring.

'Bailey, do you want to come for a walk?'

Seeing the lead, his tail immediately began to wag and he lumbered out of the bed.

'Good boy,' she said, slipping his lead on.

It was bright but chilly outside and she zipped up her jacket. She'd head for Killiney and give him a run on the beach. This time of day it should be pretty empty, she thought, as she walked briskly along, feeling her tension ease.

The tide was in and the waves were choppy, dashing against the stones on the beach, in and out, with their constant sound. Bailey barked at one or two seagulls and went down and snuffled at the water, getting his lower body wet. Labradors sure had a thing about water of any sort and she pulled him out, stepping out of the way as he shook himself off.

In the distance the huge ferry disappeared from the horizon as it made its way across the Irish Sea to Holyhead. She watched an elderly couple walk along hand in hand in a companionable silence, and a mother trying to manage a stroppy toddler further up along. She had spent so much time down here with Erin and Jack when they were younger . . . Where had the time gone?

It was a beautiful day; only a few clouds in the sky, with the early June sunshine glinting through and warming her. She loved it here and drank in the magnificent views of Dublin Bay. They lived on the south side of the bay; Dublin city itself was in the middle of the bay and on the far side, the north side, were Clontarf, Sutton, Howth and Malahide.

She'd always hoped that Erin's birth mother might have moved back to the country, or that she now lived in another county, or even country. But when Erin had told her that she had somehow uncovered Kate's married name and discovered that she lived literally across Dublin Bay from them, on the other side of the city, it was bloody awkward. Two women connected, but not connected at all; their lives lived opposite each other, one northside, one southside, with only a few miles between them across the bay.

She walked along the shore with Bailey beside her, watching the waves come in and out rhythmically, timeless, soothing and calming. She sat for a while on the old wall that led down near the beach, then, realizing that the sky was beginning to darken a bit, she set off up the beach. And as she went an idea came into her head and, quickening her pace, she headed home.

With Tom in the UK, and Jack staying in Pixie's place tonight, Nina had the house to herself. She made herself a cup of tea and put some dog food down for Bailey. Grabbing a sketchpad from the pile on the dresser, she began to work, excited as the first picture began to take shape on the page. The seashore and a simple house on the beach, a path of cockleshells, lobsterpots by the door, a window that would catch the light of glimmering blue in the distance . . .

She was in her study, immersed in her drawing, when Erin phoned. She stopped and took a deep breath, moving to sit down in the big squashy brown chair as Erin took her step by step through her first time meeting with Kate Cassidy.

'Mum, you won't believe it, but we have the same colour eyes, and freckles on our nose. We both are allergic to penicillin and the smell of heavy perfumes makes us cough.'

Nina listened quietly, trying to take it all in. A sinking

feeling enveloped her as her daughter excitedly told her every detail about her newly discovered mother.

'Kate's a bit smaller than me, and I suppose kind of young-looking and pretty fashionable. She was wearing leggings and boots and a cool Zara top.'

'She sounds lovely, like you said.' Nina tried her best not to sound the way she felt.

'I asked her about my father and what happened between them and she told me all about how their relationship didn't work out. Mum, it was great seeing her . . . seeing someone that I resemble and just looking at the photos of her kids in her sitting room. I think that I'm quite like Kevin, her second guy.'

'Erin, I'm so glad meeting her went well, truly I am.'

'Mum, I only stayed for about two hours because Kate had to go and collect Aisling from school, but I'm hoping that maybe we will meet again – but I don't know.'

'Why don't you come over here tonight, Erin? I can take something out of the freezer or cook up some pasta and you can tell me all about this meeting with her?'

'I'm dying to see you, Mum, but I'm knackered,' replied Erin. 'I think that I was so stressed out about the whole thing that it's hit me now. I haven't slept the past few nights and I just want to heat up something quick and easy here and crash. Luke said he might call in for half an hour. So if it's okay, can I come over tomorrow after work?'

'That sounds perfect, love,' said Nina brightly, 'absolutely perfect. I'll see you tomorrow then.'

She put the phone down. The change had already started. Kate Cassidy was back in her daughter's life and there was absolutely nothing that she could do about it.

She sat there for what seemed like an hour, gathering herself, listening to her breath and the regular beating of her heart. Becoming a mother changed you; it was such an overwhelming force that seemed to invade and take over every space inside you – head, heart, lungs, ribs and even the very soul, that intense love for your child that nothing could tear from you or remove bit by bit because it was indelibly bound to every cell in your body. As long as she was alive it was there, a part of her that could never, ever be removed and destroyed. No matter what Kate Cassidy did or said, she could not take that from her.

Chapter Thirty-one

NINA WAS SO RELIEVED THAT TOM HAD MANAGED TO GET HOME from England before Erin came for dinner that she hugged him madly when he came through the front door.

'Erin will be here soon,' she said. 'She's coming over to tell us all about how her meeting with her birth mother went yesterday.'

'And how did it go?' he asked, as he dumped his case in the bedroom and changed into his cords and a navy sweater.

'Very well. The two of them apparently immediately hit it off. They seem to be quite alike and Erin really likes her,' she said, her voice wobbling.

'Nina, you cannot be like this when Erin tells us,' he warned sternly. 'Erin's got to think that we are a hundred per cent behind her on this, ready to back her up on whatever she does and there to catch her if the whole thing goes wrong. Do you hear me?'

'Yes,' she nodded.

'A hundred per cent behind her – agreed?'

'Agreed.'

* * *

Nina had made a chicken casserole and somehow managed to force herself to pick at it, but she had absolutely no appetite. She could see how excited Erin was as she gave them a blow-by-blow account of arriving at the Cassidys' house unannounced and meeting her Kate for the first time. She listened as Erin told them all about her natural mother's reaction to first seeing her and almost every word that she had said.

'Mum, I know that you and Dad would really like her,' she smiled, 'because she's a bit like me.'

'And of course we love you!' said Tom.

'Yes, Dad,' she replied, hugging him tight.

Nina felt like a part of her gut was clenched shut as she tried to appear normal when all she wanted to do was scream *'Stop talking about her at my table – our family table!'*

'I only had barely two hours with her, as she had to go out to collect Aisling – I suppose she's kind of my half-sister. Her family don't know anything about me and she doesn't want to tell them. I guess she's still ashamed of having me.'

Nina didn't know what to say. She'd kill Kate Cassidy if she hurt her daughter, she really would.

'Will you be seeing her again, Erin?' Tom asked, pouring them all another glass of wine.

'I hope so . . . I know I landed myself, just turning up at her house the way I did, but maybe the next time we can arrange to meet properly and spend more time together.' Erin sounded a lot less confident about it than they expected.

'At least you two have finally met,' Nina said slowly. 'You have seen and talked to the mother that gave birth to you and she has met her beautiful daughter and no one can take that away from either of you.'

'Oh Mum, what a lovely thing to say.' Erin's eyes welled with tears. 'Thanks for being so understanding about what I'm going through. I don't know what I'd do if I hadn't got you and Dad.'

'We're here, and we are always here for you, Erin,' Tom said firmly. 'We are your parents, remember that and that parenthood is a lot more than biology.'

'I know that, Dad. And I'm so glad that I was raised by you and Mum. I like Kate, but I couldn't imagine growing up with her around. I wouldn't be the same person.'

Nina couldn't believe how mature and sensitive Erin was becoming. She was the one being stupid and feeling so threatened, when really Kate Cassidy was more wrapped up in her own family and had scant interest in her long-lost daughter turning up. Relief washed over her – Erin wasn't going anywhere. She was here at home with them where she was meant to be.

Chapter Thirty-two

KATE COULD NOT BELIEVE THE CHANGE THAT MEETING ERIN
had wrought in her life. Nothing was the same. She had talked
it over with Sally and her sister had been so supportive.

'I won't say, "I told you so", but I did tell you so – that it
would be okay! That the world was not going to come crashing
down if your daughter discovered you or met you!' said Sally,
wrapping her in her arms while Kate bawled her eyes out
crying. 'You have held it all in for so long, Kate, buried what
you must have been feeling. You have to let it go. I'm here and
I don't mind – that's what us big sisters are for!'

Afterwards she had felt so much better. The relief was immense and she did not understand how she had carried the
secrecy and weight of it for so long. She could finally put her
burden down.

'You will meet her again!' insisted Sally. 'You do realize how
much courage it must have taken for her to come to your house
after the last time?'

'I know, but I have to think of Paddy and Aisling and the

boys. What would they think? The boys will probably think I was a slapper—'

'Kate! Stop that! Your sons would not dream of thinking anything like that about their mother, you know they wouldn't!'

'Paddy would be devastated. He never asks me about the past or going out with Johnny, we never talk about it. Can you imagine his reaction if he finds out that I had a baby? It would destroy him . . . destroy us.'

'Why do you always underestimate him, Kate? I warned you when you married him that it was too soon, that maybe you were only marrying him on the rebound after Johnny, looking for a safety net after all that had happened, but I was wrong. Paddy is so good for you, sometimes I don't even know if you realize it. Do you think something that happened over twenty-six years ago is going to wreck a good marriage?'

'Well Sally, I'm not sure and I'm not taking that risk. They're my family and it's my choice.'

'I'm sorry for interfering, Kate, and trying to put my big oar in as usual,' apologized Sally, 'but Erin has come back into your life. Don't let her go again. There is no guarantee you will get her back next time.'

Kate thought about it. She did want to see Erin again, but certainly not anywhere near her home. She'd phone her and arrange to collect her, maybe, and they could go somewhere Erin wanted.

She had to admit she was excited thinking about it and rooted around in some of her old family photograph albums to find one or two family photos to copy for Erin.

Chapter Thirty-three

KATE WANTED TO MEET HER AGAIN — ERIN COULDN'T BELIEVE it. This time it was her birth mother who had made contact, and to make sure she wasn't going to be left hanging around, Kate offered to collect her at her flat and maybe they could go for a walk or get something to eat. Erin was amazed that her mother was actually the one reaching towards her. It felt good. She would arrange to meet her on Saturday and just see how things went.

'Stop looking out the window!' she yelled at Nikki and Claire, who were trying to see if they could spot Kate pulling up outside their apartment block. Getting a text message from Kate, she grabbed her jacket and left them to it.

Kate looked younger, even prettier. She had make-up on and her hair was perfectly blow-dried. She was obviously making an effort.

'Where should we go?' Kate asked.

It was dry out, but rather blustery. Erin directed her to the car park down near Sandymount Strand and the two of them went for a walk, heads bent, barely taking in the views as they had so much to tell each other. Afterwards they drove up to Sandymount Green and went for soup and a roll there, deciding to share a large slice of apple tart for dessert.

As they were eating, Kate produced some photos from her handbag. 'I thought you might like some of these,' she explained, passing them over to Erin. 'They are of my family and me when I was younger.'

Erin took them in her hands, amazed by how she felt. The faces she was looking at were all people related to her.

'That's my dad, your granddad, and that's my brothers and there's Sally and Mike on their wedding day. I was her bridesmaid – check out the awful purple dress she made me wear!'

'Who's that?'

'That's Sally and me and our Granny Anna outside her house in Furbo. She was an amazing woman. Spoke Irish fluently and had nine kids and baked her own bread.'

'What about this woman?' Erin stared at the photo. It was so weird – she could have been looking at a photo of herself taken at a different time, with a new hairstyle and vintage clothes.

'That's my mum, Julia. She was up in Dublin and a guy took her photo on O'Connell Street near the big cinema. It was taken before she married my dad. I think that you two are very alike.'

Kate was right, there was such a strong family resemblance. There was no denying it.

'And this is mammy and daddy's wedding photo. She looks gorgeous in it.'

Julia Flanagan did look beautiful and Erin felt a lump in her throat for all the parts of the jigsaw that she had missed for so many years.

'Have you one of my father?'

Kate shook her head vehemently. There were no more photos.

'Please tell me a bit about him?'

She could see that Kate was uncomfortable with the conversation. She obviously didn't want to discuss him or go back over whatever had happened between them.

'Do you ever hear from him?'

'No, we lost touch years ago – it was better that way. He moved to London. I believe that he is still there.'

'Did he get married, have a family?'

'I'm not sure,' Kate said, calling the waitress over so that they could pay their bill.

'I would like to meet him, to see him . . . He is my father after all,' Erin continued stubbornly. 'I might try to make contact with him if you have an old address or phone number or anything.'

'Erin, I'm not sure that would be wise. It could be a disappointment.'

'Thanks for the photos,' Erin said, kissing Kate's cheek. 'Here – I'll take one of the two of us!'

Ignoring Kate's protest, she quickly pressed the button on her iPhone and captured the image of the two of them standing on the Green together.

'We'll keep in touch,' promised Kate when she dropped her off, and Erin knew that she meant it.

Chapter Thirty-four

MONIKA DE BERG WAS JUST DOING A RUN-THROUGH OF THE Powerpoint presentation on some logos for a new mobile company when Alice came into the room.

'I'm sorry to disturb you, Erin, but one of your friends is on the line and she says she needs you urgently. Your mobile is turned off so she phoned through to reception. Will I transfer the call?'

Monika gestured to her to take it and Erin went outside the door.

'Oh thank God! I've been trying to get you for the past hour nearly!' screamed Claire.

'What is it?'

'Nikki's been taken into hospital. She's bleeding.'

'What?'

'She's bleeding! Her office got an ambulance for her but she's on her own now. She's like a basket case . . . Her mum and dad are gone to Amsterdam for a break and I have about eight patients lined up for me – I can't just cancel on them. Erin, you'll have to go to the hospital. She needs one of us with her, especially if it's going to be bad news about the baby.'

'But I'm not a good person for that!' Erin said. 'You're the medical person, not me.'

'That doesn't matter. She needs someone to hold her hand and stay with her, that's all, Erin. She's probably scared shit-less.'

Monika totally understood, so Erin found herself literally running from their office to the big maternity hospital on Merrion Square. The porter on duty told her where to go and Erin found Nikki in a small pre-natal room off one of the main wards with one other woman.

Nikki looked absolutely awful, whiter than the bedsheet she was lying on, and she burst out crying the minute she saw Erin.

'They're not sure if the baby is still there,' she cried. 'It could be gone.'

'Oh Nikki, I'm so sorry.'

'They did one scan but now they are going to do another to check things again. The bleeding is easing a bit . . . Oh Erin, what am I going to do if I've lost my baby?'

Erin didn't know what to say. She just pulled her chair right up beside Nikki and held her hand.

'You're not sure of anything yet, Nikki. Let's wait and see what the doctor says.'

Nikki drifted off for about half an hour, her fingers clenched round Erin's. Erin silently prayed, 'Don't let this happen! Please, don't let this happen!'

A little later a nurse came in to bring Nikki down for a major scan. She began to cry hysterically again. The nurse talked to her, trying to reassure her and calm her down.

'Can I go with her?' offered Erin. 'I'm her best friend.'

A few minutes later she was sitting beside Nikki as the ultrasound nurse began to do the scan. Nikki had her eyes closed, tears streaming down her face – it was unbearable. The doctor pushed the scanner all along her belly, up and down, backwards and forwards, as if looking for something that was missing. Nikki had her hand held so tight that the pain was excruciating. Erin could make no sense of what was on the screen.

Suddenly the doctor stopped. He moved the scanner in a small circle, round and round, and Erin thought she could see some kind of shape in outline. It looked like a foot, some bit of a bone. There was complete silence except for Nikki's sobs.

'Nicola, you can open your eyes,' the doctor said gently. 'I want to show you your baby.'

'My baby?'

'Yes, there's your baby. This is the spine,' he pointed with his finger, 'and this is the head, and in here we can just about see the heart. Look – it's pumping.'

Nikki had stopped crying for a moment, then began all over again, even more violently. The doctor turned up the machine and suddenly they could hear a really fast pumping, beating sound.

'Listen to that! That's your baby's heartbeat. I don't think this baby is going anywhere for the moment except mum's tummy,' he said.

As Erin looked at the screen she realized that she was crying too. It was the most wonderful thing ever, Nikki's baby there on the screen in front of them.

'Hello, Snoopy B,' said Nikki, touching the screen and her tummy.

*   *   *

They wheeled Nikki back up to her ward. She was going to be kept in for twenty-four hours and then could go home, but she had to promise to take it easy for the next few days.

'I'm taking it easy until Snoopy B is safe in my arms,' she insisted furiously.

Erin phoned Claire to tell her the good news and stayed with Nikki till her sister, Hayley, arrived on the train from Limerick where she went to college and Claire came in after she finished work.

'She really needs to rest,' bossed Claire, 'so in ten minutes we are all going home and letting her and the baby have some peace.'

'Snoopy B,' murmured Nikki, yawning. 'I love my Snoopy B.'

'She had a Snoopy toy when she was young and she loved it,' explained Hayley.

Erin and Claire made sure Nikki was settled before they left for home. Erin, exhausted herself, just wanted to collapse into bed.

Chapter Thirty-five

GETTING NIKKI HOME FROM THE HOSPITAL, CLAIRE AND Erin vowed to make her relax, try to get her to eat more and finally to enjoy her pregnancy. A print-out of the scan of Snoopy B took pride of position on their kitchen fridge and Nikki kissed it first thing every morning as she marked up on their calendar another day of the countdown to Snoopy B being born.

Conor, the baby's father, had made a surprise appearance at the hospital with a bunch of roses, but Nikki was adamant that one bunch of roses did not a father-to-be make.

'I've cancelled my work trips to Berlin and to Paolo Alta,' said Nikki defiantly. 'I've told Fergus that I cannot do it with the baby, and he's sending that snake-in-the-grass Derek instead. My career is probably fucked, but I don't care!'

'What about our holidays?'

The three of them had planned to go to Claire's auntie's place in Marbella for a week in July.

'I'm sorry to let you down, but I don't want to take any risks after this scare. I'm just going to go to Rosslare and chill out down there in the mobile home with Mum and Dad. I want to be near the hospital.'

Neither of the others could believe what a change there had been, with Nikki now prioritizing the baby's needs over her own and disappearing off to bed with some pregnancy book or other by ten o'clock most nights. What a change!

Erin was spending as much time as she could with Luke, as soon he would be moving to live in London full time. He kept on and on about her moving, but now with Nikki and the baby, and with her beginning to develop a friendship with Kate, this wasn't the perfect time. They would just have to do a bit of the commuting thing for a short while.

For his last weekend in Ireland in two weeks' time they had booked to go to Lough Moyne House, just outside Dublin.

'I bet he's going to propose to you,' teased Claire. 'It's fabulous there.'

'He will not!'

'He will!' insisted Nikki. 'He's probably got the ring already, and that's where Ben Murphy, the Irish rugby star, proposed to his girlfriend a few weeks ago.'

'Shut up, the two of you – it is just a romantic weekend,' she insisted, embarrassed beyond belief, 'that's all!'

Erin didn't know what to think. What if the girls were right and Luke did propose?

Did she even want him to . . . ?

Chapter Thirty-six

NINA DROVE DOWN TO THE FERN HOUSE CAFÉ IN AVOCA TO meet her friends for lunch. She'd been so engrossed working on a cover illustration for a new collection of children's rhymes and poetry that she hadn't even realized the time.

'Nina!' She could see Mags waving madly at her from a table near the back of the restaurant, overlooking the garden. Avoca's fabulous shop, garden centre and restaurants were busy as ever with a mixture of locals and visitors.

'Sorry I'm late, but I was working on something and lost track of the time,' she explained as she grabbed a menu and ordered the fish cakes and a salad. She and Mags and Dee and Carole met about once every three weeks for lunch or dinner, which was a chance for them to catch up with each other. The venues might change, but the talk was always good. They'd all been friends for years.

'Did I tell you that Dylan finally got a job?' beamed Dee. 'He was so nervous about the interview and I still can't believe he got it. But he starts next Monday, working in Newstalk, the big radio station.'

'Newstalk – that's wonderful!' exclaimed Nina. Dee's son was one of those serious political types, always campaigning for a cause, and she and her husband Billy had begun to despair of him ever finding anyone to employ him.

'What will he do there?' asked Carole.

'Hopefully he'll get to use some of what he learned in that expensive post grad journalism course he did last year,' replied Dee. 'He'll be working as a researcher on the news team.'

Everyone knew just how hard it was for graduates of every discipline to get a job or start of any kind nowadays. Unemployment figures were through the roof, so getting anyone off the family payroll was an achievement. Nina wondered how Jack would fare once he finished his degree in animation.

Mags's eldest daughter, Jess, had just moved in with her boyfriend, Andy.

'I'm just a bit worried about what will happen when he discovers the real Jess . . . They'll probably break up!'

'Don't be so pessimistic,' laughed Nina. 'He loves her and probably knows all her little foibles already.'

'That's just it – Andy hasn't a clue, the poor sod. He has no idea of how difficult she really is; the mess, the craziness, and the way she is such a grump in the morning. Poor Dan says that she'll be back home annoying us within the month!'

They all burst out laughing. Mags had five kids and Jess was the first to leave the family nest. Their house was always full of drama and action and chaos, and they all enjoyed hearing about long-suffering Dan's efforts to maintain some sort of balance in the Clinton household.

Carole told them about her husband Mike's upcoming knee replacement. 'I'm dreading it,' she admitted. 'I know that he really needs it and should have had it done ages ago, but he's such a bad patient and it's going to take months for him to get over it. He'll be out of work for weeks, but since there is so little work for architects going at the moment, that's fine with him. So I'll have him stuck at home annoying me.'

'Mike's not that bad,' they teased. 'Maybe it will be nice for the two of you to get some time together, and hopefully by the time his knee is better things will have improved a bit.'

'I had plenty of time with him last year when he got the flu. I was up and down the stairs like a skivvy with cups of coffee and hot lemon drinks and tissues and meals and newspapers. This time it will be a whole lot worse!'

Nina smiled. The girls were such fun to be around and knew they could unburden themselves with each other and not worry about it. They all loved their husbands and their kids, but nobody was perfect.

'What about you Nina? Anything going on in your life?' quizzed Mags as the waitress arrived with their food and passed around the plates.

'Tom's busy in work, away a lot travelling. Jack's got a cute new girlfriend called Pixie – isn't that some name! Erin and Luke are still going out, and thank heaven she still has her job, and believe it or not Mum hasn't caused any problems for weeks. And . . .'

She could sense them all watching her.

'And?'

'And . . .' She just couldn't hold it in any more. 'Erin has made contact with her birth mother. They've met twice already.'

'Shit!' burst out Mags. 'What are you going to do?'

'There's nothing much that I can do,' she sighed. 'Tom and I always knew that this day would come; that one day our

185

children would want to find out about their backgrounds and perhaps want to meet or reunite with their birth mothers.'

'Oh Nina!' Dee grabbed her hand and squeezed it consolingly. 'It's not going to change anything! You and Tom are wonderful parents – far better than the rest of us.'

'Erin's twenty-six now and totally entitled to do this,' Nina tried to explain and seem somewhat rational. 'She met the social worker in the adoption agency, and a counsellor, and went through things with them and then she wrote a letter to her mother.'

'Fecking hell!' burst out Mags.

Nina tried not to be critical or to appear too negative towards this other woman. 'At first her mother didn't want to meet her, but now they have met twice and seem to get on very well, and they have things in common and even seem to be a little bit alike. So now we have to wait and see what happens . . .'

They all were silent and Nina knew that they totally understood how she felt. It was stupid and irrational, but she couldn't help herself feeling betrayed and wounded by what Erin was doing.

'Erin's a good kid, Nina,' Dee said soothingly. 'You're her mum, so you know that. She's probably just curious and once she's satisfied her need to know, then she'll be fine.'

'But what happens if she and this other mother really bond and become part of each other's lives?' Nina asked despairingly.

'That mightn't happen!' said Mags firmly. 'Just wait and see!'

'But if it does?'

'Then you will have to learn to accept it,' said Carole, 'if you don't want to lose Erin.'

Nina nodded. She already knew that. At night she lay awake thinking about it, making sense of it. This woman had given Nina her child years ago, and now it might be time for her to claim that child back.

They lingered over cappuccinos and cake before heading out for a tour of the shop. Nina bought some home-made brown bread and a leek and cheese bake to take home.

'How about having lunch in that new place near me in Dalkey next time?' she suggested as they arranged a date to meet again.

'Nina, if you hear anything about Erin's mother, let us know,' begged Carole and Dee.

'And remember, when Mike is up for visitors, Tom and I will call in to see him in the hospital,' she offered.

Driving home, Nina was glad that she had told her friends. The whole situation was weighing her down, and poor Tom was getting fed up talking about it, saying that it was something that they couldn't control and they both just had to learn to accept it.

Chapter Thirty-seven

ERIN HAD PACKED HER BAG THE NIGHT BEFORE, ALL READY FOR her romantic night away with Luke in Lough Moyne. She'd checked the place out on the internet and it looked absolutely gorgeous, a real big old Irish country house overlooking a lake, with acres of grounds and a plush swimming pool and spa area, and a restaurant run by a famous, award-winning chef.

They drove down on Saturday morning and even going up its rhododendron-lined driveway she had to admit it was beautiful. Two stone lions guarded the entrance and within minutes of checking in they were in their first-floor room with its lake view, massive bed, walk-in dressing room and luxurious bathroom. It was heaven!

'Let's go for a walk up round the lake,' she suggested, 'and then come back and grab lunch in the bar.'

Luke was fully agreeable and, holding hands, they walked past the rose garden and the area known as the Lady Moyne Walk, which brought them down the steps in front of the house to a part of the garden where the herbaceous borders were in full bloom.

'My mum would love this!' exclaimed Erin admiringly, taking a photo of the most amazing display of tall blue delphiniums. 'We have them in the garden at home. Does your mum like the garden?'

'Not really. She hasn't the time, what with playing golf and bridge – they keep her busy.'

'Look how close the lake seems, and it's so peaceful.'

Luke spotted a small jetty with three boats moored. 'Maybe one of the boats belongs to the house and guests are let use them. I'll check it out with reception later.'

Tall reeds bordered the rest of the lake and, taking another path, they found themselves walking through a wooded area which brought them in a circle to the other side of the house, where a gardener was working in a kitchen garden filled with onions and carrots, runner beans, lettuce and chives, plums and strawberries, and old-fashioned gooseberries.

'Probably nearly everything we eat here will come from the gardens.' Erin thought that it was wonderful to know the produce was so healthy and fresh.

'Come on,' demanded Luke. 'I'm starving!'

The bar was housed in the old library, with a feature wall of glass that overlooked the rose garden. The menu was very tempting, but Erin was conscious that they would be eating a big meal later, so she opted for the lettuce and garden herb soup and the fish cakes on a bed of rocket, which the table beside them were having and looked lovely.

After lunch Luke was determined to take her out on the lake. It was so romantic that she couldn't help thinking of Nikki and Claire's predictions and was nervous as hell.

Luke wasn't used to boats or rowing, and after about twenty

minutes Erin was in stitches laughing as he got them stuck in a bed of reeds. Instead of laughing too, Luke was annoyed and the more he tried to right the boat the worse he made it!

'Here, let me, Luke,' she offered, trying to take the oars. 'I've spent half my childhood messing about in boats. I'll get us out of here.'

'I can do this,' he insisted. 'I'll get us out of here.' But Luke's frantic efforts at rowing and trying to push off made absolutely no difference; the small boat wouldn't budge – they were totally marooned.

'Just let me have a try?' she begged, sensing that his pride had been dented. She could tell he was annoyed as he reluctantly agreed to swap places and let her have a go.

A few minutes later, with a little bit of manoeuvring and getting a good pull on one oar, Erin had managed to turn them around so they were free.

Luke was not impressed. Not even a cheer!

She gave him one oar while she took the other, hoping to try to retrieve the romantic occasion, but Luke was in no mood to row and didn't want to explore the lake any further.

'Luke, come on – it's fun! Please stay out on the lake for a bit longer. It's such a beautiful day and it's so stunning here,' she pleaded, trying to get him to change his mind.

'I've a few calls to make back in the room,' he said importantly as they moored the boat, and he took off.

Erin stayed sitting on the wooden deck, her feet dangling in the water, watching a busy moorhen. She hated when Luke got like this; he couldn't take any teasing, or any slight criticism. She'd give him time to cool down before she went back to the room. They had booked some treatments in the spa and she knew Luke would love them . . .

*   *   *

Luke, thank heaven, had lightened up as they enjoyed a swim in the luxurious pool and then went to sit in the bubbling, romantic outdoor jacuzzi. It was paradise here. Then, to top it all, they had both opted for a de-stress relaxing massage and pedicure. What a treat! Erin was so relaxed and tired that, back in their room, she fell asleep in Luke's arms.

Waking up, she studied his sleeping face and wondered how she was going to survive without seeing him as much. She would miss their being able to just call in on each other and being able to do things spontaneously together. Luke had really surprised her by booking such a romantic retreat for his last weekend officially at home.

Forty-five minutes later she was dressed in a navy lace dress and her open-toed LK Bennett shoes, sipping Prosecco in the bar and studying the dinner menu when she heard a familiar voice.

'Hey guys!' It was Luke's friend Ronan, from Hibernian. What was he doing here?

He was with Michelle, and before she knew it they had joined them and the waiter was leading them to a table for four in the dining room.

'Bit of a double celebration!' joked Ronan. 'With Luke and I moving to the London office, it makes sense for us to share a place together until you girls move over. And take the two of you off here for the night.'

'Sure does,' smiled Erin. She'd kill Luke! He hadn't said a word to her about meeting Ronan here or about him being transferred over to London too. She couldn't believe it. So much for a romantic dinner *à deux*!

At least Michelle was nice, and the four of them soon began

191

to chat as they ordered their meal and wine. The dining room was full, mostly with couples her parents' age and one or two engaged couples who were probably checking out its potential for hosting their weddings. The waiters danced attendance on them as they worked their way through the fabulous menu and ordered another bottle of red wine.

Luke and Ronan were all excited about the move, boasting about their new jobs and their bonuses and the kind of work they would be doing instead of the more humdrum stuff they handled in the Dublin office. As the meal progressed the talk got louder and wilder and Erin wished that Luke would just shut up for a bit. Excusing herself, she fled to the ladies cloakroom and Michelle joined her there.

'When are you moving over?' Erin asked as she brushed her hair.

'I'm not,' said Michelle. 'I've no plans for going to London any time soon. If Ronan wants to see me, he's the one going to have to come home here on Friday nights. I'm working in PWC and have to finish my accountancy exams. I'm contracted to them for another year and a half at least. What about you?'

'I've got a job I don't really want to leave and a few family things going on,' confided Erin. 'Luke and I will just have to try to work out some kind of rota for getting together.'

Returning to the dining room, they saw an older man standing near their table talking to the guys. Nodding at them, he returned to his own table.

'Fecking hell! How were we to know that Gordon Leonard would be here!'

'Who's he?' asked Erin.

'The senior partner, and that's his wife with him,' explained Ronan.

'He told us to keep it down,' Luke added, 'that he didn't want the rest of the restaurant knowing the company's business!'

Erin had to smother her laughs. Ronan and Luke were like two schoolboys in trouble with their teacher.

The meal was delicious and they ended up with Irish coffees all round and then decided on another bottle of wine as they continued to chat at the table. A nightcap in the bar followed, and it was nearly one thirty a.m. before they eventually said their goodnights.

They were all a bit drunk, and when they got into their room Luke just literally stripped off and fell into bed. By the time Erin came out of the bathroom he was snoring loudly. So much for romance!

They had breakfast in bed. Later, they both went for a reviving swim in the pool before they checked out. Looking down at the lake and the gardens, Erin made a secret promise to return to Lough Moyne House another time . . .

Chapter Thirty-eight

KATE LOOKED AROUND CASSIDY'S OFF-LICENCE PREMISES. IN A few hours the place would be full, hopefully, with friends and customers coming along to sample the new Blue Ridge range of New Zealand wines that they were launching. They regularly had wine nights, French, Spanish and Italian, but tonight was a little bit different, as Paddy had actually managed to get the Irish agency for handling this new New Zealand wine brand. He had also invited a few fellow off-licence owners that he knew from different parts of the city and country to come along and enjoy the sampling and meet the guys from the Blue Ridge Winery, hoping that they may be interested in stocking it too. There would be some New Zealand food – she had trawled the internet for a few typical Kiwi treats to serve. There was New Zealand music and Paddy had organized that a few of the Kiwi players from their local rugby club would come along and perform the Haka, their legendary Maori dance.

Everyone had been roped in. Sean and Kevin had helped move some of the shelves to make space, and had shifted all the cheaper beers and minerals to the back of the shop to make space for everyone; later they would serve as wine waiters. Aisling and her friend Ruby were serving the food. Fingers crossed that the weather held so they could spill out on to the paved area in front of the shop.

A good organizer, Kate wanted everything to run smoothly for Paddy's sake. The downturn had affected business, like everything else, but Paddy had soon realized that although people might not be buying expensive wines and spirits any more, they still wanted to stay home with a good bottle of wine that was not going to break the bank. His foresight in delivering what his customers wanted, and the fact they knew they could trust him to look after them, had ensured that Cassidy's wines had stayed in business.

Once Kate was satisfied that everything was organized, she slipped home to change into a classic black linen shift dress and heels, before grabbing the food she had prepared earlier and carrying it out to her car.

Paddy was wonderful, making a point of introducing everyone and welcoming even random locals who had stumbled on the wine event by accident. Soon they were all tasting New Zealand's finest. Hamish and Erik from the winery were great, listening tirelessly to questions about their country and telling customers about their beautiful vineyard. As the crowd assembled, wine glasses in hand, the Kiwi rugby players put on an amazing display of the Haka in front of the shop to huge applause. Paddy and Hamish then got up to speak.

Paddy was always a little nervous speaking in public, but tonight he sounded calm and relaxed as he welcomed everyone and told them about these fantastic new wines from down under he'd discovered, and introduced Hamish.

Afterwards the girls passed around the trays of mini tuna

and kumera patties, down-under cheese puffs, and shrimps with a pistachio and coriander crumb, while the boys topped up everybody's glasses.

'Well done, Kate. You and Paddy have done a wonderful job. We're all loving that wine,' enthused Trish as Sean refilled her glass again.

It was all going so well and, looking over at Paddy, she could tell he was pleased. He was deep in discussion with Bobby Murphy, who had two wine shops in Cork, and Ryan O'Donnell, who had opened an off-licence somewhere on the south side.

Eventually the crowds began to drift away and Sean and Kevin and the girls began to tidy up all the wine glasses. Paddy had booked a table in Mario's, the Italian restaurant only a few doors up, and the party moved there. Hamish and Erik spent a lot of the time trying to persuade them to come out and see Blue Ridge themselves.

It was late when they eventually got home. Kate was exhausted.

'Thanks for everything today, Kate,' said Paddy, sitting down to take off his shoes and undress for bed. 'I couldn't have done it without you. Hamish was delighted with the way it went, and Bobby and Ryan have already placed orders with me – so it couldn't be better.'

'That's great.'

Looking at her husband, Kate was tempted to sit down beside him, tell him that she had had something pretty good happen to her too, and explain to him about her daughter . . . But looking at him, she just couldn't do it. She couldn't ruin tonight for him.

Chapter Thirty-nine

DUBLIN ZOO WAS ONE OF THE PLACES THAT ERIN HAD LOVED AS a kid and she had arranged to meet Kate here for a few hours. Luke wasn't coming home for the weekend, so she was at a real loose end. Tonight she was going to the cinema with a few of the girls.

Seeing Kate approach, she automatically ran to say hello to her and hug her. The zoo was the perfect place for them to walk and talk and have a coffee together.

'God, I haven't been here for years,' admitted Kate. 'Not since the kids were small. Aisling used to complain about the animals being behind bars and wanted the keepers to release them all.'

'I used to come with my mum and dad. It was always a great family day out and we'd have a picnic. Have you seen the big African savannah section?'

'No!'

'Then let's start there. It's pretty spectacular and you see the animals up close in a much more natural habitat. I'm like Aisling – I don't want to see them in cages either.'

They walked around, taking in the long grasses and lakes where the animals could roam more freely and watching a mother lion keep order as her cubs played and tumbled in front of her. The zoo was packed with families, mums and dads with children of all ages, from babies in buggies to toddlers holding hands, to young kids flying around trying to take in all the animals as they careered from the elephant section to the pets' corner, the monkey island to the seal enclosure.

Kate was quiet.

'Are you okay?' asked Erin.

'It's just seeing all these little kids toddling around with their mums makes me realize all the times I missed with you – the things I didn't do . . .'

'I didn't mean to make you feel like that,' apologized Erin, 'honestly I didn't. Don't feel guilty. I got to do most things kids do – Jack and I were spoiled!'

'I'm glad your parents are such good people. I'm so grateful to them for looking after my beautiful daughter so well.'

Sitting in the busy café, Erin asked Kate about her father again.

'Please tell me about Johnny.'

'Erin, I've told you almost everything I know. We were very close . . . and really loved each other, but it just didn't work out.'

'That was my fault—'

'No it wasn't!' exclaimed Kate indignantly. 'Johnny and I could well have broken up a few months later anyway, baby or no baby!'

'Do you ever still think of him, miss him?'

'It was awful at first – just awful. He was *the one*, my one-and-only, the guy I wanted to spend the rest of my life with, so I was heartbroken. But I guess we all get our hearts broken sometime or other . . . And then Paddy came along.'

'And you fell in love with him?'

'Well, something like that . . . He's a lovely man and they are few and far between.'

'Johnny was my dad,' said Erin. 'I keep thinking about that, and I'd really like to try and talk to him, meet him . . .'

'I told you, it's not a good idea,' Kate said, her eyes flashing. 'Why don't you believe me?'

'You didn't think that the two of us meeting was a good idea in the beginning,' Erin persisted, 'and here we are. You must have some details about Johnny you can give me so I can try to find him. You said he was from Wicklow, so I could start there. Did you go to his house and meet his parents? Someone in his family must know where he is living now.'

She could see Kate was taken aback at her insistence on trying to find out.

'You are very determined.'

'Yes, I told you I was.'

'Erin, I'll try to contact him, tell him that we've met and see what he says . . . Can you leave it with me? I promise that I'll come back to you.'

'Okay,' agreed Erin, satisfied that the first steps to find her father were now beginning to be taken.

Chapter Forty

TALK ABOUT A QUANDARY. KATE HAD NO IDEA WHAT TO DO about Erin's insistence on tracing her father. But she knew that Erin would go ahead and do it with or without her help.

Johnny's family still lived in Wicklow. His dad had died about ten years ago – she had seen his obituary in the newspaper; but his mother, Cora Devlin, was still alive. Then there were his brothers and sister, all still living in the same area. Erin would easily find him.

She needed to talk to Johnny, tell him about their daughter and how afraid she had been to meet her and what the outcome had been. He had refused to have anything to do with his baby daughter, but that had been so long ago and people change . . . maybe he had too.

She phoned Cora, who, though it had been years since they met, remembered her as Johnny's girlfriend and chatted easily to her. Cora had never been told about the baby. She filled Kate in on all the family and the twelve grandchildren she now had, and the one dote of a grandson. Johnny was away living in London, Kilburn area, and had been married and divorced twice. He was still good to Cora and came home every few months. She had always liked Kate and gave her Johnny's phone number and address.

Putting down the phone, Kate looked at the numbers and tried to get up the courage to phone him. The house was empty, the boys gone to parties, Paddy working, and Aisling gone off to Irish college in Connemara for a few weeks with a load of girls. Taking a breath to steady herself, she dialled the London code and waited nervously as it rang and rang.

'Hello! Who is it?'

His voice hadn't changed a bit.

'It's Kate.'

'Kate? Kate – after all these years . . . Are you okay?'

'Yes, I'm fine.' She was taken aback by the way he had recognized her straight away and the unexpected concern in his voice. 'I'm fine, Johnny, but there is something I need to tell you. It's about our daughter—'

'The baby?'

'She's not a baby any more. She's twenty-six, her name is Erin and she's absolutely lovely.'

'You've met her?'

'Yes. I didn't want to, but somehow she got her birth cert and managed to find me. I was in bits about it. I'm married with three kids now—'

'And you've never told them?'

'How did you guess?'

'Kate, what's this got to do with me?'

'She wants to meet her father.'

'Well I don't want to meet her,' he said firmly. 'I've never been involved and that's the way it is going to stay.'

Kate knew she could start screaming and getting upset

with him like she did before and it would make not a bit of difference.

'Listen, Johnny, I know how you must feel with me phoning you out of the blue to tell you, but can't we talk about it? She's not looking for anything from either of us. She's a great kid – you would be proud of her if you saw her, honestly you would. I am.'

He was silent on the other end of the phone – he was thinking about it.

'I'm in Dublin the end of next week. Can we meet up to talk about it?'

Kate didn't know what to say. She hadn't seen or spoken to Johnny Devlin for years.

'You can tell me about her,' he coaxed.

Going against her better judgement, but only for Erin's sake, Kate arranged to meet him on Friday evening in the bar of the hotel he was staying in along the quays. She must be mad to have agreed it and was tempted to phone him back straightaway and cancel it, but because of Erin she didn't. Their daughter was entitled to know about her father. How could they have believed that a grown adult wouldn't demand to have full information about both her birth parents?

They had both been so naïve then, never considering the consequences of what they had done and the effect it might have on their child. But that was then and this was now, and Erin deserved answers.

Chapter Forty-one

SHE MUST BE MAD, MAD, MAD EVEN TO CONTEMPLATE MEET-
ing Johnny Devlin. Sally would kill her if she ever got wind of
it. The very thought of seeing him again was nerve-wracking,
but she had to try to get him to change his mind about meeting
Erin.

After twenty-five years she wondered what he would be like.
Was he still as handsome as before? Cora had told her he was
involved in the music and entertainment business still and had
an office in central London. What would he think of her, an
ordinary housewife with three grown-up kids, who had done
nothing very special with her life except look after her family.
He'd probably find her boring.

Boring or not, she was going to dress up to show him that
she still looked good, and she calmly went through her wardrobe searching for the perfect dress.

Paddy was working late tonight and she decided to take a
taxi into town. She'd told him she was going to a reunion with
some of her old college friends, and that one of the girls was

home from Canada and staying in a hotel in town. She was just about to phone a taxi when Trish arrived.

'Do you want to come over to my place to watch *The Late Late Show*?' she asked. The two of them had got into a routine of often going to each other's house to watch RTE's big Friday-night show, having a few glasses of wine and a chat as Paddy worked late and Trish's husband did a Friday-night shift in the Call Centre he helped to manage.

'I'm just about to go out,' she said, bringing Trish into the kitchen for a second.

'Where are you off to?'

'A reunion.' My God, she was becoming such a liar!

'School is it?'

'No,' she said, knowing full well that Trish knew she'd gone to school in Galway. 'It's just a few old pals from college days.'

'Any old flames?'

'Maybe . . . I don't know, Trish,' she replied, getting embarrassed.

'Let's see what you're wearing.'

'It's my Louise Kennedy, the one I got for Sean's graduation last year,' she said, opening her coat.

'Very elegant!' said Trish. 'Exactly!'

'What do you mean?'

'For a graduation, okay, beautiful on; but we are talking cool Kate Cassidy with her perfect figure and looking still as beautiful as ever. Eat your heart out . . .'

'Shit!' said Kate.

'I'm thinking that divine dress you wore at the New Zealand wine thing. You looked amazing in it. You had those poor Kiwi men drooling over you.'

Kate belted upstairs and changed while Trish told the taxi man to wait for her.

Arriving at the big hotel near Dublin's Conference Centre she hesitated, wondering if she should just forget about meeting Johnny. But she was curious and found herself going through the glass revolving door and making her way to the bar.

The Quay Hotel, overlooking the river, was modern and bright with funky purple and green and gold couches and chairs, and clusters of people having drinks. She spotted him up at the bar and waved. Okay, he had aged, but he hadn't changed that much – she still recognized him.

'Kate,' he said, pulling her into his arms. He still smelled of the same aftershave, Eau Sauvage. 'You look gorgeous!'

'Thanks.'

'Here, let me get you a drink.'

They went and sat over at a table in a quiet corner and Kate had to steel herself not to be overwhelmed with the emotion of seeing him. His black hair was streaked with grey, his face even thinner than she remembered, and he was dressed in a rather flash jacket and a fitted black shirt. He had made an effort too.

'So this is a turn-up, the two of us meeting after so long,' he said, leaning forward. 'I didn't think our paths would ever cross again, despite what we meant to each other.'

'They probably wouldn't have except for Erin,' she said slowly, 'our daughter.'

She told him all about meeting Erin and getting to know her. 'She's so lovely, so grown up.'

'Wow! It's kind of hard to get your head around having a grown-up kid you've never seen.'

'You did see her!' she reminded him angrily. 'In the hospital.

You held her, you said she was beautiful – and Johnny, she is beautiful, and intelligent and really nice. Have you any daughters?'

'No. I have a son. He's sixteen.'

'What's his name?'

'Max, but I don't see much of him. He lives with his mum, Andrea.'

'I'm sorry.'

'Don't be. It just didn't work out. We divorced when he was about six. I got married again, but we hadn't any kids. We split up three years ago. What about you?' he quizzed.

'I'm married to the same guy, Paddy,' she said. 'We have three kids. Sean is twenty-three and Kevin is twenty and our daughter Aisling is sixteen. They are great kids, all doing well. The boys are in college and Ash is still in school.'

'Busy lady!'

'Yes, I suppose. What about you? Your mum told me that you are still in the music business.'

'Well, it's general entertainment more. I own a company called Celtic Connections. I bring over Irish acts to clubs and pubs in London and around the UK. There's quite a market for traditional musicians and bands and Irish dance troupes and comedians. The English can't seem to get enough of them.'

'Do you still organize rock gigs like you used to do in college?'

'A few in the beginning, but most of the good bands are tied up with the big promoters, so I've specialized. I'm kind of niche, I guess. Traditional music is very big.'

They had another drink and she listened as he told her about his life in London and the gigs he did with various comedians.

'Barry Byrne is probably the best. The audiences just love

him and he packs up every club or pub I put him in. Sean O'Dooling is a madman and he nearly caused a riot in Ealing in a pub there with his comments about the royals!'

The bar was getting busier and busier.

'Let's go and get something to eat,' suggested Johnny.

She hesitated, but it was really getting too noisy to talk about Erin here, so she grabbed her coat and they went outside.

'There's a nice restaurant just a few minutes' walk away,' Johnny said, 'and it should be a bit quieter.' He went to put his arm around her as they walked and she moved away from him.

Rico's was down a narrow road that ran behind the big office blocks overlooking the Liffey. Candles glowed enticingly in the window. They sat together in a small booth as the waiter fussed around and got them a bottle of wine, assuming that they were on a romantic night out.

As Johnny studied the menu, Kate studied him. He was still bloody attractive, and he knew it. He still had that nervous energy, talking fast, moving fast; the ability to be noticed and get attention. He hadn't changed! Not an iota.

She smiled when he ordered the steak – medium rare with pepper sauce and fries; it was still his favourite meal. Any time they could afford to eat in a good restaurant he'd always ordered the same thing.

She opted for the house special, chicken parmigiano, and Johnny ordered a bottle of red wine. They talked about the old days, about college, and her working in Captain America's Steakhouse, and him trying to make money by organizing gigs.

'Some of those bands were dire!'

'Remember that band from Sligo that got so drunk playing the Commerce Ball that everyone flung stuff at them?'

'The drummer could barely see the drums, let alone hit them!' he laughed. 'We had to leg it . . .'

They reminisced for ages, drinking more and more wine, sitting closer together, the attraction between them the same as ever, Johnny's arm around her, his fingers touching her bare skin. It felt so familiar being beside him, both of them reluctant to break the fantasy of it, both skirting the thorny subject of her getting pregnant.

'Kate, we had so many good times then. We were a great couple!'

'You're right, we were a great couple,' she said, taking another slow sip of her wine. 'But then I found out that I was having your baby, Johnny, and that was it. I wasn't part of a couple any more. I was on my own.'

'I'm sorry for not standing by you,' he said, reaching for her hand. 'I really am.'

'Do you know what you did?' she demanded, watching the expression on his face.

'I let you and the baby down,' he said, looking at least a bit ashamed. 'I know that.'

'I had to give my baby away – give her away!' she said, losing control. 'Can you even begin to understand what that means?'

'I'm sorry, Kate. I've always been a selfish shit, that's what Andrea said – that I didn't deserve to be a dad!'

'Why didn't you even try to be a friend to me?'

'I was scared,' he admitted. 'Scared where it would bring us and that it would tie me down, so I got the fuck out of there . . .'

'You never thought about me or the baby.'

'I was twenty-one!' he said defensively. 'I could barely keep myself, let alone you and a baby. I knew that – it was impossible.'

She said nothing. Johnny hadn't changed; he was still the same. Looking out for number one, Johnny Devlin, and God help everyone else.

'Kate, can we not fight – please.'

She stopped. There was no point to it, fighting with him over something that could not be undone. Instead she focused on telling him about Erin and how much she wanted to meet him and get to know him.

'You let our daughter down years ago; don't let her down now, that's all I ask,' she begged.

'What does she want from me?' he asked angrily. 'Didn't you tell her what happened?'

'I did – but you're her dad!'

'I don't think it's a good idea after all these years.'

'I only came along tonight to ask you one thing, Johnny – to give our child an hour or two of your time. I don't think it's too much to ask.'

'Kate, I told you already that I'm not interested in meeting her,' he argued defensively. 'She's found you and that's great, but I'm not part of the picture, so there's no point to it!'

'Johnny, I was scared too when she contacted me. I refused to meet her,' she confided. 'But now I have met Erin, it's different, honestly!'

'Kate, I'm not getting involved.' She could tell that no matter what she said he wasn't going to budge or change his mind. 'I don't want to meet her, to see her, or talk to her, and you can tell her that.'

'Okay.' She sighed, realizing that whatever there had been between them was totally gone. He felt not one scrap of decency towards her or their daughter. 'If that's what you really want, I'll tell her.'

'Good.' He looked relieved. 'I'm glad the two of us have got that sorted.'

He really was a shit! They had nothing left to say to each other. How could she have ever imagined it otherwise?

'What about another drink?' he asked.

She didn't even bother answering him, but just grabbed her handbag and coat, got up from the table and started walking to the door.

Chapter Forty-two

NINA WAS SITTING DOING THE CROSSWORD WHEN TOM CAME downstairs to the kitchen.

'You look very smart,' she said, admiring the new grey pinstripe suit and crisp white shirt, and a tie she had definitely never seen before. He'd had his hair cut a few days ago and the tighter shape of his grey hair somehow made him younger.

'I have a few important meetings in town today, so I probably won't be home for dinner,' he said quickly.

'I'm going out with Mum later, so I'll get something over in her place. Tom, is everything okay?' she ventured.

'Everything's fine, Nina, but I'm running late . . .' he said, disappearing out the kitchen door.

She listened as his car pulled out of the driveway. She had no idea what was going on with him, but she wished that, whatever it was, he would just tell her.

After breakfast she escaped to the comfort of her study. The Oscar Wilde illustrations were just about done. She was so pleased with *The Happy Prince*, standing tall on his pedestal surveying the city and its inhabitants, the detail of the little swallow flying over the rooftops, the jewels from his sword being sold, the food on a family's table. It was such a wonderful classic tale, but so very sad. She ordered a courier to collect them, as they were far too precious to risk getting lost in the post en route to her editor in London. The job had been for a small publisher, but Nina was grateful to still get some work when she considered all the wonderful new, young, upcoming artists.

She looked at the preliminary drawings she had started for *The Selkie*. She hadn't even mentioned it to Poppy, her agent, yet. It was just something she wanted to do, tell it her way. The face of the girl was almost hidden behind her long golden hair, and as she began to draw the eyes and cheeks she realized that the face she was sketching was her daughter's.

Her mother was waiting for her, anxious to be off on the promised outing to Carragh House, to see one of the famous Guinness family gardens down in Wicklow. It was only open to the public for a few days of the year.

'I have wanted to visit here for years,' she smiled, 'and I'm so glad you are the one bringing me, Nina. Lizzie is wonderful, but she has no interest in plants and gardens. The last day she took me to Mount Usher she raced me through the place. All she wanted was to sit and have coffee – but can't I do that at home?'

Nina had brought a camera and as she rambled around the huge gardens with her mother they discussed the variety of old roses growing there and the wonderful layout of the Carragh House garden with its central water feature, a large pond with a dolphin fountain. They strolled along the massive summer borders of blues and pinks and purples, which almost looked like a Monet painting. She took photos of her mother, intent and totally engaged with the beauty of the cottage-garden plants. It amazed her how her mum could name every flower, remember when she had planted each one and how well it had done. This was a person who sometimes struggled to remember her grandchildren's names!

They sat on a bench in the sunshine, enjoying a pot of tea and home-made scones with jam. Her mum was wonderful, on days like this, just wonderful . . .

'How's Erin?' May asked out of the blue.

'She's fine, Mum. But there's a lot going on with her at the moment. Her boyfriend has just moved to London and he wants her to move there, and she has recently met her birth mother!'

'What?' asked May, puzzled.

'Her birth mother. Erin and Jack are adopted.'

'I never think of that,' said May firmly. 'Never.'

'I know,' smiled Nina, 'but it's something Erin wanted to do – to find her mother. Anyway, her mother is living in Dublin and they've met a few times. Now she's even talking about trying to meet her father.'

'How awful for you, Nina, how truly awful! It must be so upsetting for you!'

'I am upset, Mum. I know it sounds terrible, because Erin is so happy to have discovered her birth mother, but I feel like I've been kicked in the teeth. I feel like I'm second best now she has her real mother.'

Her mum seemed to be the only one that really understood what she was saying.

'You can't help yourself being jealous, Nina. We are always

jealous of anyone or anything that takes our children away from us.'

'I know,' said Nina, tears welling in her eyes. 'It's so stupid, but I'm afraid that I'll lose her.'

'We never lose our children,' her mother assured her. 'Never.'

'Thanks, Mum.'

'I was jealous of Betty,' she said, very softly, 'when you were younger. I used to feel that she was taking you away from me. I couldn't compete with her.'

Nina remembered her Aunt Betty, who was the eccentric in the family, an artist who was always painting and drawing, and had even turned her hand to sculpting. Nina had loved the visits of her mum's older sister, who was living in sin with her partner, Harry, in a terraced house in Rathgar. Betty used to bring her to exhibitions by her artist friends and buy her pastels and oils and sets of brushes for birthday and Christmas presents. She was the one who encouraged her constantly to look and draw and paint. When Harry retired, her aunt had moved to a place in the mountains in Spain where the light was good and she and Harry could grow olives. She had died about five years ago, her ashes sprinkled over the olive grove.

'Did you ever say anything to Betty, Mum?'

'Why would I? She was my sister. Everyone loved her – children and animals and men!'

'I loved Auntie Betty, Mum, you know I did. But you're my mum!' she said, putting an arm around her. 'You know I love you!'

'I know, pet – and you're stuck with me!'

Back in her mother's bungalow, Nina put on a wash of clothes and checked her fridge, taking note of a few things she needed.

'Mum, do you fancy an omelette, or scrambled eggs, or pasta with a cheesy sauce?'

'The pasta would be nice.'

She looked around her mother's small kitchen. Her parents had moved here from their old house in Foxrock about ten years ago. It had been such a wrench, moving home at their age, but her dad had bad arthritis in his spine and feet, which made walking and the stairs a problem. Now May Armstrong had the bungalow to herself and she felt safe within it. Her Filipino home help, Charity, came in twice a week, and Lizzie and Nina were both living near enough to help out and keep a close eye on her.

'*Coronation Street* will be on in twenty minutes,' May reminded her. Nina laughed; their mother would never miss her favourite TV programme.

'The pasta's nearly ready,' she promised, as she tossed it in the creamy-white cheese sauce and put it out on their plates.

As she watched May eat, Nina realized that her elderly mother was right: she was entitled to feel jealous about this Kate woman, but the thing she had to remember was her mother's belief that, no matter what age you are, you never lose your children.

Chapter Forty-three

ERIN STARED AT THE JUMBLED ARRAY OF FOOD IN THEIR FRIDGE. There was hummus, cheese, eggs, rashers and sausages and that awful black pudding that Nikki suddenly liked. Where had her Parma ham and antipasti selection packet gone? She hadn't even opened it yet! Also, she was sure she had left a portion of gratin potatoes on the middle fridge shelf and that too had just disappeared. She grabbed a tomato and some cheese and two eggs. She'd have an omelette; she was too tired to bother cooking anything else. She diced some onion and gave it a quick turn in the microwave before tossing it on to the melting cheese filling of the omelette.

'Mmmm, Erin, that smells good,' murmured Nikki, appearing from the bedroom in her pyjamas. 'I wouldn't mind one of them.'

'Here take this one, Nikki. I'll make another,' she offered, placing the perfect golden omelette on a plate and putting it on to the table before her friend.

'Thanks, Erin. I don't know why, but I'm constantly starving at the moment. The smell of cooking just seems to make

216

me want food. I took that lovely cheesy potato thing of yours. I couldn't resist it.'

'It's okay, Nikki; mine will be ready in a minute or two. Eat it while it's hot!'

Nikki didn't need much telling and she had polished off the omelette in a few minutes.

'You make the best omelettes ever, Erin!' she sighed appreciatively.

'Thanks. It's the one thing I can manage that Mum showed me.'

Erin turned her own omelette on to a plate and sat down opposite her. Nikki was glowing, her skin and hair glossy. Being pregnant finally suited her.

'What are you doing for the weekend?' asked Nikki.

'Luke was meant to come over, but he's got roped into going to some big work charity thing,' she explained. 'But Lilly, one of the girls I work with, is moving into a new house up in Sandyford. She's having a house warmer, so I'll probably go to that. If you want to come along, you're welcome.'

'Are you sure?'

'Of course. You'll like Lilly.'

Erin knew that Nikki's social life had become seriously curtailed with the baby. Nights out in night clubs were a thing of the past, and it wasn't much fun watching everyone getting hammered around you while you stayed sober.

'It must be tough for you with Luke away,' sympathized Nikki.

'It is, but I've booked to go over next weekend. We try to talk or text or email each other every day, but it's not the same.'

'You'll probably have to move over there eventually.'

'Maybe . . . but not till after Snoopy B has been born.'

217

'Well, I've a very busy weekend. I'm going to my ante-natal class – lots of lying on the floor on a mat breathing – and then I'm going shopping with my mum for some baby stuff.'

'Sounds fun!'

'Sure!'

Claire and her boyfriend Donal had gone off on a romantic trip to Barcelona for the weekend. 'If any one says a word about engagement rings, I will personally bash them over the head,' Claire had threatened. 'Donal is dead broke and he has another year before he's finished all his law exams.'

'*Three Men and a Baby* is on TV tonight,' announced Nikki as she took a bite of the tomato on her plate. 'We could watch it later.'

'Sure,' laughed Erin.

Erin went into the bedroom to phone Kate. She wanted to see if there was any word or information about contacting her father.

Kate was very distant on the phone. She said she had managed to speak to him but that he had been adamant he would neither see nor talk to Erin.

'So you do know how to contact him, Kate?'

'Erin, you are only going to be disappointed,' warned Kate. 'He's not going to change his mind.'

But she pressed her, saying that a search on the internet could probably find him anyway.

'Okay!' Kate very reluctantly agreed to give her his phone number in London and his address. 'Try if you want to . . .'

Erin couldn't believe it. Another piece of the puzzle had just fallen into place. She was going to London next weekend, and now she had two good reasons.

Chapter Forty-four

ON THURSDAY NIGHT ERIN JOINED DECLAN AND MONIKA AND a big crew from the office in the Sugar Club for the launch of Lia Sullivan's breakthrough first album, *Lia*. The ethereal cover design looked amazing; Erin was so pleased with it. The publicity posters, the launch invites, the flyers for record shops and the song words also looked magical.

Lia was stunning, and when she got up on stage to sing a few of the songs from the album there was utter silence as her voice and music captivated everyone. Her tumbling red hair and white skin – her almost fairy look – entranced everyone. Erin had loved working with Lia and her manager, and with the record label that was taking the gamble in investing in this wonderful new talent. Everyone was genuinely excited and she spotted one or two big music industry people there along with people from RTE and TV3.

'Hi Erin,' smiled Lia, embracing her. 'Everyone is saying how good the CD looks and the whole package, how different it is with that old-fashioned spidery writing and the beautiful background. You just captured it all perfectly. Thank you.'

'Well it was just a matter of listening to your amazing music and getting that right feel for what you're doing, and of course being able to use the still from your video was brilliant,' smiled Erin, noticing that the video was being played on a loop system in the background in conjunction with the album.

'I'm kind of nervous about it all,' Lia admitted shyly, 'but in another way excited. I've been asked to sing on *The Late Late Show* on Friday night, which is wonderful. My mum and granny are so excited for me and are getting tickets to come along to the show.'

Erin suspected that after Friday night's live performance Lia Sullivan's career was going to take off.

She made her way to the bar to join Declan and Lilly for a drink. She was standing at the counter as the barman took her order when she heard a familiar voice.

'Hey Erin!' called Matt, coming over to her. 'How are you? How's it all going?'

She felt a bit guilty. She had texted him a few times but hadn't really given him a proper update on how things were with Kate.

Grabbing his hand, she made for the sitting area and told him all about it. He was such a good listener and so bloody kind. She also confided in him that she was going over to London tomorrow morning to try to see her biological dad.

'Declan always gives us a morning off if we attend a company thing, so I'm just taking the rest of the day off too and heading over on an earlier flight so I can go and see him.'

'Do you think that's wise, Erin? He's made it very clear that he doesn't want to see you . . . Maybe you should accept that?'

'Matt, my mother didn't want to meet me either and now we have a relationship at least. This might be the same.'

'I wouldn't count on it.'

'Anyway, what are you doing here?' she asked, trying to get him off the subject.

'I edited Lia's music video. We are already in production on her second song. We're shooting it next week down in Wexford.'

'Which song is she going with?'

'"Lover Mine".'

'I love that track!' exclaimed Erin. 'It's so beautiful. I listen to her album all the time.'

'You did a great job on the cover!'

'I know,' she said proudly. 'I'm very pleased with it and grateful to Declan for letting me work on it.'

The launch party continued for hours, with Lia and the band getting up later and playing again. Erin found herself hanging out with Matt and his friends as Monika and Declan had sloped off earlier.

It was after midnight when she realized the time and re-membered she was getting a flight in the morning – there was no way she was drinking any more.

'Good luck tomorrow,' said Matt, pulling her into his arms and holding her tight. 'If you need me, Erin, just phone me. I'm just home working on my laptop all day.'

She suddenly sensed his lips brush against her hair and felt momentarily awkward.

'Matt, thanks for listening and for everything,' she said, kissing him lightly as she said her goodbyes and headed out on to Leeson Street to get a taxi.

Chapter Forty-five

ERIN WAS TENSE AS HELL AS SHE BOARDED THE FLIGHT TO Heathrow. She hadn't mentioned anything to Luke about trying to see Johnny Devlin; she knew that he would try to dissuade her, but this was something she had to do.

She had left repeated messages on Johnny's home and office numbers, but he had not bothered to return her calls. Undeterred, she had checked out his office in Ealing and made an appointment with his secretary to meet him. Knowing that if she used her real name he might refuse to see her, she had used the name Maria Armstrong, which was her great-grandmother's name, and said it was an enquiry about a new young Irish singer that she was working with. Well, she did work with Lia and it was only a ploy to get her through his office door. Hopefully the young singer would forgive her! The meeting was arranged for two p.m.

She took the tube from the airport and, arriving far too early for the meeting, went into a local coffee shop and grabbed a salad sandwich and coffee. She was nervous and apprehensive, but there was no going back now.

222

At two o'clock she walked towards the rather ugly sixties office building where she saw the name Celtic Connections on the door. She rang the bell and a woman's voice answered and opened the door automatically for her. The office was on the fourth floor. There was a lift that was in need of a cleaning, and when she got out she went straight through the door ahead of her. A skinny girl a bit older than herself sat talking on the phone in a small reception area and gestured for her to take a seat.

'Mr Devlin will be with you in a few minutes,' she said, continuing her conversation with a friend.

Erin looked around the rather grimy office. One wall was covered with photos of various Irish musicians and comedians, as well as with posters of appearances in places such as London, Manchester and Liverpool. She stood up to get a better look at one photo of a well-known traditional fiddle player with a thin, dark-haired man. She wondered, was he her father?

Ten minutes later he emerged from his office. Erin held her breath as Jonathan Devlin introduced himself and shook her hand. Trying to control her nerves, she smiled, followed him into his office and sat down across from him. He was just like Kate had said – and she supposed still very good looking in a kind of trying-too-hard way. He was wearing a tight-fitting grey-and-white shirt and skinny jeans, and was tall and wiry, with his hair to his shoulders. His eyes were dark and he had the longest black eyelashes. His face was narrow with thin lips, and he was one of those men who look like they constantly need to shave.

'Now, Miss Armstrong – or can I call you Maria?' he smiled, his eyes running over her face and figure. 'What can I do for you, or to be more exact for this girl Lia? I have checked her out on YouTube and she is very talented. Her record company is fairly new and probably only has a few contacts here in the UK, but I'm sure I could help in terms of arranging a few appearances on this side of the water if that is what you want for her?'

Erin listened as he spoke. He still had a bit of his Irish accent and she could see he was wired and full of energy as he started to list a range of Irish clubs and pubs where Lia could sing. She couldn't imagine Lia singing in any of them. She wasn't that type of artist.

'Well, Maria?'

'I'm sorry.' She hadn't even been listening properly.

'I was talking about the Irish Club in Manchester—'

'Listen, Mr Devlin, I'm sorry, but the truth is I'm not here about Lia,' she admitted. 'I just wanted to meet you.'

'Meet me? What is this about?' he said, instantly suspicious.

'I'm Erin,' she said, looking directly at him and seeing the dawning recognition in his eyes. 'I'm your daughter.'

He said nothing for a few seconds. She could see that he was actually speechless. He was used to being the one in control of situations.

'I've left lots of phone messages trying to arrange to see you or meet you, but you didn't return my calls. So I decided I had to find a way to get to meet you here. I do know Lia and have actually worked on the cover of her new CD, so I hoped that it might help,' she explained, trying not to be confrontational.

'I don't care who you are, you have absolutely no right to come in here pretending to be someone you aren't and wasting my valuable time,' he said, standing up. 'I should ask you to leave.'

'I'm your daughter – that's who I am!' she exclaimed, not moving.

He stopped for a second, then sat back down.

'Kate told me about you, but I was very clear that I didn't want to see you. Didn't she tell you?'

'She did.'

'Then why are you here? What are you looking for? Is it money?'

Erin laughed. It was ludicrous. He thought everyone had to be after something.

'I wanted to meet you, that's all,' she said gently. 'No other motive. Just to see what my father looks like and sounds like.'

'I told Kate when we met for dinner a few weeks ago that there was no point to this, that I wasn't interested in getting involved. I made it very clear to her. I have my life here. All this happened in the past and I have put it behind me.'

Erin swallowed hard. Kate had gone out to dinner with him! Why hadn't she told her?

But Kate had tried to tell her, to warn her off . . .

'I see.'

He was looking coldly at her, silently taking in her clothes, the expensive handbag her mum and dad had given her last Christmas, weighing her up.

'I'd better go,' she said, standing up. 'I'm staying with a friend for the weekend.'

He stood up too. 'Erin, perhaps it is good that we have got to meet,' he said, grudgingly. 'Kate told me a lot about you and what a great girl you are . . . I can see that now for myself. But it still doesn't change the fact that I have my life over here and you have your life. I wish you luck in whatever you are doing and for the future, but I'm sorry I cannot at this stage become a part of it.'

'I'm sorry too,' she said, lifting her handbag. She didn't shake his hand or anything; she walked back out to the reception desk, grabbed her weekend bag and headed back down in the lift. Johnny Devlin had been very honest with her and she had to accept it.

Back out in the street she stood for a few minutes trying to compose herself. She wanted to get as far away from here as possible and found herself hopping on a tube to the city centre. Luke wouldn't be home for hours and she had no key for the apartment, so she would just have to hang around until he finished work.

Chapter Forty-six

ERIN GOT OFF THE TUBE DOWN NEAR BRIDGEPORT ROAD, WHERE Luke and Ronan had found an apartment. It was an older area and there were lots of local shops, bars and restaurants. She spotted what looked like a tea room with cakes and biscuits displayed in the window and went inside and sat down. It was quiet, with a few older women sitting talking together over cakes and coffee, and an old man ensconced near the window reading the *Financial Times* with a large slice of chocolate cake in front of him.

Erin felt sick, but she ordered a large cappuccino. She still couldn't believe the reaction she had got from Johnny Devlin. He had been direct and honest with her, even if it hurt knowing the truth. Perhaps she had been expecting too much, but he had disappointed her. She couldn't get around the fact that he had fathered her and not only walked away from Kate when she really needed him but even now, when she was an adult and wasn't making any demands on him, he was only interested in himself.

He was a selfish man, not capable of being a proper father.

Maybe she was lucky that Johnny Devlin hadn't been a part of her life, and now never would be.

Sitting there, she gradually began to calm down and relax. Okay, it was sad, so sad – but it didn't change anything. She had satisfied her curiosity and deep-felt need to know about her natural father, and, okay, it had not turned out the way she had planned, but at least she could just get on with her life and forget about him.

As she sat there she suddenly got the urge to phone her dad and called his number.

'Hi, Erin.' He sounded surprised. 'I thought you were going to London today?'

'I am, Dad. I just arrived and I phoned to see how you are.'

'I'm down at the boat,' he laughed. 'I'm trying to fix this yoke of a rudder of mine; it keeps sticking. Is everything okay?' he asked, unable to keep his concern for her out of his voice.

'Fine, Dad,' she lied, trying not to cry. 'I'll be meeting Luke in a while.'

'Tell him I said hello. When will you be home?'

'Late on Sunday.'

'The weather is meant to hold till next Wednesday. I haven't been out in her much lately, been a bit preoccupied with things; but do you fancy a bit of sailing after work on Monday or Tuesday evening?'

'That would be lovely, Dad! I'll call you when I get home, okay?'

She sat for a while, comforted by his voice – her real father's voice. At five o'clock Luke phoned and they arranged to meet an hour later.

*   *   *

Luke had suggested she made her way to the wine bar that was situated near his apartment building. It was already beginning to fill up with a post-work crowd, but Erin managed to nab an outside table where she could at least watch the world go by and chill until Luke appeared. The waitress passed her an impressive wine list and she ordered a glass of one of her favourites, a lovely chilled rosé, and the waitress put a small bowl of complimentary olives on the table. It was a lovely evening and she urged herself to relax. She had decided to make no mention of her meeting with Johnny to Luke. She was gutted, but she wasn't going to have her useless father ruin her weekend.

She was on her second glass of wine when Luke arrived. She had forgotten how good he looked in a suit and tie, and she could see lots of envious glances from girls around her as he joined her and ordered more wine. They stayed there for ages, laughing and chatting, until he finally agreed to letting her go home and change in the apartment before they headed out to dinner.

'Luke, maybe we could stay home in the apartment and get a takeaway?' she pleaded, tiredness and the few glasses of wine hitting her.

'No way! You are glamming up, and I am taking you to the best Argentinian restaurant ever! It's only about a ten-minute walk from where I live,' he laughed, taking her hand.

The street where he lived was just one big row of tall, modern apartment buildings, all glass and concrete stacked together like angled dominoes around a central plaza. His building was Number Four, and the apartment was on the eighth floor with a balcony and great views. It was smaller than she had expected, with a living room and neat galley kitchen with very little space for cooking. The living room was *über*-modern, with black-and-grey leather couches, a massive plasma TV and a small glass dining table with four chairs.

Luke was right, because if you went out on the balcony you had a massive view over that part of the city. Erin struggled to get her bearings as Luke pointed out various city landmarks to her.

She dumped her case in his bedroom and giggled as he pulled her into the shower while he changed out of his own work clothes. She really had missed him and would have been so happy to spend the time here with him.

'Maybe the restaurant can deliver?' she pleaded, wrapped in a towel.

'Tempting as it is to stay in, we are going out,' he insisted. 'I work bloody hard all week and the least I can do is go out on a Friday and have a good time. Crashing at home is not an option!'

Half an hour later, as she ordered from the Argentinian menu and sipped a mojito, she had to agree with him. The place was hopping with lots of people determined to enjoy themselves, but by midnight Erin found herself yawning, the stress of meeting Johnny Devlin catching up on her. After a few drinks she felt pretty wrecked and emotional and needed to sleep.

'Luke, let's head back to the apartment,' she pleaded over the music.

'Don't be such a granny!' he teased, showing utterly no interest in leaving the place. Then some of his friends from the office appeared and Luke insisted they join them. It was two a.m. before they finally made it home.

*   *   *

Saturday morning they both slept in and only the sound of
Ronan banging around the place woke them up. Ronan was
watching Sky Sports and they spent the next two hours glued
to a match Erin had zero interest in.

In the afternoon Luke brought her to view three apartments
in a new complex nearer his office. Each was much bigger than
the one he was sharing, but two of them had only one bedroom
and very little storage space. The rents were outrageous.

'Luke, there is no way I could afford that! Absolutely no way
I could even earn that!'

'Everyone has to pay out here for rent,' he cajoled. 'People
work hard! Play hard! And when you are our age you want to
stay in the centre – nobody wants to be doing a big commute
after working till eight or nine, or even later, most nights. So
you just have to pay up! In a year or so I think I'll probably
buy a place. It will be a good investment, as I can rent it out
later.'

Erin could see he had it all planned out, but she wasn't sure
that his plan was the same as hers.

Dinner and a night club were organized for Saturday night and
Ronan joined them.

'Has Michelle been over yet?' she asked.

'Nah, she's got lectures on a Saturday morning for the next
few weeks and it's not really worth my while going over, as I'd
have to head home on Sunday afternoon.' He didn't sound too
disappointed, and judging by the attention he was getting from
one of the girls he was chatting to up at the bar while they
waited for a table, it wasn't bothering him too much.

The night was great fun and Erin drank far too much,
trying to block out yesterday's fiasco with the man who was

her so-called father. What was it Claire called fathers like that? *Sperm donors*!

Luke paid her lots of attention and they danced and drank and danced again before eventually heading back to the apartment.

There was no sign of Ronan the next day, so they just chilled together over breakfast. Then things began to sour as Luke started to go on and on at her about moving to London.

'When are you coming over?' he demanded tetchily. 'Erin, I don't think that you are making any effort to get a job here. Why aren't you putting things in motion to make the move?'

'It's not that easy, Luke,' she tried to explain. 'You were transferred with your job, but my job in Dublin is going okay at the moment and I really like what I'm doing. Declan has been great to me and let me do all the design work for the CD and publicity pack for Lia, this great new singer. I wouldn't probably get that opportunity over here.'

'You don't know that,' he countered. 'Anyway, I thought that the reason for moving is for us to be together, that you wanted to be with me.'

'I do. Why do you think I'm here?' she teased, trying to placate him. 'But Luke, you know I've only just started to connect with my birth mother . . . It's early days, but we are friends and I do want to try to get to know her better and build on it a bit.'

'She's not important in your life!'

'You don't know that!' she remonstrated.

'We need to build lives here, careers here,' he pressed. 'Erin, the world doesn't revolve around Dublin or Ireland, you know.'

'That's where my family are,' she reminded him, 'and your family too. Mum and Dad are already all *angsty* about Jack going to Australia for the year with Pixie. If I move they'll have no one at home.'

'Thank God for Mr O'Leary and his cheap flights!' he laughed.

'I'm serious, Luke,' said Erin. 'If I do move over here it would only ever be temporary, for a year or two. But then I would plan eventually, when I have a family, kids, to move back home.'

'I'm not sure moving back to Ireland is part of the plan. Let's face it, I'm here working in the London office in a dream job – it's where I want to be. Maybe you need to think about that,' he said, getting up and going and getting a glass of juice in the kitchen.

Erin didn't know what to say. She'd had a wonderful weekend with Luke, but living day to day like this . . . she wasn't sure. He worked mad hours; they'd hardly see each other.

'Luke, you need to give me more time,' she said, following him into the kitchen and kissing him.

'Sure,' he laughed, pulling her close. 'But just don't take for ever.'

'Will you come home next weekend?' she asked.

'Don't think that's an option. One of the guys in work in my section is having his stag on Saturday night.' He shrugged. 'So I'm not going to miss that.'

'Well then, the following weekend?'

'There's a big barbecue in Marcus Stephens' home. He's one of the senior partners. It's a big thing to get invited,' he explained, 'so there's no way I can say no. But girlfriends are welcome. You should come over!'

'I'll see about the flights,' she said as she zipped up her bag and checked that she had everything.

This was the part she hated, saying goodbye to Luke. He walked her to the station where she could get the Heathrow Express. She hated leaving him like this; it might be weeks before they saw each other again. This whole long-distance thing was shit! Luke was right – she was going to have to make up her mind.

Chapter Forty-seven

KATE WASN'T SURPRISED WHEN ERIN PHONED HER AND TOLD her what had happened in London with Johnny.

'I tried to warn you,' she said, wishing that he hadn't hurt her daughter so much. Johnny's ex-wife was right: he did not deserve to be a father.

Kate couldn't help it, but lately she found herself thinking more and more of Erin as her elder daughter and wanting to protect her. She was so glad that they had found each other and she knew that she would never let Erin out of her life again. They were bit by bit becoming friends; sometimes she felt more like Erin's big sister, but she guessed that was okay too. She looked forward to meeting her, chatting on the phone, to being a part of her life.

She was at home on Wednesday, about to go out to dinner with Paddy, when he arrived home and handed her an invitation card.

'I got an advance copy of the invitation for our anniversary party to check before we get it printed,' he said proudly, passing the white-and-silver card to her. 'I think it looks great and

Liam said he can do them tomorrow. Then we can start posting them out to people to give them proper notice about it.'

Kate took the expensive card with its silver writing and studied it.

Paddy and Kate Cassidy

invite . . . . to join them
to celebrate 25 years of marriage
at their Silver Wedding Anniversary Party
8 p.m. on Saturday 20 September
at 125 Bayview Park, Sutton, Co Dublin

R.S.V.P. 5 September

Kate held the invitation. It was beautiful, so classic and perfect. Paddy always did everything right, organized everything so well.

Twenty-five years of marriage . . . She was such a fraud to deceive someone as honest as him. To have lied to him, pretended to him, to have kept so much hidden!

'Hurry on, Kate, we'll be late,' he urged. 'We can talk about it over dinner and try to agree our numbers.'

She sat on the bed, touching the writing on the card.

'Paddy, I need to talk to you.' She gestured for him to sit beside her.

He looked puzzled. 'Are you all right? Are you sick? I'll phone them and cancel it.'

'Please, just sit down. I have something to tell you,' she said, barely able to speak. What if he hated her, never wanted to speak to her again or see her? But she couldn't keep up the lie any longer.

He sat down beside her and she could see the worry and concern for her in his eyes.

'What is it?' he said, reaching for her, wanting to comfort her.

She took a breath, the sigh so big that she felt she might never breathe again.

'Paddy, I have kept something from you for so long,' she began. 'I was afraid to tell you, ashamed. I thought that you would look down on me if you ever found out.'

His eyes were intent on her face and she could see fear reflected in them.

'I had a baby the year before I met you,' she said. 'A little girl.'

'You had a baby?' He looked absolutely shocked.

She nodded silently.

'You had a baby before our Sean was born?'

'Yes,' she said, looking into his eyes. 'I gave her up for adoption. I couldn't keep her. The father and I broke up. I couldn't tell my dad or anyone. Paddy, I was stupid and scared. I talked to the social workers and the adoption agency and they organized everything for me, arranged for her to be adopted. I felt it was the best thing for her . . . and for me.'

Paddy said nothing. He didn't shout. He didn't scream at her or hit her. Just nothing, sitting there quiet at the end of their bed.

'Why didn't you tell me when we started going out?' he demanded angrily. 'When we were getting married?'

'I couldn't tell you,' she said. 'It was a secret.'

'Some bloody secret!'

'I was afraid. It was bad enough that I'd lost my baby! I couldn't have borne it if I'd lost you too, Paddy.' She sat on the bed, tears sliding down her face.

'And why are you telling me now after all this time?' he pushed. 'Why now?'

'It's because she has come back into my life. My daughter found me. Her name is Erin and somehow she got this address and came to the house. I couldn't believe it. She's twenty-six years old and lovely and intelligent and bright. I'm not ashamed of her, Paddy, or of being her mother any more.'

'Years of lies and secrets, Kate! Why didn't you trust me?'

'Paddy, I was just young and scared. I thought that you might stop loving me.'

He said nothing. He wasn't denying it.

'What about the father? Were you in love with him?'

'I thought that I was at the time,' she whispered. 'We were in college—'

'Have you seen him since, had any contact with him?' he continued, serious.

'Not for years, but Erin has been trying to contact him, she wanted to meet him. So I phoned him, told him about her. We met to discuss it. But he has no interest in Erin. He told her that when she went over to London recently to see him.'

She stopped, then went on, 'I didn't mean to hurt you, Paddy. I'm sorry. Sorry for keeping it secret. But I'm not sorry about having Erin,' she said firmly. 'I have a lovely daughter and I'm not ashamed of that.'

Paddy got up. He didn't look at her or touch her. He began to walk around the room, pacing up and down. Then he grabbed his jacket from the wardrobe and left. She listened to his steps on the stairs, and the hall door bang.

She sat on the bed, empty and drained, alone. Pulling the quilt over, she curled up. It was what she had feared for so long –

that the information would destroy them. She had delayed it for years by keeping Erin's birth a secret, but the inevitable had now happened and Paddy was gone.

She lay there for hours as the room went dark, listening to her breath and her heart and the ticking alarm clock on Paddy's side of the bed. Then she heard it – the key in the door and his heavy footsteps coming back up the stairs, walking towards Sean's bedroom, then suddenly in the darkness she felt him beside her, warm and strong, lifting her into his arms.

'It's okay, Kate. It's okay,' he repeated over and over again as she clung to him.

Chapter Forty-eight

NINA WAS ENJOYING THE SUMMER DAYS POTTERING AROUND the garden, going for walks and working up the illustration for the story she wanted to re-tell. They'd had a few barbecues with friends and family, but she so wished that Tom would take some proper time off and come on holiday. He always seemed to be busy on that iPhone of his, taking calls and answering emails and out seeing clients at all hours. He had barely been out in the boat at all, which was most unlike him, and if he did go he tended to go off sailing for hours on his own. She was hurt that he hadn't even asked her out once; okay, she wasn't the best sailor in the world, but on a good day when there were no gales blowing she enjoyed the peace and joy of skimming along the waves in a strong breeze with the wind in their sails.

Two or three times she had asked him about when they were going down to the small summer house they owned in West Cork for a break.

'Tom, please let's go down to the cottage for a few days. We both need to get away from everything and have a break.'

'I've no time for a break,' he had answered, distracted. 'I've far too much on. You go on your own if you want.'

Hurt, she said nothing. She didn't want to go on her own; she wanted him to come with her. Tom badly needed to unwind and relax. She was worried about him and whatever he had got himself caught up in.

He seemed to get texts at all hours, which he then would disappear outside to read and answer.

Taking one of his summer linen jackets to be cleaned one day, she discovered a name and a phone number in the breast pocket: 'Caroline', and a number . . .

Consumed with curiosity, she phoned the number and heard the sound of a woman querying who was on the line.

'Tom, is that you? Is that you?'

She dropped the phone.

Lizzie was back from her holidays with Myles in Portugal. They had had a great time and she called over to see Nina for lunch to show off her tan and her holiday photos.

'When are you and Tom heading off to Schull?' Lizzie asked. 'I'm surprised that you are still in Dublin.'

'We're not sure yet, but probably in a week or two. Tom's very busy.'

'Well, that's a good complaint at the moment,' said Lizzie as she tucked into her salad.

It was very hot outside and Nina had put up the parasol over the table on the patio. She had made a big dish of potato salad and chives and had served it with some cold barbecued salmon and tomatoes and lettuce from the garden.

'Mum seems to be doing fine. Charity is so good to her and having you here while I'm away means I can relax and not worry.'

Nina laughed. She and Lizzie had a sort of tag-team arrangement that one of them would always be around for their mother if the other was away.

'Are you working on anything?' Lizzie asked.

'*The Happy Prince* illustrations are finished. I've no idea when the book is coming out, but I am pleased with them. But I've started working on something new. Do you remember Granny used to tell us the story of the Selkie Girl? Well I'm trying to do a version of it. I've always adored that story.'

'Has it been commissioned?'

'No, I'm just drawing and painting it myself. It's not a very popular story, so a publisher might not even be interested in it, but I just want to do it.'

'Sometimes I envy you,' admitted Lizzie. 'You get such enjoyment from what you do.'

'But you enjoy your job too!'

'It's hardly the same thing, working part time as an accountant,' she laughed, finishing off her cup of herbal tea. 'Anyway, I'd better get going.'

'Lizzie, have you ever worried about Myles?' she found herself asking as her sister started to get up.

'What do you mean?'

'I mean about Myles and other women?'

'No,' Lizzie protested, laughing. 'Why would I? We have a great relationship and don't hide things from each other. What is this about, Nina?'

'It sounds crazy, but I'm worried about Tom. Hopefully I'm just imagining it. I found a phone number for some person called Caroline and he's bought new clothes and changed his hair and seems to be constantly away on business.'

'Nina, I think that you are wrong. Tom is old fashioned like

Myles. He wouldn't mess around with another woman! You're just imagining it. You're putting two and two together and getting five!'

'I know I'm probably totally getting things out of context,' she said, embarrassed.

'Look, I've got to run, but just talk to Tom,' advised her sister as Nina walked her out to her car in the driveway. 'He'll give you a straight answer.'

So she waited up for Tom to come home that night to talk to him. She waited and waited until it was well past midnight. When he did eventually come home, he was surprised to see her waiting up for him. He'd obviously been drinking.

'Where were you?' she demanded.

'Out.' It was the kind of oblique answer Jack used to give when he wouldn't tell them he had gone drinking with his buddies when he was seventeen or eighteen.

'Who is Caroline? Were you with her?'

'Nina, this is utterly stupid. It's very late and I have no idea what you are talking about. I was out in town with an important client. He wanted to go to Bucks, that night club place, and I went with him.'

Out nightclubbing – she couldn't believe it!

'Tom, what the hell is going on?' she demanded. 'What's happening to us?'

'I have an important early-morning meeting tomorrow and I am not talking about this now,' he said dismissively. 'I need to get to sleep. And I'll sleep in the spare room tonight. That way I won't wake you in the morning.'

Sleeping in the spare room? They never slept apart unless one of them was away or really ill. Nina couldn't believe it.

Tom wouldn't even discuss it with her. He hadn't even denied knowing this Caroline woman. Whatever was happening with him, he obviously had no plans to tell her. They had always talked things out before. If they argued they'd stay up till all hours trying to find a solution or resolution to it. But this was different. Tom was shutting her out as if she was not important to him any more.

She could hear him moving around the next-door bedroom, falling into bed, and then the sound of his deep, heavy sleep. She couldn't sleep. She was far too upset and tossed and turned for what seemed like hours. She couldn't stick this tension and fighting between them – she had to get away.

Chapter Forty-nine

AFTER LAST NIGHT'S ROW, NINA ANNOUNCED TO TOM BEFORE he left the house in the morning that she was going down to West Cork. 'Since you are far too busy to come away, I've decided to take your advice and go to the cottage myself.'

He seemed a little surprised but made no effort to stop her.

Escaping to Oyster Cottage, their West Cork hideaway, was exactly what she needed, she thought, as she packed up her bags and art materials and put Bailey in the back of the car.

The old house was about a mile's walk from the village of Schull and had great views over the sea and the surrounding fields. When the children had been younger they had usually decamped here for about six weeks every summer, but now they could come and go as they pleased. It was such a retreat; she always found it so relaxing here and a good place for working.

She was still annoyed with Tom, but she was in no mood for big fights and dramatics; she just needed time to think and this was the perfect place to do that.

The cottage was stuffy and warm when she arrived and she opened the windows to air it. Jack and his friends had come down for a few days about three weeks ago but the grass needed cutting again. The garden was bursting with wild purple and pink fuchsia and spiky, tall montbretia. It was heaven. She had stopped off and filled up with a few groceries at the local supermarket and so, switching on the radio to Lyric FM, she unpacked quickly and made herself a sandwich and a mug of tea.

Tired after the long drive from Dublin, she needed to stretch her legs and decided to go for a walk with the dog along the road up towards Colla Pier before it got dark. It felt like coming home. She could feel her tension and anxiety suddenly ease as she walked and took in the wild, rugged scenery all around her.

She slept well that night and woke refreshed to the sound of crickets in the grass. The day was already warm and the weather forecast was for a scorcher. Even though she was tired, there was no point lolling around in bed, so, bracing herself, she hopped into the rather ancient shower that they had never got around to replacing, and ten minutes later she was watching a fishing boat chug its way out to Long Island as she ate her breakfast of brown bread, home-made jam and a pot of coffee.

She spent the morning working, spreading her rough sketches all about her as she began to work on a picture of her Selkie Girl standing looking out at the sea, the wind and the waves calling her. She broke briefly for lunch and in the mid-afternoon went for a walk down towards the shingly beach a few minutes from the cottage, where they often went swimming. The tide was out and two of the Murphy kids from the ultra-modern house across the other side of the road from her were there with their minder, a young Polish girl. She laughed, watching their antics as they paddled and dipped into the chilly water.

At eight p.m. she fixed herself some pasta and texted Tom to tell him she was fine, then she worked on till almost midnight, totally undisturbed.

As the days passed she got into a routine of work, walks and short breaks. She talked to Tom twice and could sense the concern in his voice. She reassured him that she was okay, that she was caught up in work and that it was going far better than she had expected.

Down here her senses were assailed by the sense of place her story needed and she pushed herself to try to capture on paper the essence of the cottage overlooking the sea – the small home that could not hold the Selkie when the great ocean beckoned her. Her heart ached at times, and she cried as she wrote the words and drew the pictures for a story she had loved for so long.

A week passed and, barring forays into the village to buy bread and milk and supplies, and to treat herself to two books in the bookshop and have a cake and coffee with Damian Ryan, a musician friend who lived locally, she kept herself to herself.

Erin had phoned her. She had met Kate again; a friendship was slowly developing between them. Erin had shown her a photo of herself and Kate together. The other woman was young and dark and very attractive, with the exact same eyes as her daughter. Captured on camera, they looked more like sisters than mother and daughter. It had hurt Nina, seeing them together, but it was strange, as now she no longer felt as jealous and possessive about it as before. Down here, things that had seemed immense and daunting seemed to develop a different perspective.

She was sitting in a small cove sketching a seal basking on

the rocks, trying to capture the changing colour of sealskin as the water lapped around it and the light reflected on the sea. She sat there for two – no, three – hours, sensing that the seal was watching her as much as she was watching it. Eventually satisfied with what she had drawn, she walked back up to Oyster Cottage – and recognized Tom's large Jeep in the driveway.

She felt suddenly awkward seeing him. She had no idea what to say.

'How are you?' he asked.

'I'm fine – really fine.'

'This work is amazing! Nina, I haven't seen you work like this for years!'

She laughed. In the kitchen there was paper everywhere, covered in sketches and pen-and-ink drawings and paintings at various stages; it was the same in the sitting room, and she even had done four rough sketches of the view from the bedroom window at different times of the day and colour-washed them.

'It's been great. I've just been able to concentrate on what I'm doing. No distractions.'

'Do you mean I shouldn't have come?'

She shook her head. She was glad that Tom had made the effort.

'Here, let me clear a bit of space so you can at least sit down.' She made him a coffee. He looked tired – exhausted even.

They skirted around each other, making smalltalk about the kids and the dog and the family. If that was the way he wanted it, well that was okay with her. They went for a long walk together and barely said a word. Then while Tom dozed in the armchair she made them dinner – fresh hake bought early this morning down at the fish market on the harbour and new baby potatoes with salad and scallions.

'Wow, I missed you throwing a meal together,' he complimented as he tucked in.

After dinner she worked again while he went down and checked out the small cove where he often fished in the little dinghy they kept in the shed. Finishing up a few hours later, she realized that he had already gone to bed and was fast asleep. She didn't know whether to be angry with him or relieved. Undressing quietly, she slipped in beside him and within minutes the familiar, regular sound of his breathing sent her to sleep.

Next morning Tom had breakfast without her and, realizing he was gone down to the cove with the dog, she followed him. He was sitting there lost in thought, staring out at the water.

'You should put on your baseball cap,' she said softly. 'I don't want you to get sunburnt.'

For a second, as she took in his hunched figure, she thought that he seemed to shudder.

'What's happening with us?' she found herself saying aloud as she sat down on the rocks near him.

'I don't know what you mean, Nina.'

'I mean are we going the way of Vonnie and Simon?'

'What have they got to do with us?'

'Is there someone else?' she burst out. 'Are you seeing someone else, Tom? I'd far prefer that you tell me instead of pretending.'

'Someone else – how can you even think that!' he protested fiercely. 'You know there's no one else, Nina!'

'That's it – I don't know!' she retorted, facing him down.

'There's a woman called Caroline. You are off all over the place. You're on business, you're working late, you have to meet someone . . . You are down playing golf with Frank, when Frank is having dinner with Brenda in Dun Laoghaire. Excuses all the time and I have no idea where you are or who you are with. Then there's the fancy new suit and haircut—'

'But I wanted to tell you—'

'It's still need-to-know as far as you're concerned,' she accused, trying to control her emotions, 'even though I'm your wife.'

He said nothing and she could see how nervous he was.

'There is something we need to talk about,' he said finally, almost shuddering. 'You're right – but it's about the business. The business is gone. Literally collapsed.'

'What are you talking about?' Looking at him, Nina was suddenly scared.

'Harris Engineering is no more,' he said, pulling himself up straight. 'I have been doing everything in my power to try and stave it off, dealing with the banks, trying to get some new investors on board – but it's too late. The business is going to be put into receivership.'

'Oh God, Tom, don't say that! We must be able to do something, to try to rescue it—'

'That's what I have been doing. Bill put some money in and I've been trying to see if we can sell it as a going concern, keep the jobs, pay our creditors . . .'

Nina sat absolutely stunned. 'Why didn't you tell me?'

'You were dealing with that whole thing with Erin and her mother. I didn't feel you would be able to take the stress of this too, and besides, I was sure that I could somehow get it sorted.'

Nina couldn't believe it. Why had Tom hidden it from her?

'We could have talked about it.'

'Nina, I'm sixty-four years old and trying to rescue a company I set up almost thirty years ago. I had to buy a suit – do you know what it's like going in to meet bankers and lenders almost half my age? I needed to look right . . . younger . . . shave a few years off this old fogey's face and look smart. Caroline is the girl who cuts my hair,' he said slowly. 'Old Peter in the barber's shop retired and Caroline took it over. She not only revamped the place but I think decided to do a bit of a revamp on a lot of Peter's old customers, including myself.

'Do you have any idea of how hard it is out there when you are my age? I've been all over the place trying to chase up payments on contract work and get some new business in, well enough to tide us over. Frank was great. He let me use his place in Mount Juliet to bring three guys over to play golf and try to set up some financing with them. It worked, and in fact Larry Maxwell and his team will hopefully be the ones who will take over the firm if the bank agrees it. I've been buying equipment off Larry for years, so it's a good fit. They have no engineering presence and plan to implement some of the things I advise, but naturally they want to develop their own strategy and have promised to try and keep the jobs – well, most of them.'

'What about your job?'

'Bosses don't keep their job when there is virtual takeover of the company,' he said. 'With the receivers' backing they will take it over, pay off the debts we owe and then start over again doing what Harris Engineering does best.'

'Tom, I'm so sorry!' Nina threw her arms around him. 'I just cannot believe this is happening, but I'm so relieved!'

'Relieved?'

'I thought that you were having an affair.'

251

Tom laughed. 'I must have looked really good in that suit!'

'I'm sorry for being so bloody unsupportive at a time you really needed me,' she apologized. 'How could I have not seen it?'

'There isn't anything you can do, Nina. You didn't cause the Irish economy to collapse and for the recession to strike all over the world. We just have to live with it.'

'What will you do?' She couldn't imagine Tom not being a part of the company he had set up and developed.

'I'll work as an adviser for the short term, then God knows what else. I want to clear any money I owe. Pay off any creditors. I'm not one of those people who try to shaft my suppliers, so that's got to be sorted. I want to try to stay on good terms with Morten and Baz in Sweden. I feel I've let them down; Larry and the guys have their own supplier of solar-heating panels and won't use them.'

'What about money?' she ventured.

'That's the million-dollar question. My investments have crashed like everyone else's, and even my pension is half what it should be. So, Nina, I'm afraid that there is a possibility we may have to sell the house to raise some capital to live on.'

'Sell the house?' She couldn't help herself getting upset. She loved their house and had hoped that they would live there like Darby and Joan till they were much older. 'It's our home!'

'I know. The property market has crashed and I expect that we won't even get a half of what we could have got four or five years ago, but we haven't a mortgage on it. We bought the house over twenty-three years ago for what we thought was a huge amount but was in fact a song, so we would definitely make money.'

'That is if we can sell it,' she reminded him. 'O'Malleys have had their house up for sale for the past eighteen months and have had no proper offers.'

'Our house is a much nicer house than theirs.'

'But where would we live?'

'We'd downsize and move to something smaller, more manageable. You know we hardly ever use the big dining room any more, and even only use the sitting room for big family get-togethers at Christmas and a few other times in the year. You and I are rattling around the place.'

Nina didn't know what to say. Tom had obviously been working it all out in his head for the past few months without confiding in her. She should be angry and annoyed with him, but she could see he was heartbroken about the company and the possibility of them losing their beautiful old house.

They walked and talked for hours, then, both exhausted, they slept for a while. There were sausages made from the locally bred black pigs with all kinds of herbs in the fridge and they had them for dinner with some fried-up slices of leftover potato. Tom opened a bottle of wine and Nina pulled on her pale-green woollen wrap as they sat outside on the wooden bench.

'I'd better go back tomorrow, try to tie things up more,' he said, holding her hand.

'I'll come back with you,' she offered. 'We'll face it together.'

'I'm over with Larry for two days at the end of the week. Why don't you stay here and try to finish what you are working on?' he encouraged her.

Tom loved her drawings and the fact that, for the first time ever, she was taking a well-known legend and telling it in her own words.

She hesitated. 'Are you sure?'

'Yes. I'll come down here again when I get back and let you know what's happening.'

'What about Erin and Jack? They need to know.'

'I'll have a better idea of things next week. Can we tell them then?' he asked.

Nina knew that the kids would be devastated when they heard about Tom losing the company, but losing their child-hood home was even worse.

They sat up as the skies darkened, watching the sun set and the moon come up before eventually going to bed.

Next morning, still in her pyjamas, Nina made him break-fast before he set off on the long journey back to Dublin.

'I love you, Tom,' she said, kissing him.

'And I love you too,' he said, holding her tight to him. 'And that will never change.'

Chapter Fifty

IT WAS ONLY AFTER TOM HAD GONE THAT THE FULL IMPACT OF what he had told her really hit her. Harris Engineering closed down or owned by somebody else! What would Tom do? How would he survive such a drastic change in his life?

Like most men, his business and work had been the main focus of his life and the plan had always been for him to work for as long as he could in a business he really enjoyed until he was ready to retire. Now everything had been catapulted into an economic maelstrom and they had no idea how they were going to come out of it. She had always assumed that they would live comfortably as they got older and had never worried about it, but now that safety-net of ignorance was gone and Nina felt a very genuine fear of what the outcome would be.

She loved Clifton, their old three-storey house, and had always imagined living there for the rest of her life, with Erin and Jack and their children always having the house to come home to. But if Tom felt that, financially, they had no other option but to sell it, then they would have to move. It was unbearable, but she had to be realistic; their marriage and financial security were far more important than a big house. If they had to they would start over, just like they did when they were young and first married, living in their little terraced house in Harold's Cross. As a couple they had worked together and built a strong marriage, and now it was even more important that they strive together to find some sort of solution to this calamity. They were both strong and in good health and had years of life ahead of them. She still loved Tom as much as ever, despite him being so absurdly stupid trying to protect her from what was happening to the business. They were a pair and would face up to things together, and, if needs be, begin again.

Alone in the cottage in West Cork, she sought refuge in her painting. She worked from breakfast time till late in the evening, covering the pages with blue washes and lines and strokes of colours as the story took shape. The illustrations flew from her hand like magic, each picture more fluid and beautiful, as if the enormous stress she was under was actually making her retreat into work and lose herself in it totally.

At night Tom called her from his hotel and they spent hours on the phone as he told her everything that was going on. She felt for him; she could sense the pressure and desperation he was experiencing as he and Larry Maxwell and the bank began to draw up the agreements for the sale of the company. She phoned Erin and Jack and briefly told them the situation, both of them appalled by what was going on. She had been so annoyed with Tom for keeping her in the dark about things; she wasn't prepared to do the same with their children.

'Poor Dad!' said Erin, shocked to discover what was happening. 'Is there anything we can do to help?'

'There doesn't seem to be much anyone can do, but at least we can stick together as a family,' said Nina firmly.

Jack had been so quiet when she told him that she thought at first he hadn't heard her.

'That explains a lot,' he said, almost tearful. 'I've been worried that Dad was sick or something. We haven't gone out in the boat for weeks. I asked him if he wanted to go fishing and he just snapped at me and said he was far too busy.'

Nina packed up her art gear, her collection of illustrations for the story almost done, and, after a final walk with Bailey, closed up Oyster Cottage and decided to head back to Dublin. Bill, who was a part-owner of the cottage, and Charles were coming down to stay for a few days next week.

With Tom due back tomorrow night, she didn't want him coming home to an empty house and she had organized for Jack and Erin to come for dinner. The family needed to be together to discuss the situation. The company being sold or closed down would have a massive effect on everyone and Tom needed to know that he had the full support of his family.

Nina felt like everything was in slow motion as she prepared a simple meal and waited for Tom's return. He had phoned her from the airport and sounded exhausted. Studying herself in the mirror, she was determined to look well and appear collected on his arrival. Her blonde hair was washed and dried, hanging softly round her face, her skin a honey colour from long walks on the beach; and she wore a simple Betty Barclay blue-grey shift dress which brought out the colour of her eyes. Mascara, lipstick and lip gloss, a spray of her favourite summer perfume, and she was ready to greet him.

Arriving in the hall door, he clung to her and she hugged him tight. His skin was almost grey and he looked tired out, his eyes full of disappointment.

'Tom, leave your bag and come down to the kitchen,' she fussed. 'We'll have a drink and you can tell me all about it.'

'Unfortunately there's not much good to tell,' he admitted grimly.

She fixed two large gin and tonics and sat down beside him as he revealed the outcomes of the various meetings.

'The firm is going to be sold to Larry Maxwell and his group. The figure they are paying is far less than what I would have expected for the company, but that is the only offer on the table. They will take over all the assets of the business and will also assume its debts. There will be a few redundancies, as they do not want to duplicate roles within the company. On the sale, I will resign from Harris Engineering but will retain a small shareholding and for a period of four months be available to help with any transitional problems with customers and suppliers,' he explained, his voice breaking. 'And then at the end of the sixteen weeks I'm out of it.'

'Oh, Tom.' Nina didn't know what to say. 'But at least this way you will get something for the company.'

'By the time I pay off other outstanding loans for invest- ments I made in two big property ventures, there will be very little left. I'm sorry.'

'Is there any alternative to this?' she asked.

'No. There is no alternative, because the bank will just go ahead and put the company into receivership and then no one gets anything.'

Nina's pity for her husband was heartfelt. He was seeing something he had worked so hard for crumble around him.

'I feel so useless, Tom. I wish there was something I could do to help.'

'There is nothing anyone can do at this late stage,' he said bitterly. 'It's like a truck going down the mountain with no brakes – there is no way to stop it.'

'Then we have to look to the future,' she said, trying to be positive. 'If the house has to be sold, so be it – we can find a new house, a smaller house. After all, there's only the two of us really, and we don't need anywhere too big.'

'Selling now means that we'll get nothing like what we would have got a few years ago if we put it on the market,' he warned.

'I know, but we'll still get more than we originally paid for Clifton – so hopefully once you have paid off the loans we might have enough to just buy somewhere else,' she said optimistically. 'Then, fingers crossed, we can both work and between us we'll get by . . . We'll survive.'

'Nina, you're in cloud cuckoo land!' he said, exasperated. 'I'm sixty-four. Don't you realize that there is no work for someone like me except I create it myself?'

'Exactly!' she said, doing her best to be hopeful.

An hour later Erin and Jack arrived, and Erin threw herself into Tom's arms.

'Dad, I'm so sorry,' she said, flinging her arms around his neck.

Jack was stoical, saying little as Tom explained all the ins and outs of what had happened and about the expected takeover of the company.

'But Dad, why can't you stay in the company?' insisted Erin. 'It's not your fault there's been a downturn in the economy. You know the business, you love the business.'

'I know, but Larry can expand it using his existing contacts all across the UK. There is great synchronicity, as they have been one of our main suppliers. We owe them a lot of money, but in return for this deal they will get a strong foothold in the Irish market for their products.' He trailed off. 'Then they won't need me.'

'Dad, please don't do it!' begged Jack. 'The company is your life! Can't you borrow the money from the bank?'

'No, the bank is part of the problem!'

'What about Uncle Bill?'

'Bill has already helped as much as he can. I'm not asking him to put himself any further at risk financially over this!'

'Well what are you going to do then?' Erin asked.

'We are going to have to sell the house,' Tom said slowly. 'It's our only way to raise the necessary capital to pay off any outstanding loans and leave enough for your mother and me to buy a smaller place and have some money to retire on.'

'Sell Clifton?'

'Yes,' Nina said firmly. 'I know it must be a shock, and we are all upset about it, but it's the only avenue open to us.'

'I love this house,' wailed Erin. 'Jack and I don't want you to sell it.'

'It's my fault our family home has got to be sold,' Tom said, blaming himself, 'but we have to sell it. There's no choice.'

Dinner was a pretty sombre affair, but Nina could see that everyone realized how much effort was going to be needed in the months ahead.

'Dad, is there any part of the business you can salvage?' asked Jack.

'The only thing that I'll be left with are the two small agencies for Baz's solar-panel systems, which Larry's company has no interest in retaining as they manufacture similar solar-panel systems themselves. Personally I think that the Swedish ones are far superior, but they have little monetary value. I'm still friendly with Baz and Morten and they both said that they are still happy to have me continue to represent them here in Ireland.'

'Well that's something!' said Nina. She had very little under-standing of solar-heating systems, but at least it was a straw for Tom to cling on to.

By the end of the meal there was a growing sense of accepting the inevitable. Erin and Jack were both determined to support them as much as possible and not get involved in a blame game, which was what Tom had feared.

'So what happens next?' asked Erin.

'I'll talk to the auctioneers to arrange for them to come and see the house,' he said. 'The solicitors will draw up the con-tracts for the sale of the business and then . . . Well, I don't know what happens then. I wish I did, but I have no bloody idea.'

'Things will work out,' Nina jumped in, seeing the dismay in their eyes. 'They always do. Our generation is used to recessions and downturns and getting out of them. We will manage, so don't you two be worrying about us.'

'We can't help worry!' shouted Erin, bursting out crying. 'You're our mum and dad!'

They stayed talking for hours, till eventually Tom and Nina went to bed. Nina realized that Tom felt utterly defeated and was finding it extremely hard to come to terms with the sale of the company. Barring a miracle, in a few weeks Harris Engineering would be under new management.

'Tom, it's all going to be okay,' she said, leaning over and kissing him. 'We still have each other, and that's what matters most.'

Chapter Fifty-one

ERIN COULDN'T BELIEVE HOW HOT IT WAS OUTSIDE AS DUBLIN sweltered in a heatwave. Everyone was wandering around in sandals and T-shirts and sundresses, and sitting outside restaurants and cafés and bars as if they were in France, or stretched out on the grass sunbathing in the city parks, in St Stephen's Green and Merrion Square.

Trying to put her worries behind her, Erin had gone off for a week's holiday with Claire and Sinead in Marbella, to an apartment near the beach. Since then she'd been at Jenny's hen weekend in Kilkenny and gone down to the cottage in West Cork for a few day's break with Jack and her mum and dad.

She hadn't seen Luke for weeks. But at least she had made the effort and gone over to London to Luke's work barbecue thing held in one of the partners' homes. She'd flown over on the Saturday morning, as she had a work thing herself on the Friday night, and discovered that Luke was working in the office himself most of that day. In the evening they'd gone to the barbecue in Richmond. The house and garden and food had been fabulous, but Luke had been so busy schmoozing with everyone that they had barely spoken.

The partner's wife, Lauren, who was French, had come to talk to her. 'Marcus always says that all the young men and women who work for him are far too busy trying to impress each other and outdo each other!' she laughed. 'In time they will calm down and make time for their pretty girls and wives and kind boyfriends, and realize what is important – home and family. It is just a question of time!'

But then Luke hadn't bothered to come over to Dublin to visit her, even though things with her family were all up in a heap, with her dad absolutely gutted about losing his company. She and Jack were worried sick about what was going to happen and how they were going to get through it all. Neither of them had any money to help out, but the least they could do was to be there to support their parents as the house was going to have to be sold.

'Erin, will you plug in that fan, please!' begged Nikki. 'I'm sweltering here.' She was finding the last few weeks of her pregnancy really hard. She suddenly seemed to swell and puff up, and could no longer fit into anything half normal.

'Shit – I look like a blimp. What is this baby doing to me?' she wailed as Erin fastened her sandals and Claire made her another plate of sundried tomatoes and olives in oil. She hadn't put on a single pair of her expensive high-heeled shoes in weeks, as her feet wouldn't fit into any of them, and her racks of designer clothes lay forlornly in the wardrobe because her bust had got so big she couldn't attempt to put any of them on lest she burst them!

They'd made an emergency visit to Mothercare and to the expensive maternity shop Bonne Maman.

'This is outrageous,' Nikki groaned, paying a fortune for a beautiful silvery-blue dress with a scooped neckline and material that seemed to skim her bump and hips, making her so sexy-looking that Claire wanted to buy one too.

'You look like one of those Old Master paintings, all soft and sexy and curvy,' she sighed. 'But it wouldn't probably look as good on me!'

'You are welcome to borrow it any time!' laughed Nikki.

Erin knew that Nikki was trying to prepare herself for the massive change having a baby was going to bring. She was being fantastic about it, and as the weeks went by everyone was getting really excited. Now she had only four weeks to go and Snoopy B was gone head down, getting ready to be born and putting so much pressure on Nikki's nether regions that she could hardly stand and couldn't walk for too long.

'For God's sake, how long will this go on? At the rate Snoopy B is pushing down I'll be able to pull him or her out by their hair! It's so uncomfortable and I need to go to the loo every twenty minutes!'

Nikki had gone on maternity leave and was already bored, fed up with sitting around reading baby books and going on mother-and-baby social sites.

'I think I might be slowly going mad,' she said as she opened a package that she had ordered on the internet, containing breast cones and a breast pump and pads.

'Claire, maybe we should do something really special for Nikki to cheer her up,' Erin said. 'What about us having a big dinner or a baby party for her?'

'We have to do something,' agreed Claire. 'She's become a real couch momma. I found her asleep there yesterday when I came home from work and she was still in her pyjamas and hadn't even brushed her hair!'

'What about having a big baby shower for her like all the celebs do?' Erin laughed. 'You know she'd love that.'

'She'd absolutely adore a baby shower!' agreed Claire. 'We'll have lots of the girls over and make a big fuss of her and have lots of food and vino for everyone!'

'We'll make some non-alcoholic cocktails too,' added Erin.

So it was all arranged for Saturday night. Erin and Claire filled the apartment with a mixture of pink and blue balloons and lots of gorgeous baby goodies, and Claire cooked up a storm while Erin took Nikki out of the way for a few hours. She had booked a pamper treat at their favourite place in nearby Ballsbridge; afterwards they'd go for a late lunch. She had arranged a gentle massage and a special mother-to-be pamper pedicure and manicure for Nikki and one for herself.

'My feet won't know what's hit them,' Nikki said, all relaxed after her massage, as she let them soak in the soothing foot bath.

'And when we get home you are having a rest for two hours before everyone comes,' bossed Erin. 'We don't want you and Snoopy B to be too tired for the party!'

The night was so warm that they completely opened the big patio door on to their large balcony so it seemed as if their sitting room was twice the size and airy, looking out over the garden area below. They set up candles and flowers on tables out on the balcony and round the rest of the apartment, and put on music. Claire had cooked a whole load of tapas and they had made a big jug of sangria. They did a last check of the place before all Nikki's friends arrived. Her mum, Maeve, and sister Hayley were coming too.

Erin had literally just pulled on her own pretty cream-and-pink shoestring-strapped dress when the guests started to arrive. Everyone was laden with gifts for Nikki and so excited about her going to be a mum. She appeared in her silver dress to huge cheers and hugs, and was given the big chair on the balcony with lots of cushions to sit on as her friends milled around her.

'Thank you for coming, everyone,' she said, eyes shining as they all swapped baby stories and her mum told them about when Nikki was born.

'She was three weeks early. I was out shopping when I suddenly felt I'd wet my pants. I was so embarrassed, standing there with a shopping trolley with a puddle on the floor in front of me in the supermarket. There was a lady in the next line and she was so kind. She said to me, "I think that you should go to the hospital." I was mortified and told her that I was fine – I'd just had an accident and my baby wasn't due for about three weeks! Anyway, she made me leave my trolley and get into her car, and by the time we came near the hospital my contractions were so close I thought that Nikki would be born in a Ford Fiesta. They rushed me into the labour ward and about twelve minutes later Nikki was born . . . Her dad missed the whole thing, but Mary Byrne was an angel – she was with me.'

'Auntie Mary,' confirmed Nikki, 'my godmother. She's gone to Spain for two weeks with her family, that's why she's not here.'

'Nikki, don't you dare do that on us!' warned Claire nervously.

There were gambas al ajillo, chorizo and peppers, patatas bravas, calamari, stuffed tomatoes and green peppers, chicken in a salsa sauce. Everyone tucked in and Erin made a second jug of sangria and a special fizzy cocktail for Nikki before they got around to opening the gifts. It was getting darker, so they all sat down on the couches as Nikki opened present after present.

There were luxury nighties and a silk wrap for the hospital, a soothing relaxing CD, a jar of Crème de la Mer moisturizing cream, a bottle of her favourite Hermès perfume, a gorgeous Lulu Guinness toiletries bag and matching shower cap, vouchers for Day spa treatments, chocolates and a bottle of champagne for post-baby celebrations; and a divine nappy bag for Snoopy B, plus a whole load of baby gifts – baby-grows for the hospital, a changing mat, baby bath towels and a robe, a T-shirt with *Snoopy B* printed on it, a grow-bag for the baby to sleep in – 'Get Snoopy into a good routine,' advised Angie, who had been seriously sleep-deprived until she had discovered the magic of the grow-bag – and lots of other goodies. There was even a bundle of Nikki's favourite chick-flick DVDs to while away her time on the couch and a *My Baby* photo album from Lucy who worked with her.

'You've all been so good and so kind and supportive of me, especially when I am on my own,' sobbed Nikki, getting all emotional.

'You're not on your own!' the girls all promised her. 'We're all here for you and Snoopy B whenever you need us.'

Later they slipped on the DVD of *Bridget Jones* as Nikki stretched out on the couch and relaxed. Erin smiled when at almost one a.m. she realized that Nikki was asleep and snoring softly as everyone began to slip quietly away.

Chapter Fifty-two

EVER SINCE THE NIGHT SHE HAD TOLD PADDY ABOUT ERIN, things had changed. Kate realized what an absolute giant of a man she had married. He could have been nasty or mean or given out to her, but he hadn't. With Paddy Cassidy there were no recriminations, just understanding and forgiveness.

When he had gone to work the next day and she was alone, she had cried and cried; shuddering, shaking tears, crying as if a massive dam inside her had been opened, releasing all the pent-up years of loneliness and grief and loss that she had experienced, like a raging current washing and stripping it all away from her. Afterwards she had felt drained and exhausted and had slept, only waking when it was dark, and then sleeping again.

When she awoke next morning she felt tired, like she had completed some exhausting athletic feat or marathon, but as she stood naked in the shower washing herself she felt strangely energized, renewed, as if the dark hidden place within her had suddenly disappeared, gone for ever.

They went out for dinner that evening and Kate showed

Paddy her photo of Erin and told him about meeting her daughter.

'She's beautiful like you, Kate,' he said. 'And if she is anything like her mother then she must be a very special girl.'

'Thank you,' she whispered, kissing him, wondering how she had been so fortunate to have been given a second chance – not just with Erin, but with her marriage.

'Are you going to tell the kids?' Paddy asked. 'I think that they deserve to know.'

Kate was extremely nervous about her sons' and daughter's reaction to finding out that she had been an unmarried mother and that they had an older half-sister.

'I want to tell them all together,' she insisted. 'I know Aisling is around, but I want to wait until Kevin gets back from his JI in Chicago and Sean is home from holiday in Thailand with his pals. If we tell one of them, you know that they will just Facebook or email or phone each other. I want to tell them face to face. I don't want them to hear it from someone else.'

'And what about the party?' he asked. He pulled the invitation from his pocket and laid it on the table.

She looked at it and at him. This was important to him.

'I think we should go ahead and have it!' she laughed. 'We have so much to be grateful for, and I want to celebrate twenty-five years of being married to the kindest man in the world, who I love very much.'

'Then we'll get cracking on the invites!' he said, delighted.

Two weeks later, when everyone was home, Paddy told them that they wanted to talk to them about something.

'It's probably about the bloody party and us helping out,' complained Kevin, who was still jet-lagged and hungover after the best summer of his life working as waiter in a bar in Chicago for six weeks.

Kate was nervous as hell about telling them. She hadn't said a word to Erin about it. Paddy sat in the big armchair in the living room and the kids were all on the couch.

'Your mum wants to talk to you about something,' Paddy said sternly, which immediately got their attention.

Kate stood up. 'I wanted to tell you all something very important about something that happened in my life when I was much younger. I hope it won't change things in the family, but even if it does you still need to know.'

She could see that Aisling was tense, pale and hunched forward.

'When I was younger – about your age, Kevin – I was in college. I met someone and we fell in love. We hung out together all the time. Then I found out I was pregnant. I didn't know what to do. Neither of us had any money and we were both students, but I did know that I wanted to have my baby. Auntie Sally was very good to me. But the guy panicked. I was scared, but he was even more scared about us having a baby. I had a little girl that March. She was so beautiful . . . but I knew that I couldn't manage being a single mum with so little support, so I gave her up for adoption. I wanted my baby to have a proper family and parents and a nice life – things that I couldn't give her at that time.'

She could see they were stunned – trying to process this new side to her.

'Mum, you had a baby!' cried Aisling accusingly. 'Why didn't you tell us?'

'I didn't tell anyone. It was a secret,' she admitted. 'I suppose I was ashamed.'

'Why are you telling us now?' demanded Sean.

'Because my daughter, Erin, has recently come back into my life and it's only fair that you should all know about her.'

They all bombarded her with questions about having the baby and about Erin herself. She could tell they were angry with her, furious, blaming her for getting pregnant, for not having the courage to keep her baby, and for lying to them and deceiving them.

'Mum, all the times you told me that I was your only little girl you were lying to me!' Aisling screamed at her. 'I don't want a half-sister!' And she stormed off up to her bedroom, banging the door so hard that it nearly came off its hinges.

She could see that her sons regarded her differently too, both of them awkward about it. Kevin hugged her at least, but Sean made some excuse about having to meet someone and left.

'That went well!' She felt overwhelmed and near to tears as Paddy pulled her into his arms.

'Give them a chance to think about it, get used to the idea. They'll come around. Then we can organize for everyone to meet her.'

'Meet Erin?'

'Of course,' said Paddy firmly. 'She's your daughter and their half-sister – and everyone in this family will have to get used to it!'

Chapter Fifty-three

NINA CLOSED HER EYES AS DOMINICK DELAHUNT ARRIVED TO see the house. He was one of the senior partners in Delahunt's, the big auctioneering firm that was usually retained to sell larger properties in Dublin and around the countryside. With his arrival, the first steps in selling their beloved home were now being taken.

Tom was locked away upstairs in his study, while she had spent the past few days trying to get the house in order for Dominick's visit.

The auctioneer had a pad and pen and voice-recorder with him and, as she started to show him around the large living room and dining room, he kept up a running commentary of his own, which was a bit disquieting.

'What a lovely home! Warm and sunny – so many of these old houses suffer desperately from damp and are impossible to heat.' He remarked on the fireplaces, the windows, the plaster-work and woodwork, and even on the doors and door handles. He seemed to notice everything.

When Tom joined them she could see he was pleased that

Dominick had such an appreciation for their home. They walked from room to room – the five bedrooms; the bathrooms; the study; the large landing with its view of the sea; the old-fashioned walk-in airing cupboard; the downstairs that had been upgraded with a hand-painted kitchen, a large living and dining area with patio doors to the garden, and a cosy den for watching TV; and the large utility/laundry room with its old-fashioned Belfast sink and large storage area.

'A remarkable period property!' continued Dominick. 'I would think that it only needs upgrading work in terms of the bathrooms and kitchen.'

The kitchen! Nina loved their kitchen. Why would anyone want to change it?

Tom then showed Dominick all around the outside of the house and the garden, Bailey following the two of them. Tom led the way down the very back of the garden towards the old boat house. They seemed to be an age out there, and the two of them walked back up towards the house, heads bent deep in discussion. She wondered what kind of valuation the auctioneer would put on a home that was so loved!

When they came back into the kitchen where she was waiting she made a pot of coffee and produced some home-made oat cookies. She was as nervous as anything.

'Clifton is very special,' Dominick said admiringly, 'and I know how hard it must be for both of you to have to put it up for sale at this present time.'

Nina nodded, trying not to cry.

'Tom has filled me in on the reasons for the sale and I assure you that many properties on our books are being sold for broadly similar reasons, but a home is at least a form of saving which most of us have at our disposal should we need it.'

'We hate leaving it and having to sell,' Nina confessed. 'We love this old place.'

'I often feel with these big old houses that we are all only caretakers from one generation to the next,' Dominick said kindly. 'When you think of how many families must have lived here over the past hundred and forty years or so, and walked the staircase and slept in the bedrooms and sat talking around that magnificent fireplace. We might pay the mortgage, and be able to say on paper we own a house like this outright, but we never really do – we are only enjoying the privilege of minding it until another family becomes part of its fabric.'

What a lovely thing to say, thought Nina, comforted by his words and very relieved that it was Dominick who was selling Clifton.

'Well, as I was saying, a gracious property like this with its extensive gardens and location, so close to Dalkey village, the sea and the DART, is ideal, and I feel it should certainly be able to attract a lot of interested parties.'

'Has Tom explained to you that we don't want open viewings and gangs of people traipsing through the house?' Nina asked.

'Of course. I would only suggest privately booked viewings with a house like this.' He smiled. 'We would include it in the property section of the *Irish Times*, with a photograph and details, but my hope is that the paper itself might also do a piece on it for their readers. People still love reading about old houses.'

He discussed the agency's fees and then told them what he realistically felt he could achieve. Nina could see Tom was disappointed.

'I thought that we would get at least Euro 500.000 more than that!'

'We could be lucky, but I'm afraid the banks are being far more circumspect as to who they lend to and how much they will lend.'

Tom looked rather crestfallen.

'But I'll do my very best on your behalf,' promised Dominick.

'It's just that when we sell the house we hope to buy a smaller place here in the Dalkey area, if possible,' explained Tom.

'Unfortunately there are very few smaller homes for sale at present,' admitted Dominick, 'but I promise that I'll keep an eye out for a suitable property for you.'

Nina couldn't believe it when Dominick confirmed that the sale of Clifton would be advertised in a few weeks and go up on Delahunt's website then. 'We are better to wait until the first or second week in September when people return from holidays and decide to start looking at houses again and the market is refreshed with new properties. Then we will go ahead and run our sales campaign.'

Nina was relieved that at least the 'For Sale' sign wasn't going up next week.

Following Dominick's visit Tom seemed even more pre-occupied than ever and spent much of his time trying to work out the vagaries of their finances, as the sale of Harris Engineering was due to be signed. Nina couldn't bear the thought of the house being sold and almost wished that nobody would want to buy it.

'Of course someone will buy it – it's a perfect house, a good-size family home with a lovely garden and, as Dominick says, there are the coach house and outbuildings too. God knows where I'll put my boat in the winter when we've sold the place.'

'Maybe we could keep the coach house,' suggested Nina. 'It is right down the very back of the garden with hardly any connection to the house, and then you could still store your boat there. We could section off that part of the garden and courtyard area and just not include them in the sale.'

'Dominick would probably go mad!'

'It's our house, not Dominick's!' she reminded him.

They walked down the garden to see whether they could do it and, as they wandered around the old coach house with its courtyard and overgrown wasteground, they looked at each other.

'Let's look inside, Tom,' Nina said, opening the door.

Despite being neglected, the old building was warm, its stone walls dry and sealed; and it was actually much bigger than it seemed from the outside. There were the trailer for the boat and Tom's tools and his big workbench and pots of old paint, bicycles and the ride-on garden mower. There was a small bathroom and what must have served as a rough kitchen with a few presses and a sink; then stairs led up to the loft area. Nina climbed up carefully. She hadn't been up here in years. More old rubbish stored. But, again, it was dry and warm, and from the small windows you could see across the back laneway and up towards the curving slope of the coast road and Killiney.

'The chauffeur used to sleep up here, and before him the stable lads who looked after the horses,' said Tom. 'There are two good rooms with a lot more space than you would think.'

They went and sat outside on the wooden bench near the door. It was very sheltered and secluded.

'I'm going to really miss the house,' he admitted, 'but I'll miss this old place too. It's a bit of a refuge.'

Nina closed her eyes. With moving they were giving up so much.

'Tom, we are not giving this up! If we cannot afford to hold on to Clifton, at least we can keep this. Maybe we should get someone to look at it?'

'But I don't need a fancy boat house.'

'I'm not talking about a boat house,' she laughed. 'I think we should ask Mike Flynn to come over and look at it to see if there would be any potential to convert it for us. He's driving poor Carol mad, hanging around the place since his operation.'

'I'll phone him,' Tom offered, 'and I can go and collect him, because I know he's not let drive still after his knee replacement.'

The next day Mike came over to the house and disappeared off down the garden with Tom. There wasn't sight of them again until lunchtime, when Nina made soup and toasted sandwiches for them all. Tom and Mike were both excited as they explained the potential for a conversion of the coach house that would give them two bedrooms upstairs and a small bathroom, and a good-sized kitchen-cum-living space with a smaller room and bathroom downstairs. Mike was sketching furiously, trying to show her.

'Let me draw up something to give you an idea of the layout and a very rough costing. I'll work on them tonight and, if you are free, I'll get Carol to drop me over tomorrow.'

Tom drove him back home and, when they had gone, Nina tried to imagine herself living down the bottom of the garden!

Chapter Fifty-four

ERIN STOOD LOOKING TOWARDS THE AISLE AS THE MUSIC BEGAN to play and Ciara and Annie, her friend Jenny's two sisters, in their pale-pink fitted bridesmaids' dresses began to walk slowly up the aisle, followed by Jenny, eyes shining as she held her dad Frank's arm.

Jenny looked amazing in her off-white lace dress with its narrow, fitted bodice and soft flowing skirt, which showed off her fabulous petite figure; she wore a simple veil over her dark hair and carried a bunch of summer roses. She was such a beautiful bride and everyone almost cheered when her dad handed her over to Shay, who was standing in front of the altar waiting for her. They had been going out since they were sixteen, all through school and college, and everyone had always known that someday they would get married. And now today was the day. Jenny's Uncle Peter, a priest, was marrying them, so that made it even more special.

As they lit the candles and the ceremony began, Erin knew that she was witnessing two people who really loved each other make that proper commitment. Luke was in the bench beside her, looking very handsome in a tux. They had been invited to Jenny's wedding months ago and Erin had been really annoyed when Luke had begun to suggest he mightn't be able to make it over from London.

'Shay and Jenny have been saving for this wedding for years and, Luke, you are not pulling out of it with only two weeks to go.'

'Okay, okay.' He had given in, but was still complaining about the cost of the hotel they were staying in in Cork and the fact that it was such a long drive from Dublin.

Nikki had come down in the car with Claire and Donal and was absolutely glowing. She looked as if she was about to pop in her turquoise dress and open-toed shoes. Jenny's sister Annie was a nurse and she'd promised that she'd keep an eye on Nikki for them.

'We don't want Snoopy B being born down in Cork!' Claire joked.

As Jenny and Shay exchanged their vows and the rings, Erin was touched by the emotion of it all and tears slid down her cheeks. This was what marriage to the one you love meant – these promises, these vows.

When the ceremony was over they all stood to watch Jenny and Shay walk arm in arm down the church together, happiness radiating from them both as they stood at the church porch in the sunshine to meet all their guests.

'What a wedding!' Nikki said, wistfully. 'Jenny is so lucky to have found such a nice guy and married him!'

'They are both lucky,' agreed Claire, 'to have found each other.'

Erin joined the queue that was pushing towards the bride and groom, Luke standing beside her, until eventually it was her turn.

'I'm so happy for you both,' she said, giving Shay a massive hug. Then she kissed Jenny. 'Jenny, you are the most beautiful bride ever – you look so lovely today. You and Shay are just so much in love and perfect for each other. I know you two are going to be very happy.'

'Thanks, Erin,' smiled Jenny. 'It's the way it will be for you too, just you wait!'

Erin knew that when she got married she wanted her husband to look at her the way Shay constantly looked at Jenny, as if she was the most important person in the world, and to feel the way Jenny felt about Shay, that she couldn't live without him.

Everyone stood outside chatting in the sunshine and taking photos. Erin quelled her annoyance at seeing Luke off texting on his iPhone and checking his emails.

After the church they made their way to Ballyrinn Castle, near Kinsale. It was a fabulous old eighteenth-century castle that had been restored and modernized. They all enjoyed drinks in the sunshine on the lawn before moving into the huge dining hall for the meal, where Erin and Luke sat at a great table made up of all Jenny's schoolfriends. The wine flowed, the food was delicious and Jenny's dad gave a great speech about welcoming Shay into the Sullivan family and saying what a wonderful daughter Jenny was. Shay had them all nearly in tears when he talked about falling in love with sixteen-year-old Jenny and secretly deciding there and then that some day she would be his bride. The best man nearly brought the house down with his stories of his best friend's attempts over a long number of years to win Jenny's hand.

'What a lovely wedding!' smiled Erin as the band started and she and Luke got up to dance. As he held her in his arms she wondered if some day it would be them having the first dance at their own wedding, with all their friends and family along to celebrate how much they loved each other. It was strange, but somehow, even though she was in his arms, she just couldn't picture it.

They had a wonderful night, dancing and chatting to friends and keeping a very sharp eye on a cousin of Shay's who professed to adore pregnant women and was literally dancing attendance on a delighted Nikki. It was all hours before they got to bed. Luke was up at the bar talking to a group of the lads while Erin, a little tipsy, nearly fell fast asleep on a sofa.

'You two to bed!' bossed Claire, kissing her good night – or was it good morning?

They slept in and had a very late breakfast with everyone in the hotel, then set off back for Dublin. Luke's flight was at eight p.m. He was quiet on the drive home from Cork as Erin rabbited on, telling him about the upcoming sale of her parents' home and a potential new client that she might be doing some work for.

Too early to go to the airport, they went back to her apartment and, dumping their bags, she made them coffee and a toasted sandwich.

'Are you coming home next weekend?' she asked him.

'No. I've no reason to come over,' he said flatly.

'I don't know what you mean.' Erin had no idea what he was getting at. 'We can go out – go somewhere . . .'

'Erin, you've done nothing about coming to London, have you?'

281

She shook her head.

'You've no intention of it, have you?'

'I was going to . . .' She tried a feeble protest, but realized that Luke was right. He was only stating the obvious.

'No,' she admitted. 'I've no plans to move for the moment.'

'I don't like this commuting thing. It never works.'

'For some people it does—'

'Well it's not working for us!'

Erin knew what he said was true. It wasn't working. Maybe they just didn't care enough about each other to make the effort. But going back and forwards between London and Dublin sporadically every few weeks and communicating by texts and emails and phone calls wasn't enough for either of them.

'What will we do?' she said, already suspecting the answer.

'I think we should finish it,' he replied, leaning forward on the couch, his face serious. 'We both know it's not working any more. So what's the point?'

Erin tried not to cry. She did really like him – love him, in a way. But she didn't love him enough to change her life for him, even to make the commitment of going to London. And Luke – she knew that, deep down, he didn't care enough about her to make her central to his life. They both deserved better.

'I'm sorry, Luke,' she said, crying even though she tried not to. 'I know it's the right thing, but I just feel sad about it.'

They were both upset, but they promised to try to stay friends.

Erin offered to drive him to the airport, but, much to her relief, he insisted on taking the Air Coach.

'You can bring me out for an expensive dinner if I'm ever in London!' she said.

'Sure thing, and we'll try to stay in touch if I'm home,' he said, pulling her into his arms as they said goodbye.

Erin was sitting feeling numb and rather forlorn when Nikki and Claire finally arrived back.

'Luke and I just broke up,' she told them. 'I'm back to being single again.'

'*What?*'

She told them everything and they both admitted that they weren't surprised.

'I couldn't imagine you married to Luke,' said Nikki firmly. 'I couldn't see the two of you babysitting Snoopy B and bringing Snoopy out cool places.'

'Weddings are notorious for breaking couples up,' said Claire, sagely. 'They make people take a hard look at their relationship.'

'I thought weddings were meant to be great for meeting people,' laughed Nikki. 'Because I've got a hot date with Shay's cousin Paul next week. We're going to the cinema.'

'Nikki!' they both screamed.

'Shut up!' she warned, plomping herself heavily on the couch and putting her feet on the footstool. 'Nice guys are hard to meet and he is a seriously nice guy.'

Erin found herself laughing as Nikki told them all about Paul.

Chapter Fifty-five

ERIN STARED AT THE SCREEN OF HER APPLE MAC, TRYING TO turn the image around. It looked pretty good, but was still not a hundred per cent what she wanted. She wanted perfection, and for the product name and the image to jump out at you simultaneously. She was on a deadline with this; she had to have it with the client by six this evening, as their marketing people were presenting it to the directors and the board first thing in the morning. She gave it another whirl and made the image even sharper. Perfect!

'Time for coffee,' she said, rewarding herself and heading for the office coffee-maker where Monika and Lilly were already brewing up a pot. It was lashing rain outside and the water pelted against the window panes. She could see people running helter-skelter with umbrellas, trying to avoid the downpour. She chatted for a few minutes with the others and, returning to her desk, got a call from Declan to come to his office to meet a potential new client. She needed this like a hole in the head today, but Declan was the boss. Grabbing her notebook and pen, she went to join him.

'Hey, Erin, I'd like to introduce you to Brian Quinn and Matt Ryan,' said Declan from behind his massive red desk.

Erin smiled as she greeted Matt, wondering what the hell he was doing in the office.

'So you two know each other?'

'Yes, we're friends,' she said quickly, embarrassed by the way Matt said nothing about their connections.

'Brian and Matt love the work you did on Lia's album. They shot the video for two of her songs. Anyhow, they have just finished filming a new feature film and are here to talk about the possibility of us doing all the design work for the film's marketing campaign. I worked with them a few years ago on *Cromwell*, but I've told them that this time you will be the lead designer on this project. So maybe we can all sit down and talk about it?'

Shit – Erin was conscious of the time!

'I'm sorry, Declan, but I have to have something to Georgina Hill and her team very soon,' she reminded him.

'Okay then, we can just have a very brief run-through today and you can set up a meeting with the guys tomorrow or the next day,' he suggested.

Erin sat and listened as Brian, the producer, gave a very brief outline of the film, which had received some funding from the Film Board. It was yet another coming-of-age Irish film and unfortunately nothing jumped out at her in terms of market-ability.

'I'd like to see the film,' she suggested.

'I'm still editing it,' confessed Matt, 'so it's not all picture-locked yet and—'

'The guys are on a bit of a deadline,' explained Declan. 'They want to submit it to the Sundance Festival and the Cannes Film

Festival and they both require some marketing back-up. Also another thing, Erin – there is a very limited budget on this.'

Matt at least had the good grace to look shamefaced. No wonder Declan was handing the job to her . . .

'I'll do my best,' she said, 'but I really have to go. Can you send me a DVD of it the minute it's ready?'

'I'll be working on it all night,' Matt said. She could see he was already exhausted. 'I could try to have it done for tomorrow, but even if you saw a bit of it would that help?'

'Listen, Matt, let me finish what I'm doing,' she offered, 'then I'll phone you later and come over to the studio in Temple Bar and you can show me what you have got. At least I can make a start while you are working on the rest.'

'Sounds good!' said Brian.

With no time for pleasantries, Erin practically ran back to her desk. She had been talking to the girls about going to the cinema tonight but she'd text them and tell them to go without her. She would definitely be working late!

Chapter Fifty-six

ERIN HAD GOT EVERYTHING TO GEORGINA JUST IN TIME.

'I could hug you, Erin,' Georgina said when she called to say thank you. Erin hoped that the presentation would go well tomorrow and that everyone would be happy with her work on the new logos and images for O'Hara's Country Foods, suppliers of organic ham, sausages, rashers and the black and white puddings that Nikki had developed a passion for. They were a very old, respected Irish company and just needed a bit of a design upgrade to suit today's market.

She debated going home to change and get something to eat, but knew well that Matt probably hadn't eaten either. She phoned him and told him she would be there as soon as possible. En route, she grabbed them a burger each, some fries and two chocolate milkshakes from Eddie Rockets. If it was going to be a long night they needed to keep their strength up!

Matt fell on the food like a starving wolf and she watched him gulp it down. Judging by the paper cups and pizza boxes strewn about, that was all he'd eaten in days.

'Thanks!' he said, polishing off the rest of her milkshake.

'Okay, let's see this film of yours,' she suggested, knowing how hard it was to show something so rough and unready ahead of time when often your vision of what you are creating isn't fully realized on the screen the way it is in your head.

She pulled a chair over beside his screen, watching as Matt began to work and run the film. Even at a glance she could see that it was beautifully shot and lit. The story was about a boy and a girl who met when they were ten and somehow stayed in love with each other all the rest of their lives. Never being together, but never being apart. It was called *Border* and was set in a small town in Northern Ireland that literally had the border between the south of Ireland and the north running through it. The children had first met swimming in a forbidden stream and the film followed their lives over the next twenty years. It was stunning, and the music and atmosphere were almost magical, though it was set against the bigotry of the Troubles.

'Matt, it's absolutely amazing!'

'You sound shocked!' he teased.

'Okay, I am shocked that it's *so* good!' she admitted, excited to be in any way involved in such a project.

She got him to copy stuff to her laptop and the two of them worked on. Erin was searching for that one image that would encapsulate the film for viewers around the world and capture their attention. She was also playing around with ideas for the film's title sequence, which hadn't yet been done or even considered.

She went out for ten minutes and got them coffee and chocolate. Matt was bleary-eyed, and she wasn't much better. Suddenly, running back through the film again, the image of young Sarah and Sean splashing together in the water in the sunlight came to her, and she replayed it over and over again. It was much more profound than the one of the tanks and soldiers that Brian had suggested, as you could see where the stream bisected the two pieces of farmland.

Excited, she showed it to Matt to see what he thought. He sat hunched over the table, glued to the screen, his long hair all over the place, his glasses dirty. She didn't know why, but she caught his hair and pulled it back from his face, like he was a kid, and touched his hand. It was as though she had wanted to touch his skin all night.

Suddenly Matt turned and pulled her on to his lap and kissed her. His mouth was warm and he tasted of coffee, and she found she wanted to kiss him back. It was lovely. Exhausted or not, they both wanted to kiss some more.

'Wow, this is some night!' said Matt, totally deadpan, and Erin found herself bursting out laughing as they clung together in fits.

'We have to work,' he reminded her, turning his full attention back to the screen. 'But when this gets finished and edited, will you come out with me, Erin?'

'Like on a date?'

'Yes,' he said, catching her hand in his. 'Or something like that.'

Erin was knackered, but she couldn't believe it. Matt liked her – really liked her!

Chapter Fifty-seven

NINA WATCHED AS THE MEN PUT UP THE LARGE 'FOR SALE' SIGN outside the house. It was heartbreaking. It was as if the final nail had been hammered into months of horrendous change: from Tom's financial troubles to his going on to lose the entire business; Erin deciding to find her birth mother; even Jack announcing he was going off to Australia for a year with a girl they barely knew. Nina had felt that her life was tumbling down around her and that, despite her best efforts, she couldn't manage to hold on to anything. But somehow she had been able to gradually accept the change – the house being sold, Tom having at his age to start over again, Erin meeting her mother and now thinking of getting to know her half-brothers and sister, and even accepting that Jack was growing up and would take off to the other side of the world with a girl he was pretty crazy about.

A photographer had come and taken the photos of the house and garden for the sales brochure and Dominick had told her that Clifton would appear on Delahunt's page in Thursday's property section of the *Irish Times*. The house would also feature on their website.

'Then we just wait and see,' he said, sounding very positive.

Nina had spent weeks trying to strip clutter and unnecessary items from the house. How they had ever managed to accumulate so many things was beyond her. She seemed to spend all her time loading her car with items for the local charity shop or bringing things to the dump. Erin and Jack had been roped in to help and hours were spent going through boxes of old toys and books and family mementos.

'We have to get rid of stuff,' she warned. 'The new house will only be about quarter the size of Clifton, so we have no space for things we no longer need. We have to be ruthless,' she went on, hiding away a *papier-mâché* plate that Erin had made when she was about six and Jack's collection of old football cards.

The sale of Harris Engineering to Larry Maxwell and partners had finally gone through. Nina had worried how Tom would take it, but somehow, once the agreements had all been signed and the monies paid over and the debts assigned to the new owners, he had relaxed. There was nothing more that he could do for the company and the relief of it was like a huge weight being lifted off his shoulders. If they managed to sell the house for the figure Dominick felt it could achieve, then there was every chance that Tom could clear all the personal loans he had with the bank and there would be enough left to help keep them going for the coming years. They had looked at a few of the cottages and bungalows and smaller houses for sale in their area and soon realized what Dominick had meant about them having a cachet, as they were totally out of their reach and most of them needed substantial upgrading. They both recognized how lucky they were to have the coach house and that, although they would have the cost of renovating it and extending it, that was only a fraction of what buying a smaller home would cost with fees and stamp duty.

Mike had put in their plans for The Boat House to the local council and, all going well, they should have planning permission in another few weeks and then the work would begin. Tom and Mike worked well together and seemed to be forever drawing up new designs for the interior. Tom was determined to install the latest in the range of Swedish solar panels so that they would enjoy a wonderful heating system and be fully energy-efficient.

Tom and Mike also organized a local stonemason to come and build a wall at the bottom of the garden of the big house, creating a totally separate space for their mews and courtyard and garden.

'It's better that whoever comes to see Clifton realizes that The Boat House and the gardens around it are not in any way part of the sale,' he said firmly.

Nina could see he was totally immersed in restoring the old coach house and thanked heaven he had a project to occupy him. Costs were being kept to a minimum and Stephen Kelly, their local bank manager, had been more than understanding about the situation they now found themselves in.

'Downsizing is the right thing to do,' he said approvingly. 'The fact that you are downsizing to a property that you already own makes it even better. You have been very good customers here for many years, and hopefully will still remain customers of ours.' Nina could have hugged him.

Jack had been wonderful. He and Pixie had delayed their

trip to Australia for another few weeks until after the house was sold.

'I can't believe that when I come back we won't be living here any more,' he said, getting all choked up as he packed up his old Star Wars toys.

'Jack, you will always have a room in The Boat House,' Nina said, trying to control herself. 'And all your stuff will be stored with us. I promise you'll have a lovely new home to come back to, judging by the plans your dad and Mike have for the place.'

'Are you sure, Mum?'

'I'm sure,' she promised. 'Home is wherever we all are together – remember that.'

Chapter Fifty-eight

ERIN WAS DISAPPOINTED; SHE HADN'T HEARD FROM MATT IN two weeks. He obviously hadn't really meant what he said about asking her out. She was kind of gutted about it as she hadn't thought he was that sort of guy.

'Listen, it's far better he didn't phone,' consoled Claire. 'You two are friends and you'd only destroy that.'

'You might end up not liking him and thinking he's a creep if you went out on a proper date with him,' offered Nikki wisely.

Erin had tried to convince herself that they were right.

Then Matt had phoned and asked her to come to dinner – and she had said yes . . . yes . . . yes!

They arranged to meet on Friday evening in Delaney's in Temple Bar. Erin smiled when she saw him. Matt had not only washed and brushed his hair, but it looked like it had been cut a bit. And he had shaved! He was wearing black trousers, a freshly washed and ironed pale-blue denim shirt and a jacket. He looked great and the minute he met her he kissed her. Whammy!

'You've dressed up!' she smiled.

'And you've dressed down, but you look gorgeous,' he smiled, catching her by the waist.

Erin was wearing skinny jeans and a string top under a loose second-hand Miu Miu silk top. She had left her hair straight down and worn less make-up than she would normally use on a first date.

They had one drink in the bar and then he brought her down along the quays. He refused to be drawn on which restaurant they were going to for dinner. Eventually he stopped outside a beautiful, tall Georgian house overlooking the River Liffey and, going up the steps, he rang the bell. She could see candles flickering inside the tall windows.

A waiter appeared and opened the door, then led them up the stairs to the first-floor dining room. It was magnificent, with candelabras lit over the fireplace and antique sideboards. He showed them to a table for two in front of the tall window and Erin gasped to see the quays and river stretched out below them.

'Oh Matt, this place is fabulous! How did you ever find out about it?'

'One of my friends knows the chef,' he explained. 'The River House only opened a few months ago and everyone is raving about the food, and I wanted us to always remember our very first date . . . so I thought we should come here.'

Erin looked at him. He was serious. Matt was talking already as if they were a proper couple. It was strange, but she felt it too.

The menu was amazing and everything they ordered was perfect. Each of them tasted the other's food. For someone who normally lived on pizza, Matt was actually a real foodie. The head waiter had recommended a really good wine and they finished off their meal with a glass of mellow port, watching the shimmering city lights reflected in the darkness on the water below.

Afterwards they held hands and walked back up along the river together, kissing every now and then.

'I want to see you tomorrow, Erin,' Matt said, staring into her eyes. 'And the day after that and the tomorrow after that and all the tomorrows you want . . .'

Erin looked into his face, knowing how much he meant it.

'I want that too,' she said as he slipped his arms around her and held her close.

Chapter Fifty-nine

'I'M SO SCARED AND NERVOUS — MAYBE I SHOULDN'T GO . . .'
Erin worried.

'Of course you are going,' insisted Matt firmly. 'They are your half-brothers and sister. You have to meet them.'

'I'm not sure about this,' she admitted, panicking. 'Meeting Kate is one thing, but to go and meet her family! They will all probably hate me. Resent me . . . I would have hated some strange girl coming along into my life claiming to be my sister!'

'Give them a chance,' advised Matt. 'I'm sure that it's a really big thing for Kate, inviting you to their house to have tea with them and meet everyone.'

'But maybe it's too soon?' she worried.

'Didn't she say that Paddy is okay about it?'

'Yes, but the kids might be different. They might think I'm trying to gate-crash their family . . .'

'Then you make it very clear to them that you're not, and that it is not on your agenda,' said Matt, serious. 'You don't want to upset them or make them feel you are usurping their positions.'

'I would never do that.'

'*I* know you wouldn't,' he said, kissing her, 'but *they* don't.'

On Friday evening Erin came to Kate's house. Matt insisted on dropping her off as she was too nervous to drive herself. She tried to relax as Kate introduced her to Paddy and Sean and Kevin and Aisling. It was weird, but she could see the resemblance between them all straight away.

At first everyone was awkward, as if treading on egg shells, but Erin remembered what Matt had said and, once they realized that she had absolutely no intention of intruding in their lives, they began to relax a bit. Paddy was so lovely – the complete opposite to Johnny; no wonder Kate had married him. He was so nice to her despite everything . . .

'Erin, I can't believe you and Aisling have the same eyes!' he marvelled.

'My mum calls them "witchy eyes",' laughed Erin.

Sean and Kevin were a bit shell-shocked and tongue-tied at first, but gradually they began to give her a bit of a chance and actually talked and listened to her. They were nice guys and were dead impressed to hear that she had designed the cover for the new singer Lia's album.

Only Aisling wouldn't come near her or speak to her, making it very clear that she certainly didn't want her there, but Erin supposed that was to be expected. It was only when Erin started talking about her own mum and dad and family, and how much they meant to her, that Aisling let her guard down a bit.

As they sat round the table eating and talking, and little by little getting to know each other, Erin could see Kate's eyes shining, happy that they had all finally met.

Paddy opened a special bottle of sparkling wine and poured a glass for everyone.

'We all want to welcome Erin tonight, and I hope that this will be the first of many occasions that she visits this house and we all get together.'

'Thanks,' replied Erin, recognizing that, for Kate's sake, they did genuinely welcome her. 'I was very nervous about coming to meet you all, but I'm so glad I did and that we've met. Kate told me a lot about you, how she had a lovely family, and now I've met you all – you are great, just like she said.'

'Well, Erin, you'll come to visit again?' said Kate, a little nervous.

'Yes,' smiled Erin as Paddy poured her some more wine. 'I'd like us all to get to know each other, if that's okay.'

'Okay!' came the voices, even Aisling's.

'That was a very definite okay,' thought Erin, relieved, as she texted Matt from the taxi on her way home. Despite their initial reluctance, Kate's family actually wanted to try to get to know her and have some kind of relationship with her. It was far more than she had ever dared to hope for.

Chapter Sixty

KATE LOOKED ALL AROUND THE HOUSE AND GARDEN. EVERY-thing was perfect. She couldn't believe it! Even the weather had stayed dry and warm for their Silver Anniversary party, which was a real bonus. A large gazebo with fairy lights had been erected in the garden and there were cloth-covered tables and chairs and parasols set up all over the lawn, with paper lanterns hanging from all the trees and branches. Paddy and the boys had really gone to town, and their suburban home had been transformed into something magical and pretty like you'd see in a film. There was a bar area and a food-serving area, and Kevin had spent days loading up music for the party on his iPod and setting up speakers.

Cassidy's Off-Licence were, of course, supplying all the wines and beers and champagne for the night, but for once Paddy had put his foot down and organized a caterer that he worked with to do the food. Their staff, in their crisp white uniforms, moved silently around the house checking that everything was under control.

Kate couldn't believe it as she ran upstairs to get ready.

Paddy had surprised her with breakfast in bed and a beautiful diamond eternity ring, while she had given him a vintage bottle of Bordeaux and the holiday pack for their upcoming wine holiday, which he spent an hour perusing. The kids had all clubbed together and bought an expensive professional family photograph session. They had never been able to afford to get one done and it was the perfect present.

Kate had had her hair and nails done earlier and now she slipped into the expensive cream dress she had found in the designer boutique out in Malahide and which Trish had insisted she buy. Paddy was wearing a linen jacket and the new chinos he had treated himself to.

'Looking good, Mrs C,' he said, pulling her into his arms.

'And you are looking very handsome too, Paddy,' she replied, kissing him.

Downstairs she could hear some of the guests beginning to arrive, so, spraying some of the lovely new perfume Trish had given her, she went down to greet them.

All her family were coming tonight, even her elderly dad, who was driving up from Galway with her brother Eoin and his wife. Dermot Flanagan was gone very deaf, but Eoin had got him a good seat where he could see all that was going on.

Aisling looked amazing in the black-and-silver handkerchief dress she'd found in some vintage shop in Camden Street. Sean had surprised them by coming along with a girl called Tina, who he informed them was his girlfriend!

'He kept that one well hidden,' murmured Paddy, then chatted away to her.

So many of their neighbours and old friends were there and Kate was delighted that they had left no one out. Everyone was mingling and having fun and enjoying the warm evening as the waiters topped up their glasses.

Kate had invited Erin, but she wasn't sure if she would come. It was hard for her to be confronted with a big family group when she didn't know most of them and her relations had no idea about her.

Kate floated around saying hello to everyone. She couldn't believe it that one of her oldest friends had come from Canada, and that Paddy's sister Grainne and her husband Peter had come all the way from Hong Kong.

'We don't have a lot of family get-togethers,' laughed Grainne, 'so of course I'm going to make the effort!'

The caterers were just about to start serving the food when Kate noticed that Erin had arrived. She looked amazing in a fitted emerald-green dress, her hair down straight, and she had brought along Matt, the guy she had told her about. He sure looked one of those arty types with his scruffy hair and black jeans, but she could see he had Erin's fingers laced through his as they stepped out into the garden.

Sally burst into tears when she met Erin and insisted on a massive hug to make up for all the lost years! Poor Erin didn't know what to do.

Then Kate led Erin down to her dad and, sitting beside him, introduced him to his granddaughter. She had tried to explain about having Erin to him a few weeks ago when she had gone to stay in Glenalley, though she wasn't exactly sure how much he had taken in. But seeing the two of them talking together tonight was more than enough for her.

The food was delicious and everyone was having a great time. Paddy was ensuring everything ran smoothly and, once the desserts had been served, he had stood up at the top of the patio steps and called Kate over.

'On behalf of Kate and myself I would like to warmly welcome you all here tonight and thank you for being part of this very special occasion as we celebrate our Silver Wedding Anniversary and twenty-five years of being very happily married! Many of you were at our original wedding. Our marriage has brought us many things – our two wonderful sons, Sean and Kevin, and our beautiful daughter Aisling. It has brought us friendship and love and a home, lots of good friends and neighbours, and a business that we have both worked at building together. So tonight I would like to thank my wonderful wife Kate for saying "I do" twenty-five years ago and making me the happiest man on this earth. If it is possible, I love Kate even more than I did back then twenty-five years ago!'

Everyone cheered and clapped and Kate's eyes welled with tears. She hated public speaking, but tonight she had to say something. She stepped forward.

'I would like to say to Paddy that, walking up the aisle twenty-five years ago, I married the man I love. I love him even more now. Paddy, you are a man in a million. Thank you for the wonderful life we have made together. I'm so glad that we are married. I love you and always will!' Overcome, Kate threw herself into his arms. Paddy laughed as he wiped away her tears.

'Why are you crying?' he teased.

'I'm so happy!' she said as he kissed her to loud cheers.

The party went on for hours. Kate had never enjoyed anything like it. She kicked off her new high heels, as they were cutting her feet, and sent Aisling to retrieve her old reliable ones. She introduced Erin to most of the family and to some of her friends. Erin was a bit shell-shocked with all the attention.

Then, as people began to drift away, Paddy and Kate danced together, with eyes only for each other as they stayed in each other's arms, swaying to the music, and the years drifted away from them under the moonlight.

Chapter Sixty-one

'ARE YOU SURE YOU'RE OKAY?' ERIN AND CLAIRE BOTH ASKED Nikki as they got ready to go out for the night.

'I'm fine,' she said, looking enormous as she sat with her feet up watching Saturday night's *X Factor* on the TV.

'We've both got our mobiles on if you need us,' Claire reminded her.

'Stop fussing, the two of you!' laughed Nikki. 'Dr Murphy told me that most first-time mothers go overdue, so nothing is going to happen tonight, I promise you!'

Erin felt reassured. She and Matt were going to the Film Centre to the screening of a documentary that one of his friends had made, and Claire and Donal were going to Milano's for dinner.

'Be good,' laughed Erin, kissing Nikki.

Erin and Matt had just come out of the film and she had switched her phone back on when she saw the message.

'Musketeers to the hospital. Meet you there. Snoopy is about to be born. Hurry! Claire'

'Shit!' she yelled at Matt. 'Nikki's having the baby! We'd better get a taxi.'

Matt remained his usual calm and collected self as Erin got the jitters. Having a baby was something she knew absolutely nothing about. She'd avoided looking at all the films, diagrams and books that her biology teacher had shown them in school about an actual birth as they had made her feel queasy, and now Nikki was expecting her to be there!

Matt paid the taxi man as she ran upstairs towards the labour ward. Thank heaven Claire was here already. Everything was controlled and calm and peaceful there; the only person out of breath and panicking and alarmed was Erin!

'Your friend Nicola Byrne has been moved into the delivery room as she is about to have her baby,' a midwife explained, making her sit down. 'Claire is with her and she is doing really well.'

'Can I go in and see her please?'

'I'm afraid we can only let one person in the delivery room – that is hospital policy.'

Relief washed over Erin that it was Claire, medically trained and the rock of good sense, who was with Nikki, not someone useless like her.

'Please can you tell her that I'm just outside?' she asked as the midwife disappeared back inside with a doctor in tow.

Erin paced up and down, praying that everything was going well for Nikki and little Snoopy B.

Suddenly a nurse came back out. 'Erin, is it? You can come inside for a minute to see Nicola and her baby.'

Erin couldn't believe it and practically stumbled through the door. There was Nikki sitting up in the bed, holding her baby in her arms. Erin began to cry. It was wonderful – beautiful. Nikki's baby was fine and Nikki was fine.

'Come and look at her, Erin!' called Nikki proudly. 'Take a look at Milly B, my little girl.'

Erin studied the baby's perfect face and head and mop of dark hair, just like her mum's, and her tiny button nose. She touched her with her finger and the baby grabbed on to it.

'Oh, Nikki – she's so pretty and cute!'

Claire was drooling over her too, and Erin took the opportunity to give Nikki the biggest hug ever.

'I'm so proud of you, Nikki, and you are going to be the best mum in the world ever!'

Erin could have stayed all night looking at baby Milly and talking to Nikki, but the nurses sent her and Claire outside as they would be transferring Nicola and her baby downstairs to a ward. Matt, delighted with the good news, gave Erin a kiss and said he'd talk to her later. The girls were both stunned by the arrival of little Milly into their lives. She was having two godmothers, Nikki insisted.

Nikki was moved into a six-bedded room and, even though she was tired and pretty exhausted, Erin had never seen her so happy and elated in all her life.

Down in the hallway, as they prepared to leave the hospital, they met Nikki's mum and dad, all emotional as they arrived to meet their first grandchild. Conor Lynch had also arrived in a panic. Claire told him the good news about his baby daughter as she introduced him to Nikki's parents. Watching them, Erin was glad that, hopefully, little Milly's dad would play a part in his daughter's life.

Chapter Sixty-two

NINA STOOD IN THE DRIVEWAY OF CLIFTON AS THE REMOVAL men loaded their furniture and possessions into the enormous van. She still couldn't believe that Dominick Delahunt had somehow managed to find a buyer and that their beautiful house had been sold. Despite the awful market, they had got a very fair price and Dominick assured them that the people who were buying their house were a lovely family. So much for hoping the sale of Clifton would take months and months!

It was all so final, stripping the house out room by room and saying goodbye to a home they had dearly loved and filled with so many memories. She was feeling so raw and emotional about it that she was a mess, and had to keep hiding her tears from the poor removal men.

They had spent days packing boxes and crates and labelling everything. Tom had some sort of system going with stuff that was being put into storage, stuff that was being kept in her mother's house or Lizzie's or Bill's, and stuff that was going to a charity shop or to the St Vincent de Paul, and woe betide anyone who got things mixed up!

Some of their bigger antique pieces of furniture had been sold at an auction in Sandycove, but the people who were buying the house had asked if they could buy their dining table and chairs and the massive sideboard, so it was a relief to think of the original dining set remaining here in the old dining room for another generation to enjoy.

One of the removal men asked her where her arts materials were going and she took them from his hands and put them in the boot of her car. She wasn't risking them getting lost.

Erin was doing a sweep of upstairs, Lizzie was in the kitchen making tea for everyone and even Vonnie had insisted on pitching in with the packing and moving. Dominick Delahunt had called in briefly and assured them that if they found anything of theirs left behind, he would ensure it got to them.

'You will only be living the other side of the garden wall,' he laughed as he wished them well with their move.

Nina had had a long, boozy, tearful girls' lunch last week for her friends, her last in the kitchen, and they had had a family farewell dinner a few days before Jack went to Australia. She had been too upset to go to the airport, so Tom had brought him. He'd met Pixie's mum and dad there, surprised to discover that they were farmers from Roscommon, upset too that their little Philomena was heading off to Sydney with Tom's son.

'They're lovely people,' Tom declared, 'and it's good to know that she's a farmer's daughter! I'm not half as worried as I was, because her dad told me that they'll definitely be home next year.'

Nina couldn't believe how much stuff there was in the van. Tom was checking everything and talking to the foreman. It looked like that was everything in their consignment almost; just Tom's desk and lamp and filing cabinet to come. The two of them watched as two of the men lifted the heavy desk into the van and then pulled up the door.

'That's it,' said the removal man, coming over to ask Tom to sign the form.

They both stood watching, overcome, as the van with all their possessions drove out of the driveway of Clifton and down the road. A part of their life here in this lovely old house was over. Nina was glad of Tom's arm around her as she was overwhelmed with sadness.

Lizzie shoved a last box in her car, which was packed to the roof, and she took off for their mother's place.

Vonnie had her little car packed out too. 'I'll put the stuff in my garage till you need it,' she said, hugging them both.

'Let's go back inside,' suggested Tom. 'Have a last look around the place.'

The house seemed so empty, hollow, the low autumn sunshine creeping in at the windows and through the empty rooms. Tom wanted to check something upstairs.

'Take your time,' urged Nina as she walked from room to room, sensing the atmosphere, the spirits and ghosts of the old house around her.

'Are you okay, Mum?'

Erin was standing in the family room, the toy press, bookshelves, the couches, everything, gone. She looked like she'd been crying.

'Sad,' admitted Nina, sniffing and reaching for a hanky. 'Just very sad to be leaving this house . . . I really did love living here, you know.'

'Me too,' said Erin, falling into her arms and tearful again.

'There are just so many memories here,' continued Nina. 'Your dad carrying me over the threshold and nearly doing his back in . . . you running around and learning to cycle your little pink tricycle there in the hall . . . and you and Jack putting on your puppet shows here in this room, entertaining us with "The Three Little Pigs".'

'Uncle Bill was the Big Bad Wolf!' laughed Erin, remembering. 'At Halloween we used to paint all the windows and make this place like a spooky castle.'

'Remember Christmas dinner in the dining room and the massive Christmas tree in the bay window in the living room,' reminisced Nina. 'We won't fit one like that in The Boat House!'

'I know,' said Erin gently.

'So much is changing, I feel like I'm losing not just this house but a part of myself too. Your poor dad has lost the business, Jack's taken off to Australia, and even you have found your mother – the person most in the world like you . . . Everything has changed.'

'Mum, I know I've met Kate and my half-brothers and sister, and it's great – but they are not my family! You and Dad and Jack and Uncle Bill and Granny and Lizzie are my family. You are where I belong,' insisted Erin.

'Oh, Erin.' Nina didn't know what to say.

'Kate is nice and kind, and the more I get to know her the more I really like her – but she doesn't feel like my mum. How could she? I've got a mum. I've got you. With Kate it's more like we are friends, or like she is a much older big sister. Even though she gave birth to me, I don't think it could ever be more. I have the best mum ever and nothing or no one can ever change that!'

Nina stood on the bare floorboards totally overcome as Erin clasped her shoulders and held her tight.

'Mum, I'm never going to leave you . . . Don't worry.'

Nina believed every word her daughter said. The little girl she and Tom had raised in this house had somehow turned into such a warm, caring, beautiful young woman . . . their daughter.

'Are you two having a weepy session?' interrupted Tom, coming into the room.

Nina nodded, but she could see Tom had shed a few tears alone upstairs himself.

'Come on, let's say goodbye to this lovely old place,' he said huskily as they walked from room to room in silence. Then Tom closed the front door of Clifton firmly after them as they walked down the front door step and on to the gravelled drive-way.

'Come on!' he said gently, taking her hand. 'I told Lizzie that we wouldn't be too long.'

'I'll see you there,' said Erin as she got into her car and drove away.

Nina took a deep breath. It was finally time to say goodbye and let go. Looking back, she smiled. She could tell the old house was waiting, waiting for another story to begin . . .

Chapter Sixty-three

ERIN AND MATT DROVE OUT TO DALKEY. ERIN EXPERIENCED A pang of regret as she passed the gates of her old home. Clifton had been bought by a wealthy American couple. He worked in IT and they were putting on a huge extension to the back of the house and apparently doing lots of work on it, so it wouldn't be ready to move into until the end of the year.

'It's up here.' She pointed out to Matt the laneway that led to her parents' new home, The Boat House.

Her mum and dad had only moved in a few days ago, but already were entertaining and inviting everyone to come along for drinks to celebrate new beginnings. The Boat House looked absolutely amazing and bore no resemblance to the rundown place where her dad stored his yacht and tools and junk. Her parents both loved the new place; they were like a young couple starting out again.

There was a small driveway and even from the front doorway you could see right the way through the house and its glass windows to the courtyard and back garden.

'Wow, this is really something,' said Matt as he grabbed the wine and side of oak-smoked salmon they had brought for the party.

Her dad opened the door and warmly welcomed them. A few days ago the hall had been full of boxes and packing crates, but now it had been transformed. Her dad looked more relaxed than she had seen him in years. He and Mum had spent practically all of the last three months down in the cottage in West Cork and it had done him a power of good.

'Matt, come and let me give you a tour of the place,' he offered. Erin smiled. Her dad was so proud of what they had done, and of the solar-heating system and solar panels they had installed which he was telling everyone about.

'And wait till you see Nina's study! It's up in what would have been the old loft, but it's a perfect place for her to work and paint in terms of light, and that window gives her a view of the sea.'

Erin joined her mum in the kitchen. Nina was looking elegant as ever in a simple black dress, her blue eyes shining as she moved around her new kitchen.

'Can you believe me working in a modern kitchen like this, Erin? It does almost everything except cook! I just touch a press with my finger and it opens.' Erin watched as she demonstrated.

'Where's Matt?'

'He's getting the tour with Dad.'

Erin was pleased that Matt got on so well with her mum and dad. They already considered him part of the family. She and Matt had moved in together at Christmas and were renting a tiny, red-brick two-up two-down in the heart of the Liberties, Dublin. It was a sweet little house, and they loved it and the fact that, even if they were working late on something, they could still be together under the same roof.

Nikki had gone to stay with her parents after Milly's birth

and was still living there. Her mum was great and Milly adored her granny. Nikki didn't plan to move out until Milly started crèche when she was about one, and then she'd get a place of her own.

With Nikki's moving out, Claire had asked if it was okay if Donal moved in to the apartment with them. Erin liked him and, before she moved out herself, she observed the two of them living together and could see how happy he made Claire. They were a great couple and Donal had confided in her that he was saving for '*the ring*'.

Music played in the background as Erin grabbed a glass of wine and went over to say hello to her granny and Auntie Lizzie and cousins. Uncle Bill was raving about the mews house and what a wonderful job Tom and that architect friend of his, Mike, had done.

'I believe the two of them are beginning work on a number of conversion projects together, and Tom even has Charles and I considering installing one of his eco-friendly solar systems to heat up our place, which can be like Siberia at times.'

Erin laughed and went around saying hello to everyone, noticing that her mum's friend Vonnie had a man in tow.

'He's our auctioneer!' whispered Nina.

Her dad appeared and stood in the middle of the glass-surrounded room, and opened a bottle of champagne.

'Thank you, everyone, for coming along today to a launch of sorts – the launch of The Boat House, a new home for Nina and me, and a place I hope where all of you will consider yourselves very welcome. This year has been a difficult year, as most of you will know, but, like a good ship, we have come through the storms to a peaceful spot here in The Boat House. I would like to thank those of you who helped: our daughter Erin, our son

Jack who is in Australia, and, most of all, my ever-patient wife Nina. She is a truly wonderful woman and in the middle of the calamity managed to write a book and is having it published in the autumn! I thank her for guiding this old sailor home from the sea.'

Everyone gave a cheer. Erin was so proud of them – her mum and dad. She loved them so much. It had been a hell of a year for her, too: breaking up with Luke; finding Kate and getting to know and like her; and, best of all, meeting Matt.

Erin looked at him talking away to her granny. She was already madly in love with him and wanted him to be part of her life for ever.

Oh no, thought Erin, her granny had him deep in conversation. Now she was proudly showing him her rings. Poor Matt. She could guess what was coming next. She'd better rescue him.

'When are you two getting married?' asked her granny so loudly that half the room could hear.

Appalled, Erin wanted the ground to open and swallow her. If she and Matt broke up it would be a hundred per cent her granny's fault!

'May, I promise that you will definitely be one of the first to know when I put a ring on your beautiful granddaughter's finger.'

Erin couldn't believe what she was hearing, what he was saying. He was always so honest.

Matt grinned and slipped his arm around her.

'I meant it,' he said.

'I know,' she laughed, hugging him. 'That's why I love you.'

'I love you too,' said Matt, pulling her closer and kissing her as everyone around them cheered.

Marita Conlon-McKenna is one of Ireland's favourite authors. Her previous novels include *The Matchmaker* and the number one bestsellers *The Magdalen* and *Mother of the Bride*. She is the winner of the prestigious International Reading Association award and is a regular contributor on Radio and TV. She lives in Blackrock in Dublin with her husband and family.